The Lazarus Strain

The Lazarus Strain

KEN MCCLURE

First published in Great Britain in 2007 by
Allison & Busby Limited
13 Charlotte Mews
London W1T 4EJ
www.allisonandbusby.com

A catalogue record for this book is available from
the British Library.

10 9 8 7 6 5 4 3 2 1

ISBN 0 7490 8158 9 (Hardback)
978-0-7490-8158-4

ISBN 0 7490 8015 9 (Trade Paperback)
978-0-7490-8015-0

Typeset in 11/16 pt Sabon by
Terry Shannon

Printed and bound in Wales by
Creative Print and Design, Ebbw Vale

KEN MCCLURE was an award-winning research scientist with the Medical Research Council of Great Britain. His medical thrillers have been translated into twenty-one languages and all are international bestsellers. He lives and works in the village of East Saltoun, near Edinburgh. *The Lazarus Strain* is his nineteenth novel.

And thus I clothe my naked villainy
With old odd ends stolen out of holy writ;
And seem a saint, when most I play the devil.

WILLIAM SHAKESPEARE (1564 – 1616)
King Richard III

PROLOGUE

In 1918 up to forty million people died of a disease that circled the globe – more than died in the Great War itself and more than died of bubonic plague in the epidemic that swept across Europe in the 14th century. They died of a particularly virulent form of pneumonia, which caused their lungs to fill with blood and mucous until they could no longer breathe and effectively drowned in their own secretions. In the United States, the disease affected so many people – one quarter of the entire population – that in certain areas there was a shortage of coffins and gravediggers. Panic was such that travel between certain towns and cities was banned without certified permission. The epidemic alone was responsible for lowering the average life expectancy in the USA by ten years. The disease was influenza.

> *I had a little bird,*
> *Its name was Enza.*
> *I opened the window,*
> *And in-flu-enza*
>
> CHILDREN'S SKIPPING RHYME FROM THE TIME.

It is estimated that one fifth of the world's population was affected by the influenza pandemic of 1918 – 1919, its spread mediated by troops returning home from the war in Europe. Of those American soldiers who fell in Europe, half their number succumbed to influenza rather than enemy fire.

The great influenza pandemic is now beyond living memory to all but a handful of the world's population but the disease itself is as familiar as the common cold. In fact, the two viruses are often confused – particularly by those seeking to excuse their absence from work – flu sounds just a little more serious than a cold.

Influenza breaks out every winter but is not considered a deadly disease – except perhaps for the very frail or very old – but it still retains the potential to wreak havoc as it did nearly a century ago. The flu virus is a master of disguise, constantly changing the structure of its protein coat and challenging the human immune system in being the equivalent of a moving target. These almost annual changes lead to a situation where the virus will be more virulent in some years than in others – 1957 and 1968 were particularly 'bad' years although both pale into insignificance when compared to the ravages of the 1918 strain.

In recent times it has been possible for scientists to study and 'reconstruct' the pandemic strain from biological material recovered from the preserved tissue of dead American soldiers who died of flu after returning from the First World War. The wisdom of doing this has been questioned in some quarters and although the scientists concerned claim that such studies will help them to understand the virus better, there are those who suggest that creating a monster in order to understand it is irresponsible in the extreme.

There are also arguments over the level of containment necessary for experimentation with such a dangerous virus and unease expressed over the decision of certain workers to downgrade the requirement from BL-4 (the highest level of containment possible – requiring workers to wear full-cover body suits and hoods – to BL-3, a lower grade involving 'half suits'. The argument against downgrading is simple: if a laboratory worker should contract the disease and take it out of the lab, flu is so infectious that it would spread like wildfire. If the transport systems of 1918 permitted the virus to reach every corner of the globe, how much more convenient would it find travel in the 21st century? Once the genie is out of the bottle, they maintain, global disaster must surely follow.

The existence of the 1918 strain – even if held in secure laboratories – brings the spectre of terrorist threat into the equation. Pandemic flu would be a fearsome weapon in the hands of those whose only motive is the destruction of Western society. A flu pandemic would disrupt the functioning of the entire civilised world.

As with all virus-caused disease, prevention is better than cure. Antiviral drugs are still in their infancy and nowhere near as effective as antibiotics are in the fight against bacteria. Antibiotics are ineffectual against viruses – although misunderstandings about this still arise. People suffering from viral disease are often prescribed antibiotics, leading to the belief that this is to combat the virus. It is not. The antibiotics are given to prevent secondary bacterial infection moving in and causing complications e.g. bronchitis or streptococcal throat infection. When it comes to fighting viral diseases, tender loving care and the antibodies present in the body's immune system are the only weapons in the human armoury.

It therefore follows that prevention through vaccination – wherever possible – is the best way to tackle viral disease. Vaccination has proved very effective in wiping out killer diseases of the past. Smallpox has been completely eradicated and polio is no longer the scourge it once was. Influenza however, with its ever changing protein coat presents the vaccine designer with special problems. A vaccine effective against last year's flu virus might well prove useless against this year's variant. This leads to annual decisions having to be made by medical authorities over which strains to include in the vaccine for the following winter. Best guess science.

These decisions have to be made early in the year because of the long process involved in flu vaccine production. The chosen virus strains (typically three) have to be grown up in fertile chicken eggs – some 90 million of them – over the course of several months before being harvested and processed prior to distribution into injection vials for the immunisation of between 12 and thirty million people. Approximately one week after vaccination, the B-cells and T-cells of the human immune system will be ready to do battle with the flu virus – provided the scientists guessed right.

* * *

THE LAZARUS STRAIN   15

Whatever the merits of the scientific study of the 1918 strain, one outcome has been to illustrate just how little genetic difference there is between it and the avian flu viruses that have been causing havoc in bird populations in South East Asia in recent years. It has even been suggested that the 1918 virus itself arose from a mutation in a bird flu strain, which enabled it to cross the species barrier. There is little comfort to be gleaned from further research that indicates that there is actually very little in the way of a species barrier to prevent avian strains crossing to human hosts and cases of avian flu in the human population are already being recorded. Many scientists now believe the re-emergence of a pandemic flu strain to be inevitable; a case of when rather than if. They warn that every effort should be put into vaccine design with this in mind.

While scientists may disagree about many things concerned with the flu virus, there is general agreement that time is not on our side. An effective vaccine is the only conceivable defence against the threat of another pandemic – whether it materialises through natural mutation of a human strain, genetic variation of an avian strain or through malicious intent. But the will and the resources to come up with one have to be in place. Flu vaccine production is an expensive, risky business at the best of times and unpopular among the dwindling number of pharmaceutical companies willing to take it on. The commercial risks are great and compliance with the myriad regulations surrounding production very demanding. There can be no guarantee that a '1918 strain', reconstructed specifically for vaccine production, would provide protection against the variant of the virus that finally appears. The slightest of antigenic changes in that virus might render such a vaccine useless.

In addition to this uncertainty, it is not unknown for production problems to arise during the long and delicate manufacturing process of flu vaccine. If such problems cannot be eliminated quickly, there will almost certainly be neither the time nor the resources necessary to start over, leaving the pharmaceutical company facing large losses without compensation.

In October 2004, Chiron, a major flu vaccine supplier based in Liverpool, encountered a problem with bacterial contamination in the vaccine they were preparing for the following winter. Despite their best efforts, the company failed to eradicate it and the British authorities were forced to withdraw their license. Forty million doses had to be destroyed without recompense.

As Chiron had been one of only two manufacturers contracted to supply flu vaccine to the American market by the US Food and Drug Administration, the USA suffered a severe shortage of flu vaccine in the winter of 2004 – 05 – something that even became an American election issue with Senator John Kerry accusing President George W. Bush of failing to protect the vulnerable of US society. Ironically the UK government had licensed six companies to provide flu vaccine so the shortfall was not as marked in the UK.

It is against this factual backdrop that the fictional *The Lazarus Strain* has been written.

CHAPTER ONE

Norfolk
England
October 2004

'You know, planting beech hedging was quite the daftest thing I ever did,' said David Elwood, kicking off his Wellingtons at the kitchen door. 'I seem to spend half my life picking up leaves. It's autumn every month of the year!'

'I know dear,' replied his wife, Mary, who had heard it all before. 'Why don't you sit down and read your paper and I'll make us a nice sandwich for lunch. Cheese or bacon?'

'Bacon please, dear. Should have planted conifers like any sensible person... But no, that man at the garden centre assured me that the leaves stay on beech hedging...it'll give you beautiful golden leaves throughout the winter, he said. What he didn't mention was that I'd be up to my knees in beautiful golden leaves from October to May...'

Mary smiled as David grumbled his way through to the living room. She liked the beech hedging; in fact she liked everything about the cottage they had moved to in Norfolk when David had retired some six years ago. She knew that he liked it too despite his grumbles. The garden kept him busy and that was fine because it prevented him having to face up to the fact that he had little else to do. He might complain – and he did, incessantly – but looking after the garden and doing maintenance work about the place gave him a sense of purpose and, as a retired lecturer in electrical engineering with little or no outside interests or hobbies, this was important. She had reading and knitting to occupy her but come the end of the bowling season in October, David had nothing. 'Coffee or tea?' she called out.

'Tea please,' came the reply.

'Mary put six rashers of bacon under the grill and turned it to high before slicing open three rolls – two for David, one for her. She was on a diet but when it came to a choice between grilled bacon and low fat cheese spread on a Sunday, the diet was flexible. She buttered the rolls and switched on the kettle, popping two teabags in the teapot before pausing to look out of the window at the garden while she waited. She shivered as a cloud passed over the autumn sun and a cool breeze wafted in through the open window.

She leaned over to close it when suddenly, the daylight was blocked out by a dark form that moved in front of the window and an incredibly strong, black hairy hand shot in to grasp her arm and she cried out in pain and alarm.

Her scream was stifled by a second arm reaching in, gripping the back of her neck and slamming her head down on the draining board. She was stunned by the impact but not knocked unconscious: she was even aware of the bacon starting to splutter under the grill as she slumped slowly down to the floor. She lost her spectacles on the way down and could only vaguely make out the black figure who, by now, had come in through the window and was beating her with his fists and making loud screeching sounds.

'David!' she managed to call out before more blows rained in on her and she suddenly became aware of the teeth of the thing that was attacking her: they were big and yellow and pointed. She curled up into a foetal ball, still trying to call out her husband's name but her throat had tightened with horror.

Quite suddenly the thing seemed to lose interest in her and turned away. It now seemed fascinated by the spluttering bacon. Cautiously she felt out along the floor and retrieved her spectacles. 'David!' she called out as she saw that she had a large monkey in her kitchen. The animal ignored her: it was intent on trying to reach its paw under the grill.

'What on earth...' exclaimed David Elwood as he opened the kitchen door to be confronted by his wife lying bleeding on the floor and a monkey screeching in pain as it burned itself on the grill. 'Get out of it!' he yelled as the animal started to career around the kitchen, scattering pots and pans, furious at the pain in his burnt paw. David waved his arms ineffectually as he tried to give chase but the animal evaded him with ease and leapt up on to a high shelf to turn and bare its teeth at him.

'Be careful,' cried Mary. 'It's vicious!'

'Get out of here, Mary,' said David quietly, moving cautiously between his wife and the animal. 'Get out and phone the police...'

Mary dragged herself slowly across the floor and reached up for the door handle just as the animal launched itself and sank its teeth into David's shoulder. Both fell to the floor, the animal screeching and David yelling out in pain and cursing incoherently as the pair of them rolled over in a tumbling fray of fur, limbs and blood.

Mary didn't phone the police; instead, she pulled an umbrella from the stand in the hall and returned to the fray to help her husband, pausing only to open the kitchen window wide before starting to the beat the animal across its back with the handle of the umbrella while holding the pointed end. 'Get out of here!' she screamed. 'Get out of our house! Do you hear me? Get out, you disgusting animal! Get out!'

The animal lost interest in David and turned to face up to Mary but then thought better of it when she caught it with a blow across the face which sent it tumbling to the floor. It leapt up on to the draining board and sprang out through the open window, to run, still screeching, on all fours across the lawn disappearing into the shrubbery.

Mary knelt down beside David to assess the damage. He was bleeding profusely from the bites on his shoulder and also from multiple scratches on his face. 'You *are* in a mess, love,' she said, hugging him for a moment. 'Come on. Let's get you cleaned up.'

'Did you call the police?' asked David.

'No… I was busy,' replied Mary.

David looked up at her sheepishly and smiled. 'Of course you were, love,' he said and gave her hand a squeeze. 'I think we could both do with a bit of cleaning up. Whoever said nothing ever happens in Norfolk?'

'You, I think,' snapped Mary, betraying the edginess she felt. 'I'll give them a call now.'

Mary got up but paused to take another look at David's

wounds. 'This shoulder of yours is going to need proper medical attention and an anti-tetanus shot. I don't think either of us should drive. I'll get them to send an ambulance as well.'

Mary got a predictable response from the police. 'A what?'

'A monkey of some sort, a big one. It came in through the kitchen window while I was making lunch.'

'Of course it did, Madam.'

'Don't you "of course it did" me,' snapped Mary. 'My name is Mary Elwood; I live at Bramley Cottage in Holt and I am not in the habit of making hoax calls to the police, or any other organisation, come to that. My husband and I have been attacked by a monkey. We would like the police in attendance and an ambulance for my husband; he's been bitten.'

'Yes, Madam.'

By three in the afternoon, Norfolk Police had had three more calls about the sighting of a monkey and no information about a missing animal.

Inspector Frank Giles looked at the reports and said, 'This one records a sighting of a monkey in Weybourne at ten past twelve.'

'Yes, sir.'

'But the Elwoods were still under attack in Holt at five past.'

'I see what you mean, sir.'

'Even a monkey with a Ferrari couldn't have made it to Weybourne in five minutes.'

'No, sir.'

'So there's more than one of them. I take it you've had no joy with zoos and wildlife parks?'

'None of them admit to anything missing.'

'No reports of Michael Jackson moving into the area either, I suppose.'

'No sir.'

'That was a joke, Morley.'

'Yes sir.'

'Any ideas?'

'No sir...unless...perhaps a circus happened to be passing through the county...'

Giles shook his head. 'I think you'll find that circuses don't actually use animals any more,' he said. 'The PC mob got to them. I think they entertain the crowds these days with origami and card tricks.'

'Yes sir.'

'But research labs do...' said Giles as the notion came to him. '*They* use animals and there's a research institute in the area.' He got up and walked over to the wall map. 'Here, between Holt and Cromer on the A148. I can't remember the name of it though...'

'The Crick Institute.'

'That's it, the Crick Institute. Get on to them and see if they've lost any monkeys.'

Giles was still examining the map, head held to one side, when Morley returned to say that there was no reply from the Crick Institute.

'No research on Sundays, eh? Well, they must have a note of key holders in case of fire etc. Call one of them.'

'Should I get them to check their animals?'

'No, ask them to meet us there. We'll go over ourselves. It's a nice day for a drive.'

Sergeant Morley slowed the car as he saw a figure running towards them waving his arms. 'What have we here?' he murmured.

Giles opened the window on the passenger side and the running man stopped at the side of the car to rest one hand on the sill and the other flat on his chest as he fought to get his breath back.

'Take it easy now,' said Giles.

The man, a portly figure in his late fifties with a ruddy complexion and wearing a green quilted jacket and corduroy trousers, pointed behind him and gasped, 'We've been hit. These animal rights loonies have done us over. Bastards!'

'Us?' asked Giles.

'The institute, the Crick; I'm the key holder you contacted, Robert Smith, not that you need a bloody key for the place any more; the doors are wide open. The windows are broken and there's paint all over the walls. Bastards.'

Giles got out and opened the back door of the car to usher Smith inside before climbing back in himself and radioing for back-up. Morley turned into the drive leading up to the institute and drove slowly up to the front door.

'Scared they're still there?' said Giles.

'No sir, Mr Smith's already been up here, just looking for any movement in the bushes, sir.'

'I didn't go inside the building, mind you,' said Smith from the back, leaning forward to rest his elbows on both of the front seats between the two policemen. 'One look at the outside was enough.'

'See what you mean,' said Giles as the institute building came into view.

'What a mess,' murmured Morley.

'What kind of people do this?' complained Smith.

'What do you do at the institute, Mr Smith?' asked Giles.

'I look after the animals; clean their cages, see that they're fed and watered; generally cared for and that.'

'So you would have been in earlier today?'

'No, Professor Devon said that he would be coming in himself today; he would feed them so I could have the day off. Apparently his wife was going to see their daughter in Manchester this weekend so he decided to work.'

'That was decent of him,' said Morley.

'He's a real gentleman is Professor Devon, one of the old school if you get my meaning.'

'So he might actually still be here?'

'Bloody hell, I didn't think of that,' exclaimed Smith. 'I suppose he could. If those bastards have...'

'You'd better come in with us, Mr Smith. Just don't touch anything.'

Smith hesitated at the door and said, 'I'm not sure that we should go in... I mean, they work with some dangerous stuff in there, suits and masks and all that...'

'He has a point, sir,' said Morley.

Giles nodded. 'Better get a biohazards team over here. What about the other key holders?'

Morley looked at his notebook. 'Mr Smith was top of the list...'

'That's because I just live at the foot of the drive,' explained Smith. 'It's usually the fire alarm going off for no good reason. Anything else and I call the professor or one of the scientists, Dr Cleary or Dr O'Brien or one of the others.'

'I've got a Doctor Cleary on the list,' said Morley.

'Try him.'

Morley phoned Cleary while Giles turned to Smith and asked, 'Is it possible to get to Professor Devon's office without going through any of the labs?'

'Absolutely, it's just off the main corridor, along to the left.'

'Maybe we could risk that then,' said Giles. 'Just in case he's still in the building.'

'Cleary will be here in fifteen minutes, sir,' said Morley.

The three men got out of the car and paused to read the graffiti on the walls before kicking away some of the broken glass from the steps.

'Walt Disney's got a lot to answer for,' said Giles, turning his head sideways to read some of the writing around the entrance. 'Some of these buggers seem to think that the animal kingdom lives in peace and harmony singing happy jungle ditties.'

'Instead of ripping each other to pieces you mean,' said Morley.

'Survival of the fittest, the fastest, the strongest and no quarter given.'

'Nature red in tooth and claw,' said Morley.

Giles gave a surprised sideways glance at his sergeant. 'Didn't know you were a Kipling man.'

'Some things stick from school, sir.'

'They do,' agreed Giles. 'With me it was Christina Rosetti. "Earth stood hard as iron, water like a stone"...every time I walk across the park on a winter's day... Well, shall we make a start? We can at least check out the Professor's office while we wait for Cleary and make sure he's not lying there injured. We'll also get some idea of what sort of mayhem these fuck-wits have caused this time?'

'If you think it's safe, sir,' said Morley.

Giles surveyed the open door and broken windows and said, 'What was in there is already out here...'

They found the entrance hall strewn with broken glass, much of which had come from a glass-fronted notice board that had hung in the hall listing staff members and their room details. The walls were daubed in red paint. 'Murdering bastards' seemed to be a recurring theme as they moved along although 'Animals have rights too' was also popular.

'Professor Devon's room is just along here,' said Smith leading the way.

Giles knocked on the door but predictably there was no response. He turned the handle and looked inside. The room was empty and appeared to be undamaged although untidy with masses of files and papers arranged in piles on the desk and floor.

'Looks like the Prof had already left when these bastards appeared on the scene,' said Smith.

'I hope so for his sake,' said Giles. 'It wouldn't have been much fun watching your lab being smashed up before your eyes.'

'This'll break his heart,' said Smith.

The sound of wheels on gravel heralded the arrival of two

police patrol cars, followed a few moments later by a Fire
Brigade biohazard team. Giles filled them in on the situation
and suggested that everyone wait for Cleary who could
appraise them of any likely danger. They didn't have long to
wait. Giles was explaining the situation to Smith when a green
Land Rover Discovery swung in through the gates and a tall,
fair-haired man in his thirties got out.

'I'm Nick Cleary. What a bloody mess!'

'Well, they haven't been too shy about stating their views,
I'll give you that,' said Giles as he watched Cleary turn his
head this way and that to read the daubing on the walls. 'Mr
Smith thought there might be an element of danger about
going inside although we have checked out Professor Devon's
room just in case he was still here.'

Cleary looked surprised so Giles added, 'The professor told
Mr Smith he was coming in to work this morning.'

'Ah,' said Cleary. 'Not too surprising I suppose. He seems
to work all the hours there are these days.'

'About the danger...' began Giles.

'We do work with pathogenic microbes,' said Cleary.
'Several. The viruses are kept in a locked deep freeze in bio-
lab 3. The lab itself is locked and the doors are air-tight.
Pathogenic bacteria are kept in freeze-dried vials in a safe in
the same lab.'

'Windows?'

'No windows in the bio-lab. It's an inside room with a
filtered air supply under negative pressure,' replied Cleary.

'Then we should check out the integrity of that room first,'
said Giles. 'Perhaps you could brief the bio-hazard team on its
location in the building?'

'I'll go in with them if you like,' said Cleary.

'You should talk to the Fire Chief.'

'I'll do that.'

'Before you do, what bugs are we talking about here, sir?' asked Giles.

'Maybe we can leave off worrying about that until we see if there's a problem?' said Cleary.

Giles nodded his understanding. 'But if you find security of either of the microbial stores has been breached...'

'The public will have a right to know. You're quite right. But if that's the case I suspect the matter will be taken out of both our hands.'

'A comfort,' said Giles. 'There's another problem: we had reports earlier today about monkeys being on the loose in this part of the country...'

'Jesus,' said Cleary. 'They let the monkeys out?'

'Liberated them is how they would see it. Perhaps you could advise us of the risk involved?'

'I don't use primates myself; that was Tim Devon's province and the room was always kept locked. But I don't think he had any animal experiments running. Chances are they are perfectly healthy monkeys although that's not to say they can't be dangerous. You can get a very nasty bite.'

'Someone already did,' said Giles. 'But you don't think there would be any other hazard involved?'

'I can't be absolutely sure; you'd really have to ask Tim that. Have you managed to contact him yet?'

'Not yet. Sergeant Morley is still trying.'

Cleary went off to talk to the Fire chief and Giles found Morley. 'Any luck?' he asked.

'Still no answer,' said Morley.

'Shit,' muttered Giles. 'I'm beginning to think we should hit the panic button on this one.'

'Why?'

'To guard our arses. I'm beginning to see "Police Delay Puts Public at Risk." headlines.'

'You think the monkeys were infected with something?'

'The trouble is we don't know for sure and Devon seems to be the only one who can tell us.'

'I'll keep trying.'

'I'm going to give him until they've examined the microbial stocks. Even if the stores are intact, if we still haven't made contact with Devon I'm going to blow the whistle.'

Giles and Morley returned to the car to wait.

'What happens if they do find the virus store has been breached?' asked Morley. They were watching the bio-hazard team make last minute adjustments to each other's suits before trooping in single file into the institute. Giles noted that Cleary was with them.

'Depends on what bugs they've been storing there,' said Giles, 'and what their characteristics are. Some viruses are highly infectious, others not. Some are stable in air, others are not. Some diseases are contracted by breathing in the virus, others you have to ingest them. All these things have to be taken in to consideration. At least that's what they said on the course... Personally, I'm a run-for-the-hills man.'

'Surely a place like this wouldn't be working with anything really bad. I mean, smallpox or plague or anthrax, anything like that?'

'There's not much point in designing vaccines against harmless things,' countered Giles.

'But surely if they were working with dangerous bugs they'd have better security, wouldn't they? Fences...guards on the gates.'

'Let's not take that for granted.'

'So this could turn into a real nightmare?'

'Let's just say our best chance of avoiding such a nightmare lies in the microbe stores being intact and everything in them being present and correct.'

'Looks like we're just about to find out,' said Morley as the first of the bio-hazard team appeared in the doorway. Both men got out of the car.

He saw cause for optimism when one of the team waved away the men responsible for operating the mobile shower and decontamination facility. 'It's looking good.'

It was obvious that the bio-hazard team were relaxed when they removed their helmets; they were laughing and joking with each other.

Giles approached Nick Cleary who grinned and said, 'They didn't get through the door to BL3. Everything was secure. Mind you they've made an appalling mess of the rest of the place. It's going to take months to get back to normal. Any word from Prof Devon yet?'

'Still nothing. Did you check the animals?'

'No, I thought we'd better come straight back and tell you folks about the microbe situation.'

Giles nodded. 'Maybe we could take a look at the animal house now? See what's missing.'

Still wearing his bio-hazard suit but without the helmet and visor Cleary led the way along the corridor and down some stairs into the experimental animal facility. As they came to the first door Cleary said, 'This is the mouse house.' He looked in through the glass window set in the door and cursed under his breath.

Giles looked in to see chaos. Several stacked columns of mouse boxes had been pushed over on to their sides, spilling their occupants out on to the floor. Mice were clambering over everything, investigating everything and nothing, their fur matted with wet sawdust and blood from cuts sustained from the glass water feeding bottles that had been smashed on the floor. 'Will this cause big set-backs?' he asked.

'All the experiments running will be ruined,' replied Cleary. 'We can't possibly tell which mouse came from which box.'

They moved on to the next room. 'Same mess here,' said Cleary. 'Guinea pigs all out of their cages.'

Giles counted some thirty guinea pigs on a floor littered with animal feed and sawdust: many of their wire cages had been deformed by being smashed against the wall and jumped on, judging by a number that had been flattened. 'But they didn't release anything into the wild,' he said.

'Doesn't look like it,' agreed Cleary.

Giles exchanged a glance with Morley that conveyed relief.

CHAPTER TWO

The last door had Primate House written above it. It was slightly ajar. 'Jesus,' said Cleary as he pushed it fully open and entered. 'All gone.'

Giles noted that the door lock appeared to be undamaged as he joined Cleary inside. 'How many?' he asked.

'Six,' said Cleary. 'Tim told me a couple of weeks ago that the primate house was full.'

There were three large cages along each side of the room; their iron-barred doors hanging open apart from one at the far end which was still closed. There was absolute silence in the room apart from the hum of a ventilation fan but the smell of the previous inhabitants lingered on. Giles wrinkled his nose as he turned to Cleary and said, 'We can't take the chance. I'm going to call a major alert.'

'I really don't think...'

Cleary was interrupted by Morley, who had walked up to the far end of the room. The Sergeant suddenly let out a yell followed by, 'Jesus fucking Christ! What the...'

The two men spun round just in time to see Morley throw up on the floor. They hurried up to the cage with the closed door.

'Oh, God in Heaven,' said Giles, his eyes opening like saucers.

Cleary put his hand to his mouth and turned away.

The naked body of a man was sitting in the cage. He was clearly dead and had been badly mutilated. His eyes had been burned with a liquid that had also burned his cheeks as it flowed down over them and he was holding a crudely painted cardboard sign which said, "See how you like it!"

'Is this Professor Devon?' asked Giles.

Cleary nodded, still holding his hand to his mouth.

While they waited for the forensic team to arrive outside, Giles asked Cleary, 'Do you think you could have a look through Professor Devon's things to see if you can get an idea of what the animals might have been infected with? We need to know quickly.'

Cleary looked uncomfortable. He said, 'It's not something I'm keen on doing. I know he's dead but some of Tim's work was covered by the official secrets act and I don't know where I'd stand if I were to start rummaging through his things...'

'We need to assess any risk to the general public as quickly as possible,' insisted Giles. 'We can sort out the paperwork later.'

'You're right, of course,' said Cleary. 'I'll do what I can. But as I said before, I'm almost certain there will be nothing to worry about.'

'Don't you know what each other was working on?' asked Giles.

'No, not really,' said Cleary. 'Until recently we all did, but then Tim got involved in politics and told us that he was no longer able to make all his experiments public, so to speak.'

Giles and Morley looked at each other and Cleary quickly

added, 'It was nothing to do with germ warfare or anything like that. Tim was coopted on to some big government vaccines committee and it was a condition that he could not speak openly about his work, not even to his colleagues. You know how the government likes secrets.'

Giles nodded. 'It's a good way of keeping your fuck-ups out of the public eye,' he said.

'A cynical but possibly accurate view,' said Cleary with a smile. 'I'll get started in Tim's room.' As he made to go back inside the institute he turned to Giles and said, 'You will remember that you asked me to do this? I mean if men in grey suits turn up and ask what the hell I'm doing, going through my boss's desk...'

'You have my assurance,' said Giles. 'For what it's worth,' he added under his breath as he watched Cleary disappear inside.

Morley appeared at his side. 'Local radio has put out a warning telling people not to approach the monkeys but to phone the police. Manchester Police have located Mrs Devon and given her the news.'

Giles nodded. 'Then we can let the murder go out on the evening news. I want to nail these bastards. I really do.'

'Sorry about what happened in there,' said Morley sheepishly.

'Don't ever feel ashamed of that,' said Giles. 'It's when you start looking at that sort of thing with indifference that you'll have cause to worry.'

Giles broke off and walked towards the front door as he saw the police pathologist coming out. She was dressed in white coveralls and had a gauze mask slung loosely at her throat. 'Well, Madge, a bit out of the ordinary, eh?' he said.

Dr Marjorie Ryman smiled and said, 'Not exactly what I needed after Sunday lunch. Poor man had a pretty horrible death.'

'Cause of death?'

'With the usual provisos, a venous cannula through the heart following extensive torture with a scalpel and bleach.'

'Thanks Madge. I won't quote you until you've done the PM.'

'I know you won't, Frank, that's why we're friends.'

A green Rover 75 came up the drive and caught Giles's attention. He knew that its driver must have satisfied the policeman on the gate but he couldn't work out who it might be. A tall figure wearing a dark business suit and carrying a briefcase got out and started walking towards the cluster of vehicles and personnel round the entrance to the institute. 'Who's in charge?' he asked.

'I am. Who wants to know?' replied Giles.

The man showed Giles an ID card and said, 'Nigel Lees, Department of Health. I came as soon as I heard.'

'And your connection with the institute?' asked Giles.

'Professor Devon was on our vaccines advisory committee.'

'Ah,' said Giles, remembering what Cleary had said. 'So you might be in a position to tell us exactly what Professor Devon was working on and what sort of risk the escaped primates might present?'

'Indeed I am,' said Lees. 'Nothing to worry about. Tim was working on next year's flu vaccine.'

'Flu?' exclaimed Giles. 'Not rabies or bubonic plague?'

'Nothing like that,' smiled Lees.

'So the worst thing these monkeys can be carrying is flu?'

'Quite so,' said Lees.

'Well, that's a relief,' said Giles. 'I was worried when I heard that Professor Devon's work had to be kept secret from his colleagues...'

Lees seemed to sense immediately that he might have been underestimating Giles' intelligence. 'Ah, yes,' he replied. 'Well, the secrecy was necessary for technical reasons.'

'Technical reasons?' repeated Giles, intent on not letting Lees off the hook.

'How much do you know about flu vaccine, Inspector?'

'Only that my mother seems to get it every winter,' replied Giles. 'The vaccine, that is, not the flu.'

'The problem with the flu virus is that it keeps changing its antigenic structure,' said Lees.

Giles looked blank.

'In essence, this means that a vaccine effective against flu one year will not necessarily be effective against it the following because the virus will have changed its structure to protect itself. This is further complicated by there being more than one strain of flu going around in any given year.'

'I see,' said Giles.

'What the boffins have to do is make an informed guess as to what the three most likely strains are going to be and design a vaccine accordingly.'

'Why the secrecy?'

'Commercial reasons.' replied Lees. 'It's only fair to the pharmaceutical companies contracted to manufacture it.'

'I see,' said Giles. 'Thank you, Mr Lees.'

'Not at all, Inspector. Now, if I might have access to

Professor Devon's office, there are some papers I must recover.'

'Of course,' said Giles. 'Dr Cleary is looking through his papers at the moment.'

'What?' exclaimed Lees.

Giles noticed the sudden change in Lees' demeanour and found it intriguing. 'At my request,' he added. 'I asked Dr Cleary to do this in order to establish as quickly as possible what the escaped animals might be carrying.'

'Well, that will no longer be necessary,' snapped Lees. 'Will you show me to Professor Devon's office, please?'

Lees and Giles found Cleary sitting at Devon's desk reading through a pile of papers. Giles introduced Lees and Cleary got up to shake hands. Lees did so perfunctorily and said, 'I don't think we need trouble you any longer, Doctor. I've told the inspector what he needs to know.'

Giles noticed that Cleary was embarrassed at being dismissed like some errant schoolboy. He said, 'I told Mr Lees that I had asked you to do this. Did you have any luck, Doctor?'

Cleary looked at Lees and then at Giles. Lees knew that Giles was looking for verification of what he'd already told him but chose not to say anything.

'Tim appears to have been working on...flu virus, Inspector,' said Cleary.

'So I understand,' smiled Giles, although he had noted the pause in Cleary's reply. 'I apologise for putting you to all that trouble but I hope you both understand that it was imperative for us to know what danger the public might be facing.'

'No trouble,' said Cleary

'Of course,' said Lees.

As they left Devon's office Giles and Cleary came across the forensic team removing Devon's body from the premises. They paused to allow the white-suited pall bearers to pass by.

'I still can't believe it,' said Cleary, still clearly upset. 'I suppose you must see a lot of this, Inspector?'

'Not exactly like this, sir,' said Giles. 'This is a bit special.'

'What did they hope to gain? People are hardly going to flock to the animal rights cause when they hear about Tim's murder, any more than they were a few weeks ago when they stole the corpse of an old lady in Staffordshire. They're just sick, these people.'

'You may well be right,' said Giles. 'Extremist organisations always attract the sick and the inadequate. The cause doesn't really matter too much to them and in this case, the tail may have started wagging the dog.'

'A frightening thought.'

Giles and Cleary watched as a dark coloured van with blacked-out windows took Devon's body away.

Giles cleared his throat and asked, 'I take it you didn't find any indication that the professor might have been working with any other virus, did you sir? I mean it was just flu?'

Cleary seemed to take a long time to answer but when he did it was just to say, 'No, Inspector, just flu virus.'

'Good,' said Giles. 'Then we can all sleep safely in our beds...'

'Yeees...'

'But?'

'No buts Inspector, of course we can. About the animals...'

'What about them, sir?'

'What will you do?'

'The public have been warned not to approach them and to report any sightings to the police. After that we'll leave it up to the usual agencies to bring them in, RSPCA, PDSA. Don't suppose monkeys'll fancy Norfolk too much with the nights getting colder...but then I suppose they're smart enough to start looking for a billet indoors should the need arise...' Giles watched for a reaction from Cleary.

'Better warn the public to lock all doors and windows,' said Cleary.

'Really, sir?' said Giles.

Cleary looked at him. 'They can give you a nasty bite, Inspector,' he said but he knew he'd been tested.

'Were all the monkeys infected with...flu virus, sir?' Giles asked.

'As far as I could make out; it was a six animal experiment. Four animals had received Tim's experimental vaccine and had then been injected with flu virus – challenged, we call it – one had received the vaccine alone and the remaining animal, the virus alone.'

'What was the purpose of the last two?' asked Giles.

'They're what we call control animals,' said Cleary. 'One was a vaccine control to make sure the vaccine itself did not cause illness and the second was a virus control to demonstrate that the live virus was in fact alive and could cause infection. You always need controls to validate an experiment.'

'I see, sir. Is there any way of knowing which animal is which when they are recovered?'

Cleary looked doubtful. 'I think not,' he said. 'We wouldn't know which cage an animal had come from and they wouldn't have labels round their necks. Mind you... Smithy might be able to tell.'

'The man who fed them?'

'Yes, the Professor's notes state which animal was given what by name – they all had names, you see. Smithy might be able to recognise them when they're brought in.'

'Good,' said Giles. 'That might be useful.'

'I don't often feel queasy in my job,' said Marjorie Ryman. 'But I'll have to admit to it this time. For sheer, bloody minded cruelty this takes the biscuit.'

Giles looked down at the body on the table and screwed up his face.

'I mean, I can see the point of humiliating the man by stripping him and putting him in a cage like an animal. To a lesser extent I can even understand the thing with his eyes – although not with bleach – because of what's gone on in animal experiments in the past. But the systematic mutilation of his body with a scalpel by the looks of it... I fail to see the point they were trying to make.'

'Pure unadulterated sadism,' said Giles. 'I take it you were right about the cause of death? You usually are.'

'Yes, it was the cannula through the heart.' She held up the long, hollow needle that had been found in the cage beside Devon. 'I was rather hoping I wasn't because I hoped he'd died before they got round to that but no, it looks as if he was alive throughout the rest, God have mercy on him.'

'Thanks Madge,' said Giles. He found he had little heart for any further conversation.

'What now, sir?' asked Sergeant Morley.

'Home. We grab a few hours while our colleagues bring in every animal rights bozo they can lay hands on and the whole county goes on monkey watch.'

'What do you tell your wife when you've had a day like this?' asked Morley as they walked across the yard.

'I don't,' said Giles. 'We have an agreement. After fifteen years she can tell by my face what kind of day I've had and what size of a gin is required. She puts it down on the table and I say, "Thanks love," and that's the end of it. We talk about other things, inconsequential things like the meaning of life and the origin of the universe.'

'And that works?'

'Tonight she'll be leaving the bottle.'

David Elwood grunted as he manoeuvred himself into bed, hampered by having one arm in a sling. His wife pulled up the blankets and made a fuss of tucking him in. 'How's the pain?'

'It's fine; the pills are dealing with it. '

'Fancy some hot chocolate?'

'That would be nice, dear.'

'Telly on?' asked Mary, pausing by the portable television, which stood on top of a chest of drawers at the foot of the bed. '*Panorama's* on. Mind you, it's just about finished but I think there's a spooky film after it.'

'I think I've had enough spooky nonsense for one day,' said David.

'Perhaps we both have,' said Mary. 'I only hope they catch these swine. What they did to that poor Professor was just plain evil.'

'World's full of fanatics these days.'

Mary left the room and returned a few minutes later with two mugs of hot chocolate. She placed one on each of the bedside tables before going over to the window to draw the curtains. Something caught her attention in the garden and she held back the curtains with both hands while she pressed her nose to the glass.

'You've not found another monkey out there, have you?' said her husband.

'No, dear,' replied Mary. 'I think it's a spaceman with a gun...'

CHAPTER THREE

Home Office
London

'Gentlemen, the Home Secretary has asked me to convene this first meeting of the *Earlybird* sub-committee of the Joint Intelligence Committee in response to information received. As you are all aware, the JIC set up *Earlybird* in the wake of the Butler Inquiry and in accordance with its mandate to set up committees and sub-committees as it sees fit. *Earlybird* is seen as an appropriate vehicle for the early discussion of security alerts to those not directly concerned with the security of our nation but who, nevertheless, might be regarded as interested parties and who might have an input to make – thus broadening interpretation of such alerts.'

The Home Office minister turned to a man wearing army uniform and said. 'Colonel Rose, as the current information emanates from Defence Intelligence Services, perhaps you would care to take over?'

'Thank you, Minister, and good morning, ladies and gentlemen. In recent weeks DIS have correlated from a number of impeccable sources information that leads us to believe that al-Qaeda are becoming increasingly active in the UK.'

'Would these be the same 'impeccable' sources that gave us weapons of mass destruction and 45 minute deployment?' asked John Macmillan, head of the Sci-Med Inspectorate. The comment attracted glares from several of the others round the table.

'I think that was uncalled for, John,' said the Home Office minister.

Macmillan acquiesced with a slight hand gesture, which did not quite amount to an apology.

'Please continue, Colonel.'

'On the face of it, we appear to have been successful in diverting a 9/11 style attack on Canary Wharf and a planned second offensive on Heathrow Airport.'

'You've made arrests?'

'We have had a number of suspects undergoing interrogation for the past two weeks,' replied Rose. 'As a result of these interrogations we were able to reach certain conclusions.'

'Then congratulations appear to be in order.'

'Unfortunately, we think not,' said Rose. 'In fact, we think we've been had.'

'How so?'

'None of the people we picked up are, in our view, capable of planning or executing such attacks. Without exception, they were all low-level operatives, foot soldiers who knew very little...except for the targets.'

'And that makes you suspicious?'

'It makes us think that we have been fed false information. We now believe that al-Qaeda have sacrificed a number of foot soldiers, fresh from their training camps, in an effort to create a diversion. But the million dollar question is for what? What are they going to do while we sit congratulating ourselves on smashing a planned attack that never was?'

'Are you absolutely sure that you're reading the situation correctly, Colonel?' asked a commander in the Metropolitan Police. 'I mean, can you afford to ignore any threat to Canary Wharf and Heathrow?'

'That is not up to me,' replied Rose. 'I can only offer DIS's reading of the situation.'

'And that is why we would like your input, ladies and gentlemen,' said the Home Office minister. 'To a certain extent, al-Qaeda's success on September 11th 2001 has played against them. You can't really follow up something like that with a few car bombs and a couple of home videos. To maintain credibility they have to top 9/11 in terms of impact on public consciousness. Or at least equal it. Now that President Bush has been re-elected the pressure is really on them to do something sooner rather than later. Are they really going to try for a second 9/11 or do they have something else in mind...equally big?'

'We need more information. Do we have any?'

'No,' said Rose. 'The people we're holding know nothing.'

'You're sure of that?'

'We're sure.'

'Well, I don't think we can completely ignore the threat even if DIS does think it's a bluff,' said the London Fire Brigade representative.

'Deciding what to ignore is of course, a perennial problem,' said the Home Office minister. 'But with so many threats coming in on an almost daily basis...difficult decisions have to be made. We can't give priority to all of them.'

'We can still heighten security at Westminster, airports, military establishments...' said the police commander.

'We're just covering our backsides by doing that,' said John Macmillan. 'If Colonel Rose is right about the threat being a diversion – and I for one believe that he is – it will do nothing at all to help determine what al-Qaeda really has in mind.'

'But of course, a general heightening of security would...' began the Home Office minister.

'With respect sir, every time we hear about any kind of threat we get declarations of 'heightened security'. Maybe I'm missing something here but shouldn't it already be at a very high level? In fact, shouldn't it already be at the highest level possible?'

'As I see it, it's a question of manpower,' said the police commissioner. 'Given enough resources we can increase presence in all key areas and if my recommendations for changes to Westminster security arrangements were to be accepted instead of being obstructed at every...'

'They just might be able to stop any Tom, Dick or Harry climbing Big Ben whenever he feels like it or waving to the crowd from the balcony at the palace. No, I was thinking more about the limitations of our security measures rather than contemplating more of the same,' said Macmillan.

The room went deathly quiet.

'Maybe you should say what's on your mind, John?'

Macmillan took a deep breath as if knowing he was about to go into battle against insurmountable odds. 'When all's said and done, security measures are really all about trying to stop what already happened yesterday,' he said. He paused to allow the expected snorts of disapproval fill the air and then subside.

'Go on,' said the Home Office minister.

'Cockpit doors are locked on September the *twelfth* not the tenth – which would have been a damned sight more useful – shoes are examined at airports the day *after* the shoe bomber appears on the scene. It's a depressing fact but security is all about locking stable doors the day after the horse has bolted.'

'Well, none of us has a crystal ball,' said the Home Secretary.

'No, but perhaps we should recognise that 'security measures' as we know them have their limitations. At best, they might stop the same thing happening again but are the opposition really only intent on repeating past glories? I think not. Does anyone really believe that Bin Laden has been sitting in a cave planning a carbon copy of the 9/11 operation? Of course not. They will have moved on. They will be dreaming up new, imaginative ways of causing mayhem while we content ourselves with 'heightening security'. And from what Colonel Rose has said, it very much sounds as if they are about to embark on one of them if they haven't already done so.'

'So what do you suggest?' asked the Home Secretary.

'We must think like the opposition,' said Macmillan. 'In addition to rings of steel and gun-toting policemen we need people with imagination and vision who can put themselves in the terrorists' position, people who can look at a given situation and imagine the worst possible scenario arising from it.'

'I think the intelligence services already cover this,' said Colonel Rose.

'I don't think they do' said Macmillan. 'JIC certainly appoints people with good analytical brains who, in conjunction with the intelligence services of our allies, analyse and correlate information gathered on the ground and from the airwaves and appraise it...but only if it is considered relevant in the first place.'

'Of course,' said Rose. 'Where's the problem?'

Macmillan sighed and took a moment to get his thoughts in order before saying, 'There's no problem with that except that it's *applied* research. Someone has already decided where the starting point is and what the end product should be.'

'Sorry, I'm not with you,' said Rose. There were nods of agreement.

'I suppose what I am highlighting is the difference between applied research and blue-sky research.'

'I take it by "blue sky" you mean, research for the sake of research and nothing else?' said the Home Office minister.

'Exactly. It may sound self-indulgent in these focused times but throughout history that is exactly where most of man's advances in knowledge have come from: simple human curiosity being given its head: an intelligent person notices something interesting or unusual and picks away at it until an explanation is found. If we'd always been restricted to applied research we'd be sitting here wearing nylon bearskins and carrying very sharp axes.'

The Home Office minister smiled and said, 'So we should all adopt the Sci-Med approach to investigation; is that what you're suggesting John?'

'Not exactly, Minister, it's really a different way of looking at things I'm advocating,' replied Macmillan.

'You've lost me,' said the police commander.

'And me,' agreed several others.

The Home Office minister explained. 'The Sci-Med computers are programmed to collect and collate information from the world of science and medicine in this country and pick up on any unusual trends or traits. Once identified, John's team of investigators take over and pick away until they see if there's anything to worry about. Is that right, John?'

'In a nutshell, yes, Minister,' said Macmillan, deferring to the man who officially represented his boss, the Home Secretary. The Sci-Med Inspectorate came within the jurisdiction of the Home Office although it was permitted to act independently when it came to investigations.

'Well, we've certainly had cause to be grateful in the past to Sci-Med for what they've come up with out of the blue – if you'll pardon the pun,' continued the Home Secretary. 'So you are suggesting a similar approach for the security services, is that correct?'

'Yes, Home Secretary, I suppose I am, in addition to their normal modes of operation they should broaden their horizons – think laterally – give rein to their imagination.'

'Interesting concept.'

'And doomed to failure,' said Colonel Rose.

'Why so?'

'Sci-Med only looks at things pertinent to science and medicine and only in this country. The intelligence community operates on a global scale. Any attempt to use the Sci-Med system would founder on the sheer volume of information we collect, sir – the same problem that overwhelmed the Nimrod air reconnaissance programme, if you remember: it collected too much information to analyse.'

'It was logging every car on the M1, as I remember,' smiled the Home Office minister.

'That's where people come in,' said Macmillan. 'Human intuition: computers don't have that: they can't decide what's interesting and what's not. Everything is given equal billing. You need people with imagination to pick out the cherries from the stones.'

'That's what JIC people do,' said Rose.

'With blinkers on,' said Macmillan. 'They're told what to look for.'

'Blinkers have their place if they stop a horse from being distracted by irrelevance.'

'But you've already decided what is irrelevant before anything appears,' said Macmillan.

'Gentlemen, I think if we spend any more time arguing along these lines we'll end up discussing Zen Buddhism and the meaning of life,' said the Home Office minister. 'I think what John's been saying is very interesting but perhaps it should be considered again in less fraught times. What we have to consider right now is how we should be reacting to a possible but undetermined threat if the DIS interpretation of recent events is correct.'

'The Met of course will be put on heightened alert,' said the police commissioner.

'As will my people,' added the fire chief.

Macmillan just shrugged.

'Well, I think that is about as much as any of us can do at this stage, ladies and gentlemen,' said the Home Secretary.

'You will of course be kept informed of any developments as and when they occur.'

'And when the unexpected comes to call, God help us all,' murmured Macmillan.

Macmillan left Downing Street and returned to the Home Office where he closed his office door and slumped down into the chair behind his desk to stare up at the ceiling for a few moments. He knew he should have been more circumspect about criticising traditional security measures but frustration had got the better of him as it did every time he saw the armed police wandering around the concourse at Heathrow. Just what the hell did they think they were going to do with automatic weapons in a crowded hall? The intercom buzzer interrupted his train of thought and his secretary, Jean Roberts, said, 'Steven Dunbar is here.'

'Send him in.'

'Sounds like a bear with a sore head,' whispered Jean Roberts to the tall man in the dark blue suit and Parachute Regiment tie. 'Careful as you go.'

Dr Steven Dunbar, medical investigator with the Sci-Med Inspectorate, smiled and walked into Macmillan's room as he had done so often in the past. He liked John Macmillan and would be ever grateful to him for rescuing him from the prospect of a dull career in either the pharmaceutical industry or in-house medicine when his service career had ended.

He had known well enough when the time had come for him to leave the armed forces in his mid thirties that an army career with the Parachute Regiment and Special Forces, in which he had become an expert in field medicine, had done little to further his chances of climbing the career pole in domestic medicine. He had simply missed the boat. There was little or no demand for a doctor with the skills of a commando or the ability to operate on wounded comrades in the jungles of South America or the deserts of the Middle East.

Fortunately for him, John Macmillan had appeared on the scene to offer him the job with the Sci-Med Inspectorate where he would be employed as a medical investigator in an organisation he had never heard of but to which he had taken like a duck to water.

Sci-Med operated as a small independent unit within the Home Office. Its function was to monitor events developing in science and medicine in the UK and spot early indications of possible problems or crimes that the police might not have the necessary expertise to either see or investigate. Sci-Med investigators were either medical or science graduates but with many other skills acquired in the course of widely varied careers. New graduates were not recruited to Sci-Med. It was Macmillan's view that they didn't know enough about life. All Sci-Med people had to have demonstrated high levels of intelligence and resourcefulness in other walks of life and had to have, above all else, that most valuable of attributes in Macmillan's book – common sense in abundance.

'How are you?' asked Macmillan.

'Refreshed and relaxed,' smiled Steven. 'Unlike you by the look of things...'

'I've just been to a top level security meeting,' said Macmillan. 'Apparently al-Qaeda are getting restless. Intelligence suggests they're going to mount a big operation but we don't know what and we don't know where.'

'Sounds like a challenge,' said Steven.

'Apparently, we are 'heightening security',' said Macmillan ruefully.

Steven smiled. He knew that this was a particular hobby horse of Macmillan's. 'Be extra vigilant about nail scissors on Boeing 747s, you mean?'

'That sort of thing,' agreed Macmillan. 'Confiscate one passenger's pen knife while all the others trot on board with glass bottles full of duty-free. What would you rather face, someone with a broken bottle or a pen knife?'

'Luckily, neither eventuality is too likely,' said Steven.

'Just as well when common sense is in such short supply, but that's what 'heightening security' usually boils down to – confiscating more bloody pen knives.'

Steven remained silent while Macmillan worked through his frustration. Eventually he looked up from his desk and said, 'Sorry, I'm getting a bit carried away. None of this is of any direct concern to us. Did you have a good leave?'

'I did,' replied Steven. 'I was up in Scotland with my daughter. It's been a while since we could spend a decent amount of time together.'

'Good. I suppose she's not a baby any more?'

'Just moved up to Primary 2,' said Steven.

'God, how time flies. How is she getting on? Stays with your sister in law and her husband, doesn't she?'

'Yes,' confirmed Steven. 'She's happy. She's turning out to be everything I'd hoped she'd be. I can see so much of Lisa in her. It's uncanny.'

'Well,' said Macmillan somewhat uncertainly, 'I trust you can take some comfort from that.'

Steven smiled and put Macmillan at his ease. 'I can.'

Steven's wife, Lisa, had died of a brain tumour shortly after Jenny's birth and since that time Jenny had lived with Lisa's sister, Sue, and her husband Richard and their own two children, Robin and Mary, in the Dumfriesshire village of Glenvane in Scotland.

'I understand you have a job for me?'

Macmillan nodded. 'I take it you are aware of the attack on the Crick Institute in Norfolk by animal rights extremists, the one resulting in the murder of Professor Timothy Devon?'

'It was on every front page in the country,' said Steven.

'Apart from the murder of an eminent scientist and the damage they caused to the labs, they released a number of lab animals into the wild,' said Macmillan. 'Primates.'

'Ah,' said Steven.

'When it emerged that Professor Devon was on the UK vaccines advisory committee...'

'You started wondering what the monkeys had been injected with?' said Steven.

'Precisely. But I was assured that nothing dangerous had been involved...'

'And that there was no cause for alarm,' completed Steven with a smile. 'Where have I heard that before?'

'When I asked exactly what the animals had been infected with, the institute spokesperson declined to tell me without reference to something he called "higher authority". I asked him to call me back when he had such authority but nothing's happened so far.'

'Were all the animals recovered?'

'In a manner of speaking. The army was called in to shoot them.'

'The army?' exclaimed Steven. 'Why the army?'

Macmillan shrugged.

'Were they successful?'

'I understand they got five out of the six.'

'So one on the loose...but of course, nothing at all to worry about.'

'That's why I want you to go up there. It's a messy business but the question for us is: is it a dangerous mess?'

'Are the animals known to have been in contact with any members of the public?'

'One attacked an elderly couple in Holt. The man received bites to his shoulder and was treated in hospital. He was released and appears to be none the worse for his experience.'

'So there may be nothing to it,' said Steven.

'I'd like your assurance about that,' said Macmillan. 'The Crick is a civilian establishment, not military, so the attitude of their spokesperson might just have been typical civil service reluctance to say anything about anything – assume that the day of the week is a secret until some higher authority gives you permission to reveal it.'

'I'll have a poke around,' said Steven.

'Jean has prepared a file for you on Timothy Devon and the institute.'

'Good, I'll not pretend that I'm familiar with the man's work.'

'He was an expert in vaccines,' said Macmillan. 'Not exactly headline grabbing stuff but in recent times, with all the talk of biological attack and our preparedness to deal with such an attack – or lack of it – vaccination schedules are very much in the minds and on the lips of our political masters. There is general concern over our ability to vaccinate the population if a biological attack should occur. It's the sort of thing that could become an election issue.'

'As it did in the US last year.'

Macmillan nodded. 'I think we can be sure that that would not have been lost on the government here,' he said.

'On the other hand, I didn't notice *us* running out of flu vaccine last year,' said Steven.

'Apparently, we license a greater number of suppliers,' said Macmillan.

'Maybe there's a lesson there for the Yanks,' said Steven.

'The Americans didn't license thalidomide,' said Macmillan.

'*Touche*,' said Steven.

CHAPTER FOUR

Steven read that Timothy Devon had been fifty-eight at the time of his death. He was married to Joan, a former fellow lecturer in Biochemistry at the University of Warwick and was the father of two daughters, Julia and Imogen, aged 22 and 24. He had been head of the Crick Institute for eight years having previously worked at Warwick and before that, at the Institute of Virology in Glasgow. He had recently become a grandfather when Julia, who lived in Manchester with her graphic designer husband, Ben, had given birth to a son, James Timothy.

The forensic photographs of his body were horrific. Despite the awful sights he had seen in the course of his professional life, Steven still found himself grimacing while examining them. It was impossible not to imagine the hell the man must have gone through before death had come as a merciful release, just as it was impossible not to question if concern for animal welfare could ever have justified such barbarity in the mind of any normal person. Steven concluded not. The people who had done this to Devon were sick in the head: they were sadists entirely without conscience. There was some awful difference between seeing damage done to a human body in the heat of battle and that applied coldly and dispassionately by a torturer. It might be argued that both arose as the result of human failing but the latter was so much more difficult to come to terms with.

Devon had been an acknowledged expert on vaccines and had acted as an advisor to successive governments and on several occasions. Like many academics called on by government on an *ad hoc* basis, his profile had generally been low but a recent rigorous defence of the MMR vaccine had brought him into public consciousness, particularly when he had attacked the science used to question its safety and the scientist who had expressed these doubts. The spat had attracted wide press attention and the government had subsequently appointed him to their vaccines advisory committee, a position he had used to warn of the dangers of losing public confidence in essential vaccination programmes. Doubts about vaccines given to soldiers in the Gulf War and the scare over MMR had done much to damage such confidence, he had argued. Government had to address that problem and look to the future in order to anticipate further needs. At present, the nation in his view would be ill-equipped to deal with a measles epidemic let alone a smallpox or anthrax attack.

The Crick Institute, as Macmillan had indicated, was a Scientific Civil Service establishment with twelve members of scientific staff and eighteen technical and ancillary staff. Its broad general mandate was to design and test vaccines in accordance with perceived national requirements.

Steven made his own notes of its location and of the staff he might want to talk to. At the head of the list was Dr Nicholas Cleary who had been one of the first on the scene and who had gone in with the bio-hazard team to check the integrity of the institute's microbe stocks. He also wanted to speak with the policeman in charge of investigating the case, Inspector Frank Giles, and to talk to the police pathologist, Dr Marjorie Ryman. He was particularly interested in establishing who had been responsible for calling in the army to deal with the escaped animals. And why? There had been no indication of this in the file.

Collected press cuttings showed that the public in general had been outraged by the murder of Timothy Devon and feelings against the animal rights movement in the country was running high – a situation fuelled by a tabloid press who were also getting on the backs of the Norfolk Police with their demands for an early arrest. 'Blinded with Bleach!' screamed *The Sun*. 'Tortured to Death in a Cage' trumpeted *The Mirror*.

Efforts by 'responsible' leaders of the animal rights movement were clearly failing in their attempts to distance themselves from what had happened at the Crick: the public simply didn't want to know. Animal activists were all being tarred with the same brush. Moderate public opinion, that might until recently have had some sympathy with the aims of the animal lobby, were now turning away in disgust. People who could dig up the grave of an old woman and steal her body in an effort to blackmail her family into closing down their laboratory animal business – an outrage that had happened only a few weeks before in Staffordshire – and who could torture and murder a quiet academic were quite beyond the pale.

The broadsheets had also involved themselves in the case with readers' letters suggesting that feeling was running almost as high among the country's chattering classes. Steven found one particularly interesting cutting, an article taken from *The Times*, in which an expert on terrorism had claimed that the UK had become the equivalent of Afghanistan when it came to training animal rights activists. The British activists, he maintained, were the al-Qaeda of the animal rights world. This made Steven consider for a moment before concluding with a wry smile that this situation would not have escaped the attention of MI5 chief, Liz Manningham-Buller and her colleagues at Thames House. He wondered just how many security service personnel had already penetrated the animal rights movement. Not too many in Norfolk, he concluded ruefully.

He closed the file and saw that it was getting dark outside. It was four o'clock on a late November day and there was a slight drizzle in the air that was forming halos round the street lights. He'd been sitting in the library for three hours and now, he decided, it was time to go home, home to the flat he'd been away from for the past two weeks. He had flown down from Scotland that morning and gone directly to the Home Office to see Macmillan.

The flat would be cold and silent in the way it always was after he'd been away for more than a couple of days and the heating had been turned off. That first moment when he opened the door always served to remind him of how alone he was in the world. It was a moment he couldn't avoid and it was always the same. Time would stand still as he thought how different life might have been had Lisa lived – he would imagine a scenario of light and warmth, full of smiles and news from Lisa and chatter from his daughter Jenny about her day at school but instead he would be standing perfectly still in darkness, feeling the cold, still air of the flat on his cheek and facing the fact that Lisa had gone for ever and Jenny was hundreds of miles away, telling someone else about her day at school. As always, he would quickly turn on all the lights, switch on the central heating and generally seek distraction in noise from either the radio or television and the moment would pass. Until the next time.

Steven's flat was near the Thames but not quite on the waterfront. It was one street back but he could see the river and some of its traffic through a gap in the buildings opposite. He could see this from his favourite seat by the window which he plumped himself down in after pouring himself a large gin and tonic. He needed a plan of action: the water, gas and heating had all been turned back on but it would take a while for the flat to heat up and for there to be enough hot water for the bath he was looking forward to. He decided that he would go out and pick up some take-away food from his local Chinese restaurant, The Jade Garden, where he was a once-a-week regular customer; he hadn't developed a liking or aptitude for cooking. The cupboards were bare, as was the fridge: he would have to pay a visit to the supermarket and stock up on packet meals but that could wait until tomorrow.

'Yes sir...no sir...couldn't agree more, sir... I'm sure we will sir...very good sir.' Giles put down the phone.

'Chief Super?' asked Morley.

'Wishing us well with our inquiries,' said Giles.

'That was nice of him...' Morley faltered as he saw the sour look appear on Giles' face.

'If we don't crack this and get the Press off his back real soon he's going to have us both on school crossings for the foreseeable future.'

'It's not for want of trying; we interviewed nearly thirty animal rights suspects today,' said Morley.

'All of them adamant that the Crick affair was nothing to do with them or their responsible, law-abiding organisation and most of them with alibis.'

'You have doubts?' asked Morley.

Giles shook his head. 'No, it takes a special sort of nutter to do what these bastards did to Devon and none of that lot fit the bill. They might be up for a bit of placard waving and hunt sabotage, maybe even stretch to car scratching and tyre slashing but cold blooded murder? Nope. We're looking for outsiders. Our only hope is that they are not complete outsiders...'

'How do you mean?'

'I'm hoping they at least made contact with local activists for information, if for no other reason.'

'And that these locals contact us?'

'You got it. I'm counting on them shitting themselves when they find out just what they've been accessories to. It's my guess the weakest link will already be in a bad way, unable to eat or sleep, conscience screaming at them to get it off their chest. He or she will want to contact us and tell all. The strongest on the other hand will argue the case for saying nothing – just keep your trap shut and they can't possibly touch us...just keep your nerve...keep your nerve.'

'Who'll win?' asked Morley.

'The desire to confess will be strong. But going down for

life is a powerful deterrent however bad they're feeling.'

'We need a break.'

'That's right. Someone who notices their brother or sister, their boyfriend or son or daughter falling to pieces before their eyes for no known reason. Loss of appetite, constantly watching the news on telly, jumps down your throat at the most innocent of inquiries.'

'Let's hope he breaks soon,' said Morley.

'I think the Chief Super just might agree with you on that,' said Giles. 'By the way, there's a bloke from Sci-Med in London coming to see me in the morning, a Dr Steven Dunbar.'

'What about?'

'Just a general chat about the Crick business, I'm told. Sci-Med takes an interest in everything concerning science and medicine. Devon's death must be right up their alley.'

Giles was woken at 3 a.m. by the phone ringing. He found the receiver at the third fumbled attempt.

'There's been a murder, sir. The body of a man has been found in a lay-by near Melton Constable. It was discovered by a young couple who'd gone there to...'

'Play chess,' interrupted Giles. 'Has Dr Ryman been told?'

'On her way, sir.'

'Anything else I should know?'

'Yes, sir. The dead man is Robert Lyndon, known to his pals as Stig. He was a known hunt saboteur, arrested three times over the past two years for breach of the peace.'

'Was he now?' murmured Giles, getting out of bed and cradling the phone between neck and shoulder. 'Was he one of the ones brought in for interview yesterday?'

'No, but he was on the list. He wasn't at home when we called first time around.'

'Tell Sergeant Morley I'll meet him there.'

Giles pulled up his collar as he stepped out of the car and walked over to the taped off area of lay-by. Marjorie Ryman, in white coveralls was already there, kneeling by the body: the scene was lit by portable lighting being run off a noisy generator. 'We can't go on meeting like this,' he said as he squatted down beside the Pathologist.

'What?'

'Nothing, what have you got?'

'Male, early twenties, stab wounds, been dead three to four hours but...'

'Don't quote you. Murder weapon?'

'I'd say something small, clasp knife possibly, that sort of size.'

'Carried out here?'

'No, definitely somewhere else and then the body was dumped here. There's very little blood on the ground so that means there's plenty of blood around somewhere else. The abrasions to the left side of his face and the tears to his clothing suggest he was dragged along the ground – possibly after being pulled out of a car.'

'Thanks Madge. As always, you're a star.'

'Go get 'em, Batman.'

Sergeant Morley joined them.

'Better late than never, Sergeant,' said Giles.

'Sorry sir. I was at a friend's house...up in Cromer...I got here as quickly as I could.'

Giles made a play of looking at his watch and Marjorie Ryman hid a smile at the younger man's embarrassment.

'Could this be the weak link you were looking for, sir?' asked Morley.

'That's my fear,' said Giles. 'Someone thought he couldn't be trusted to keep his mouth shut...so they shut it for him.'

'Poor bastard.'

'Dr Dunbar is here to see you, sir,' announced Sergeant Morley, holding back the door to allow Steven to step inside.

Giles got up from behind his desk and shook hands.

'You had a rough night, I hear,' said Steven.

'Another murder,' said Giles. 'And not unconnected with the first by the look of things.'

'How so?'

Giles explained his thinking. 'Needless to say, we're trying to establish who Lyndon was with last night.'

'I hope you get the break,' said Steven.

'I'm not quite clear about Sci-Med's interest in all this,' said Giles. 'Apart from the fact of course, that a well-known academic was the victim.'

'It's not so much that,' smiled Steven. 'We're more concerned with the escaped animals and what they might have been used for.'

'Ah,' said Giles. 'Now I understand. I was told it was an influenza experiment. Have you any reason to believe differently?'

'Flu?' exclaimed Steven.

'That's what the man said.'

'What man?'

'A suit from the Department of Health named Nigel Lees. He turned up at the institute while we were all there. I was a bit concerned myself about what the animals might be carrying but he reassured me there was no risk to the public.'

'So who called in the army?'

Giles smiled as if anticipating the question. 'Funny you should ask that,' he smiled. 'Not me. I thought broadcast warnings to the public and the involvement of the RSPCA and PDSA would cover the situation but apparently someone thought different.'

'But you don't know who?'

Giles shook his head. 'You could ask Mr Lees.'

'I think I just might,' said Steven. 'As I understand it, five of the animals were shot but one hasn't been recovered?'

'That's my understanding too,' agreed Giles.

'Do you know what happened to the dead animals?'

'They were taken back to the institute for incineration.'

Giles looked at Steven and then asked hesitantly, 'The fact that you're here...and the fact that the army was called in... I mean, you don't suspect the flu story was some kind of a cover-up, do you?'

'I don't think anything at the moment,' said Steven. 'I'm trying to keep an open mind but I'll keep you informed if I find out anything.'

'Same here,' said Giles. 'I take it you're going over to the institute?'

'On my way there now,' said Steven.

'They'll still be cleaning up. They made a right mess of the place.'

* * *

Steven drove over to the Crick Institute, thinking about what he'd learned. Not a lot. He hadn't really thought the police would know who had called the army in and Giles was probably right about it having had something to do with the man from the Dept of Health – Lees, the same man who had told Giles that the animals had been part of an experiment involving influenza. Shooting them seemed a bit extreme...but in these litigious times, playing safe was probably the right option. On the other hand, why get the army to do it? Surely police marksmen would have been first choice in any civilian situation? British governments were always reluctant to involve military personnel...unless it was deemed absolutely necessary.

Several workmen were occupied in attempting to remove the spray paint daubing from the wall of the institute with high pressure detergent guns as Steven walked up to the entrance. Tradesmen were also much in evidence inside the building: two joiners were repairing the Reception area and an electrician was engaged in replacing smashed light fittings. Steven tiptoed through the mess on the floor to where he could see a young woman sitting at a computer console in a small office. He tapped his knuckles lightly on the door. 'Steven Dunbar. I think Dr Cleary is expecting me.'

'You know, it's like working in the middle of a building site,' smiled the woman as she picked up a green phone and dialled a three digit number before saying, 'Dr Dunbar is here.'

The woman came to the door of the office and pointed along the corridor to the left. 'Go right along to the end and turn right. Nick's office is the second on your left.'

Steven passed a number of glaziers replacing corridor

windows: he could smell the putty. He found Cleary's office without trouble.

'How can I help?' asked Cleary after initial introductions were over.

'It's my understanding that you work on vaccines here,' said Steven.

'That's right, we try to anticipate what might happen in the foreseeable future with regard to bacterial and viral outbreaks and try to make sure that the public can be protected should the need arise.'

'So what sort of things do you work with?'

'I hate to be a pain...but could I see your warrant card?'

Steven smiled and took out his Home Office ID and security clearance.

'Thanks. I personally work on anti-bacterial vaccines rather than anti-viral ones, in particular, tuberculosis. TB has been making a bit of a comeback of late and the government's been considering prophylactic measures. The BCG vaccine has been around for a long time and we've been looking at possible alternatives, so that's my main interest although I'm also involved with meningitis vaccines too.'

'So you don't all work on the same projects?'

'No, we try not to overlap too much although there is still plenty of collaboration going on.'

'So, what sort of microbes would be held in the institute,' asked Steven. 'You've mentioned TB and meningitis; what else?'

'Let's see, Diphtheria. A number of Clostridial strains and Brucella abortus. That's about it for the bacteria.'

'And what viruses?'

'Measles, mumps, rubella, flu.'

'How about bio-weapon microbes, smallpox, anthrax, plague?'

'Nothing like that,' said Cleary. 'We don't have a license for handling BLR-4 requiring pathogens. Labs with highest level of containment possible are Porton Down's province.'

Steven nodded. 'Did you know what Professor Devon was working on?'

'No, I didn't.'

Steven noted that Cleary's body language changed when he said it. He moved uncomfortably in his seat. 'Was there any reason why not?'

'It was a technical thing,' said Cleary. 'Tim had been coopted on to some high-powered government committee and complete confidentiality was required.'

'So you have no idea what experiments he was engaged in?'

'Well...actually, yes. After they discovered Tim's body and the fact that several animals were missing, the policeman in charge of the investigation, Inspector Giles, asked me to go through Tim's things to see if I could find out what he'd been working on. He was concerned about any potential threat the escaped animals might be carrying.'

'So you found out from Professor Devon's papers what he was working on?'

Cleary nodded but Steven noticed that he broke off eye contact. 'Tim was working with flu virus. He was working on a vaccine against it.'

'Do you still have these papers?'

'No, I understand they were removed by a man from the Department of Health,' said Cleary.

'Ah yes, Mr Lees?'

Cleary nodded. 'You know him?'

'No,' replied Steven. 'Inspector Giles told me about him earlier.'

'He confirmed what I had already found out, that Tim had been working on a flu vaccine...but...'

'But what?'

'Oh nothing,' said Cleary with a dismissive gesture of his hands.

Steven watched the man for a few moments, wondering what he might be holding back, before saying, 'Dr Cleary, if you have any reason to suspect that these animals might be infected with something other than flu virus, I would strongly advise you to tell me...'

'It was definitely flu virus,' said Cleary.

Steven again milked the ensuing pause to see if anything else was forthcoming but Cleary stared him out.

'Were all the animals infected?' Steven asked.

'Four were being tested for vaccine efficiency after being challenged with live virus; the other two were experimental controls.'

'One with virus alone, one with vaccine alone?'

Cleary nodded. 'That's right.'

'Do you know which animals were recovered?

Cleary hesitated. 'There was no official way of knowing once the animals had been released from their cages...'

'But?' asked Steven, picking up on the use of the word 'official'.

'Smithy, the man who cleaned and fed the animals, claimed he could tell them apart. When the soldiers brought in the corpses he claimed to know which one was still missing. Unfortunately, it was Chloe.'

'Chloe?'

'Chloe was the live virus control animal.'

'Injected with virus but given no vaccine?'

Cleary nodded and said, 'I'm not sure how reliable that information is...'

'Well, maybe Chloe will die of flu out there,' said Steven.

'If Norfolk in November doesn't get her first,' said Cleary, relaxing a little. 'Perhaps you'd like to meet the rest of the staff?'

CHAPTER FIVE

Cleary led the way to the staff common room where makeshift attempts had been made to clean up the place and an electric kettle had been pressed into service as a substitute for the coffee machine which had been destroyed during the mayhem.

'Only instant I'm afraid,' said Cleary.

Steven smiled and took the mug of instant coffee and was introduced to the staff members in turn. He had expected them to display the usual range of human emotions in the circumstances but the degree of violence used against Devon was subduing them so there were no angry tirades against the animal rights movement or pompous assertions about the value of animal experiments in saving human lives. He could sense that people were evaluating their own position in the scheme of things and a more popular theme was the need for better security in the future.

'It's crazy they could just walk in here,' said one man, a sentiment no one was going to disagree with although one person, later introduced to Steven as Dr Pat O'Brien, did point out that the microbial storage areas had remained secure throughout. 'Woops, pardon me for speaking,' he said when a silence ensued. 'I always suspected looking on the bright side was a flawed philosophy,' he murmured to Steven.

'Paddy works on meningitis vaccines,' said Cleary.

'And this is Dr Leila Martin,' said Cleary. He pronounced the name the French way. 'Leila is a visiting research fellow from the University of Washington. She was working with Professor Devon. She too is an expert in the field.'

Steven shook hands with a good looking woman in her thirties with jet black hair, a smooth olive skin and dark brown eyes that seemed to appraise him without seeming intrusive.

'Forgive me, Dr Dunbar, but I'm afraid I have no idea who or what Sci-Med are,' she said.

Steven gave her a brief outline of Sci-Med's function.

'Ah, you're a scientific policeman.'

'Sort of,' he agreed with a smile, thinking that only a French accent could make the word 'policeman' sound sexy. He wanted to tell her that but instead said, 'Have you worked on influenza virus for long, Doctor Martin?'

'I did my PhD on it.'

'You must find it fascinating.'

'I find its capacity for antigenic change fascinating,' said Leila. 'It's one of the biggest challenges to be faced when it comes to vaccine design. It's a sort of scarlet pimpernel of a virus, always moving, always changing its appearance and characteristics.'

Once again Steven found the French accent delicious. 'Sounds like something the scientific police should be hunting down,' he smiled.

Leila smiled politely.

'Professor Devon's death must be a huge blow to your research efforts?'

'Tim was a lovely man. He knew more about flu virus than anyone else on Earth but he was a true scientist: he shared his knowledge with others unlike so many others these days who rush to the patent office as soon as they have a result. Because of Tim's openness it will be possible for others to carry on where he left off.'

'At least that's something,' said Steven. 'And you personally, will you stay here or go back to the States?'

'It's too soon to say,' said Leila. 'I need time to think. This has come as such a tremendous shock to everyone.'

'Of course. Well, whatever you decide, I wish you well.'

Steven moved on to chat to some of the others about their work before Cleary eventually escorted him to the front door. Steven handed him his card and looked him directly in the eye. 'Let me know if you think there's anything else I should know.'

'Of course,' said Cleary.

Steven sat in the car for a few minutes, trying to decide whether or not his investigation was over. The institute hadn't been licensed to carry out work on the highly dangerous bacteria and viruses normally associated with biological weapons and the escaped animals had not been carrying anything more dangerous than flu virus. Five of the six beasts were already dead and the other probably wouldn't last long in the wild. End of story...or not, because there was no denying that he did feel uneasy about something. Nothing the police or Cleary had told him had given him cause to feel this way. It was just a feeling that he wasn't in full possession of all the facts. Someone was holding something back and that someone was Nick Cleary.

There had been something about Cleary's body language during the interview that had aroused his suspicions. He felt sure the man had been considering telling him more but had changed his mind. It might have been something important: equally, it might not, but a small seed of doubt had been planted and Steven had the kind of mind that nurtured such things to maturity. He still had to talk to Marjorie Ryman, the police pathologist, but it seemed unlikely that she would be able to offer him reassurance or wipe away the unease.

Marjorie Ryman was at work in the post-mortem room when Steven arrived. One of the mortuary technicians spoke to her over an intercom link in the reception area: she asked him to put Steven on. After apologising for still being busy at the time they had arranged to meet she gave him the choice of joining her in the PM room or of waiting until she had finished – she thought about forty minutes. He chose to join her rather than wait – a trip to the supermarket was still on the cards. He was shown into a small adjoining room by the Technician where there was a row of pegs along one white-tiled wall with green, surgical gowns hanging from them. Below them and underneath a wooden slatted bench, Wellington boots were lined up like troops guarding a royal route.

'Size?' asked the Technician.

'Eleven,' replied Steven.

Steven slipped off his shoes and put on the boots he was handed before standing up to slip his arms through the sleeves of the green gown being held out to him by the Technician, who then secured the ties at the back. He declined the offer of gloves, saying, 'I won't be that involved.'

He entered the PM room, wrinkling up his nose at the smell. 'Dr Ryman?' he asked.

'Come in, Dr Dunbar. Sorry I'm still up to my eyes but the police are anxious to have the report on this one and it just seems to have been one thing after another today,' said a pleasant, endomorphic woman in her early forties with dark hair that was just beginning to grey and intelligent eyes that seemed to reflect a confident but pleasant personality. 'Otherwise we could have had tea and biscuits in my office.'

'The murder victim from last night?' asked Steven, joining her at the furthest away of three stainless steel tables on which the pale corpse of a young man lay with its chest cavity already opened up.

'This is the fellow,' agreed Ryman. 'Dead before his twenty-fifth birthday...'

There was a pause during which the gurgle of water sluicing down the drain on the table seemed to offer up a mocking requiem.

'Inspector Giles seemed to think there might be a link between this murder and that of Professor Devon at the Crick Institute,' said Steven.

'So I understand,' said Ryman. 'But there's no pathological reason to think that, so I couldn't really comment. Suffice to say their deaths were very different. This chap was killed in anger after a short, violent knife attack. Prof Devon was subjected to slow deliberate torture over a period of several hours before being killed suddenly and efficiently by someone who knew exactly what he or she was doing. It takes some skill to puncture the heart with one thrust from a venous cannula. Can I ask why Sci-Med is interested in these deaths?'

'It's more the escaped animals that caught our attention,' said Steven. 'And what Prof Devon might have been using them for.'

'Oh, of course, the monkeys,' said Ryman with a knowing smile. 'I should have realised. One of them actually bit someone I understand?'

'A man over in Holt,' said Steven.

'Hope it wasn't carrying anything too nasty.'

'Only flu,' said Steven.

'That was a bit of luck,' said Ryman. 'I keep thinking it can only be a matter of time before one of these people releases something really nasty into the wild. They don't seem to consider what "freeing" the animals means when they start throwing open the doors of research labs.'

'They probably think it's a *Tales of the Riverbank* world out there. All the animals will nip down to Toad Hall to attend a lecture on social responsibility with regard to the spread of infectious disease.'

'You sound like Frank Giles,' said Ryman with a smile. 'He's a sarcastic bastard too.'

'Must be the job,' said Steven.

'Tell me about it,' said Ryman, gesturing to the corpse on the table. 'Strikes me, we've all come a long way from Walton's Mountain.'

'So what kind of person does what they did to Prof Devon?'

'Not my province,' said Ryman. 'I deal with the dead not the living and in this instance, I'm glad about that. I don't even want to think about the kind of minds behind that one.'

'That bad?'

Ryman stopped working and looked directly at Steven. 'I

was physically sick when I wrote the report.'

Steven nodded and said, 'Well, the general feeling seems to be that the animal rights brigade has gone too far this time. Any public sympathy they might have had has all but evaporated. That can only help the police catch whoever was responsible.'

'I really hope so,' said Ryman. 'And when they do...they should melt the key.'

Steven thanked her and turned to leave. As he got to the door, Ryman said, 'G'night John-boy.'

Steven smiled and turned. 'G'night Elizabeth.'

'I wish,' said Ryman, already back at work inside the chest cavity.

Steven walked slowly back to the car, giving the light breeze that had sprung up time to eliminate any traces of the PM room that might be clinging to his hair and clothes. He hated the smells associated with pathology, including that of the bloody awful air freshener they all tended to use. Even after all these years the sickly sweet smell of formaldehyde brought back images of cadavers stored in tanks of the stuff for medical students to hone their skills on.

'And so farewell, Norfolk...' he murmured as he started heading south, thinking about what he would tell John Macmillan in his report. No cause for alarm; the apparent secrecy surrounding Devon's work had just been routine bureaucracy. Devon had been working on nothing more sinister than an influenza vaccine...unless of course... Nick Cleary knew different.

'Damnation,' said Steven as the lingering doubt about

Cleary came back to haunt him. He tried arguing himself out of the sinister possibility that the animals had been infected with something more dangerous by considering the member of the public who'd been bitten by one of the animals but who had been released from hospital and was safely back home. He was absolutely fine...wasn't he? This last doubt pushed Steven over some inner threshold. He turned the car through 180 degrees at the next roundabout and started heading back into Norfolk. He was on his way to Holt. He had to see for himself.

It was just after seven when Steven slowed the car and came to a halt in the main street of Holt where he rummaged through his briefcase on the passenger seat until he found the page from the file with the Elwoods' address on it. 'Bramley Cottage, Holt,' he muttered out loud. He'd have to ask. It occurred to him that he could kill two birds with one stone by getting directions at the local chip shop while he picked up something to eat. He was starving: he hadn't eaten since breakfast time.

'Yes mate, take the third on your right and go straight up the hill. There's a narrow opening on your left – just opposite the end of speed limit sign. Bramley is the second cottage along it. There are only three.'

Steven thanked the man and returned to the car to eat his fish and chips. They tasted good and he wolfed them down in no time at all, using a handful of moist tissues from the glove box to clean his hands and face when he'd finished and hoping that he wouldn't smell too much when he got to the Elwoods' cottage.

Bramley cottage was in darkness when he finally drew up

outside it and he thought he saw disappointment on the horizon. He went through the motions however, and walked up the winding path to knock on the door with the heavy brass knocker which, he could see in the light coming from the neighbouring bungalow, was fashioned in the shape of a frog. As he expected, there was no answer but he tried again just to make sure: they might be very early bedders. There was no answer to the second knock but it did however alert the neighbours to his presence and one – a small woman wearing overly large glasses and carpet slippers fashioned as furry rabbits, came out to say, 'I'm afraid the Elwoods are not at home. David's been taken ill.'

Steven looked blankly at the woman. 'David's been taken ill' was the last thing he wanted to hear. He wanted to be told that David was down the pub or out playing bingo. He wanted to be told that David had made a complete recovery and was enjoying life to the full. He did not want to hear that David had been taken ill.

'Did you hear me? I said David's been taken ill,' repeated the woman, coming closer and peering up into Steven's face.

Steven pulled himself together and smiled. 'Oh dear,' he said. 'Nothing serious I hope?'

'I really can't say,' said the woman. 'Mary said she thought it was something to do with that dratted animal that attacked him. Anyway he's in hospital and Mary went with him.'

Steven swallowed. This was going from bad to worse. 'The same hospital as before?' he asked hoarsely.

The woman shook her head. 'No, I wanted to send him a card but Mary said she didn't have an address yet. She said they'd been very good about things and that they were going to make sure that David got the best of medical attention. They told her she could stay with him in what they called their guest suite and it was all going to be at their expense.' The woman drew even closer and added conspiratorially, 'Somewhere private, I think.'

'You don't know who 'they' were by any chance?' asked Steven.

The woman shook her head and said, 'Didn't think to ask. The institute, I suppose. I mean, it was their animal and they should take responsibility for it, don't you think?'

Steven gave a non-committal nod and said, 'It must have been very alarming for everyone round here.'

'I'll say,' said the woman. 'You don't see men with guns running round your garden every day.'

'Of course,' said Steven who had been meaning the escaped animals, 'I'd forgotten about the soldiers.'

'Soldiers?' exclaimed the woman. 'More like spacemen if you ask me. They scared the living daylights out of me and Sam, I can tell you, creeping round the gardens like that.'

'Spacemen...' repeated Steven, struggling to appear normal when even more alarm bells were going off inside his head.

'You know...these suits they wear...makes 'em look like spacemen.'

'I don't think I do,' said Steven. 'Can you describe these suits, Mrs—?

'Jackson, Molly Jackson.' She went on to give a reasonable description of something Steven reluctantly recognised as a bio-hazard suit.

'It all sounds very exciting,' he said calmly but his pulse rate had risen markedly. No one had mentioned in the report that the soldiers had been wearing bio-hazard gear...or more importantly, why.

'Frankly, I think we've had enough excitement round here, thank you very much,' said Molly. 'I liked it fine the way it was.'

Steven returned to his car and put his head back on the restraint. 'Sweet Jesus Christ,' he murmured. 'What's going on?'

Charlene Lyndon made an appeal on the early evening news for information about the murder of her dead son. She came across on screen as an unattractive woman in her forties with a weight problem due to bad diet and a make-up problem due to bad taste. Her hair was dyed jet black which contrasted badly with her pallid white skin and painted scarlet lips. Her cheeks were smudged with mascara runs from her tears.

'Robert was a good boy,' she said, reading with difficulty from a card in front of her while her T-shirted husband sat beside her like a stuffed toy, the word 'love', tattooed on the fingers of his right hand, clearly visible.

'He was always helping people... He would do anything for anyone... Someone must know something about what happened to him last night... I'm pleading with you... Come forward and tell the police what you know... My son didn't deserve to die like that... No one deserves to die like that...' She put down the card and buried her face in her hands.

'A good boy?' said Morley when it was over and the Lyndons had been ushered away.

'They all are to their mothers,' said Giles. 'She didn't see what her little boy and his mates did to Timothy Devon.'

'You still think Lyndon was part of that?'

'Lyndon was an ineffectual little prat who couldn't hold down a job or get a girlfriend. He was a known hunt saboteur who probably didn't give a shit about animals but found some kind of acceptance – like many of these buggers – in a common cause – basically anything that brings them into conflict with the establishment that's giving them such a bad time as they see it. He was weakest link material if ever I came across it.'

Morley nodded. 'So what do we do now, sir?'

'We wait for the phone to ring and pray we get lucky.'

Thirty minutes after the broadcast went out they got lucky. Morley came into the room. 'This sounds good. The landlord at the Four Feathers pub in Swaffham thinks he recognised the dead man on the telly as being one of two men drinking in his pub last night. He remembers them arguing.'

'Bingo! Get your coat.'

Gerald Stanley Morton, the licensee of the Four Feathers pub was a large man without an intellect to match but, in keeping with the undemanding standards of the times, saw his role in helping the police with their inquiries as coming pretty close to stardom and the achievement of celebrity status. Not quite 'I'm a Celebrity Get Me Out of Here', more a case of, 'I'm a Nonentity; get me in front of a Camera,' as Giles was to put it later. The Press were already in evidence when Giles and Morley arrived.

'What the fuck are *they* doing here?' exclaimed Giles as he caught sight of the scrum.

'Morton must have called them.'

'Arsehole!... Park round the corner.'

Morley parked the unmarked car round the corner from the pub and the two policemen walked back to where Morton was talking to the Press.

'I'm sorry, gentlemen,' he was saying. 'But it would be most inappropriate of me to divulge anything to you at this time without first saying what I have to say to the police. I can however reveal...'

'Fuck me; the bugger must have heard someone say that on the telly once.' said Giles as they approached. 'Prat!'

'Mr Morton! I'd prefer if you revealed absolutely nothing right now, if you don't mind,' said Giles, raising his voice. 'Police,' he added, holding up his warrant card. He walked purposefully through the reporters as if pausing weren't an option and they parted like the Red Sea. 'Let's leave press conferences until later, shall we, Mr Morton? Much later.'

CHAPTER SIX

Despite his size, Giles ushered Morton inside his pub as if the big man was a schoolgirl being seen over the road. Meanwhile Morley dispersed the reporters by telling them there would be nothing further for them and warning them about obstructing the police in a murder inquiry.

'Where can we talk?' asked Giles.

'Through here,' said Morton, leading the way through the back.

'Just what the fuck was that all about?' demanded Giles.

'You know what the Press are like,' replied Morton.

'*I* might but how the fuck do *you* know?' stormed Giles. 'That lot didn't just drop in for a pint did they? Somebody rang their bell.'

'All right...my missus thought we should give them a ring,' said Morton, moving his shoulders uncomfortably as if he had a column of ants marching along them.

'Why?'

Morton wriggled in embarrassment. 'Wanted to see our names in the papers I suppose.'

Giles looked incredulous. 'If any one of these buggers out there prints something that fucks up our inquiry, you'll get your name in the papers all right because I'll throw the book at you, along with the shelf it's sitting on.'

'You've no right to talk to me like that,' said Morton. 'I'm a law-abiding citizen doing my duty. Maybe I've got nothing more to say to you now...'

Giles, a full head shorter than Morton, looked as if he couldn't believe his ears. He walked slowly towards the big man and said menacingly. 'What did God give you instead of a brain?' He prodded Morton. 'An extra big belly?'

Morley noticed that Morton had started to sweat.

'You've got one chance my friend and that is to tell us exactly what we need to know to find the man who was in here with Stig Lyndon last night. Otherwise you can start looking out the suit you're going to wear in court. Dark blue always goes down well with the jury, I'm told.'

'All right, all right.' Morton held up his hands in capitulation. 'I'll tell you what I know.'

'And them nothing,' said Giles, gesturing over his shoulder with his thumb.

Morton nodded. 'All right, all right. There were two of them, the bloke off the telly and a bigger bloke with longish red hair. The bloke off the telly...'

'Lyndon,' said Giles.

'Yeah, Lyndon, right. He seemed to be in a right funk about something and the other one was trying to calm him down, telling him to relax an' that.'

'Did you hear any of the conversation?'

'Bits and pieces; they were sitting over there by the window. I picked up the occasional thing when I was collecting glasses but not much.'

'Every word you heard,' said Giles.

'The bloke Lyndon said something like, "never meant for that to happen". The other guy said, "Course not".

'What else?'

'Lyndon said something about not being able to live with it.'

Giles looked at Morley and Morley nodded and said, 'The weakest link.'

'What?' asked Morton.

'Nothing. What else was said?'

The red-haired bloke said, 'All you have to do is forget it ever happened.'

'What did Lyndon say?'

'Just shook his head.'

'Anything else?'

'Later on, Lyndon must have said something that upset the red-haired guy because he started threatening Lyndon.'

'Saying what?'

'Couldn't hear,' said Morton. 'I was behind the bar then. It was more the way he was behaving and the look on his face. You can tell when someone's coming the heavy. But I did hear him say there was no fucking way he was going down for something like that.'

'Anything else?'

Morton shook his head. 'That's it.'

'You've been a great help, Mr Morton,' said Giles as if nothing had ever happened between them. 'Perhaps you could give Sergeant Morley here a more detailed description of the man with red hair. Every pimple if you please.'

Giles left Morley with Morton and went outside to talk to the waiting reporters. 'There will be no further statement from either Mr Morton or the police this evening,' he said. 'And it would be a great help to us if you would wait until we *are* ready to make a statement. Anything else might jeopardise our inquiries.'

Giles maintained a neutral expression but there was no denying the inner relief he felt when the throng started to break up and drift off. 'Any last questions put to him were parried with, 'Maybe tomorrow, gentlemen.'

'Got the description?' Giles asked Morley when he got in the car.

'Pretty good one too,' said Morley.

'Good, because there will be no going home for us tonight. Any mention of the Four Feathers in the papers tomorrow and Ginger Rogers will head for the hills. We've got until morning to find him. Let's start with the Lyndons.'

Charlene and Robert Lyndon snr. were watching a video of Charlene's earlier broadcast when the two policemen arrived. 'Look at my mascara, what a sight!' exclaimed Charlene with her back to them, seemingly mesmerised by the sight of herself on the screen as her husband showed in Giles and Morley.

'Char, the police are here.'

Charlene turned round. 'Oh hello, I tell you what, if you want me to do another one,' she said, turning back to the screen, 'maybe the make-up people in the studio could help out. I look a right sight...'

'We're rather hoping that won't be necessary, Mrs Lyndon,' said Giles. 'We have a lead that we hope is going to help us find your son's killer.'

'Did Robert have any friends with long red hair?' asked Morley.

'Red hair? I don't think so. Did he Bobby?'

'Did he have any friends?" would be a better question,' said Lyndon with a shake of the head.

'"Of course he had friends,' said Charlene. 'You know what kids are like, Inspector.' Charlene turned on what she thought might be a smile denoting affectionate remembrance.

'He was twenty-four, Char. He wasn't a kid and he didn't have much in the way of friends,' said her husband.

'He was our son!'

'There was a bloke with red hair came to door for him once. Couple of months ago,' said Lyndon. 'Something to do with some fox-hunting thing they were going on. He didn't come in or anything but I'm pretty sure I heard Robert call him, Kevin.'

'Can you remember anything else about him? What he was wearing?' asked Morley.

'Scruffy bugger, one of them wax jackets that had seen better days, stripey jersey, scarf, trousers with lots of pockets.'

'Thank you Mr Lyndon; you've been a great help. You too, Mrs Lyndon.'

'If you need me to do another broadcast, just ask, Inspector. I don't want any other mother going through what I've been through.'

'Thank you Mrs Lyndon, you've been very brave.'

'What do you think, sir?' asked Morley when they got outside.

'Sometimes I think I'm on the wrong planet, Morley,' said Giles.

'Yes, but about this Kevin, I mean.'

'Update the computer search. We're now looking for a red-haired Kevin arrested in the past for offences connected with hunt sabotage.'

'There's something very wrong,' said Steven. 'I'm convinced of it.'

John Macmillan looked over his glasses. 'Oh dear,' he said. 'I was rather afraid you were going to say that. Any idea what?'

Steven took a moment to compose his thoughts while the rain pattered on the windows behind Macmillan on a dull, wet afternoon. 'A junior minister from the Department of Health – a man named Lees – turns up at the Crick Institute hours after Devon's body is discovered and assures the police that the monkeys Devon had been using were part of an experiment being carried out by the professor on a new flu vaccine. One of Devon's colleagues, who had earlier gone through Devon's papers at the request of the police, comes to the same conclusion: Devon had been working on flu virus.'

'So far so good.'

'But someone – neither the institute nor the police – calls in the army, tells them to don full bio-hazard gear and hunt down the animals with guns. They kill five and incinerate the corpses almost before they hit the ground.'

'A bit over the top, I agree,' said Macmillan. 'But not necessarily suspicious. Any politician worth his salt would explain that away under care and concern for public safety and an opportunity for the army to try out their equipment under field conditions.'

Steven nodded and continued, 'One of the escaped

animals bites a pensioner in Holt.'

'Who is taken to hospital but is sent home after routine treatment for animal bites,' said Macmillan.

'I went to his house last night. He's no longer at home and neither is his wife who also came into contact with the animal. According to a neighbour, David Elwood is ill and has been admitted to some hospital where his wife is staying in the guest suite. The neighbour didn't know which hospital or even where it was but Mary Elwood confided in her that Harry was going to be well looked after and she got the impression that it might be "private".'

'Ah,' said Macmillan, leaning back in his chair and making a steeple with his fingers. 'And now the familiar smell of rat drifts into my nostrils too.' He leaned forward and picked up his pen to turn it end over end on the desk in front of him. 'So who do you think is being economical with the *verite* over this situation?'

'Difficult to say but I got the impression that Cleary, the colleague who went through Devon's papers, found out more than he was letting on. He seemed uneasy about something he'd read in them.'

'Didn't Devon confide in his colleagues?' asked Macmillan.

'Apparently he couldn't. He was obliged to keep certain aspects of his work secret since his appointment to the Vaccines Advisory Committee. Government regulations – at least that's what he told his colleagues.'

'Can't imagine why unless he was working on something really nasty,' said Macmillan.

'The Crick isn't licensed to work on high grade pathogens,' said Steven.

Macmillan and Steven exchanged glances which became telepathic in the ensuing silence.

'Surely not,' said Macmillan.

'Please God, not,' said Steven.

'They couldn't have been that stupid,' said Macmillan with more hope than conviction.

'It wouldn't just have been a breach of license conditions,' said Steven. 'Cleary told me that the Crick did not have the required BLR-4 lab facilities for working with real killer bugs,' said Steven.

'Or the security for keeping out intruders by all accounts,' added Macmillan. 'I suggest you have another word with Dr Cleary. Give him a hard time if you think he's holding back and I will seek out your man at the Department of Health. Lees, yes?'

'Nigel Lees.'

'Call me later. We'll compare notes.'

It was just after three in the afternoon when Steven turned into the grounds of the Crick Institute and saw that the efforts of the workmen to remove the graffiti from the walls had been less than successful. At best the words had been smeared so that they were no longer legible but what had once been a pleasant if unremarkable building now looked as if it were part of a run-down council estate. He said as much to the girl on the reception desk, which had now been re-installed.

'I know,' she said. 'It's the rendered surface that makes it so difficult to clean. I think they're considering painting over it but they can't decide on which type of paint to use.'

'If a committee is involved, that could take some time,' said Steven.

The girl smiled and gave a knowing nod. 'I hope you haven't come to see Dr Cleary,' she said. 'He's off sick. His wife called in this morning.'

'As a matter of fact, I have,' confessed Steven. 'And I've come a long way. Nothing serious I hope?'

'His wife, Shirley, called in this morning to say he had an upset stomach so it doesn't sound too serious. Something he ate, she thought.'

'What do you think about my chances of being able to visit him at home?'

The girl shrugged in a non-committal way.

'You wouldn't happen to have an address handy, would you?' Steven prompted with an encouraging smile.

The girl appeared uncertain. 'Actually...' she began.

Steven interrupted her. 'You're about to say that you are not allowed to give out that kind of information and quite right too.' He took out his warrant card and said, 'But in this case, you are. I assure you...'

'Well, if you say so,' said the girl. She typed a succession of small bursts into her keyboard and came up with, '25 West Shore Road, Sheringham. The house is called Four Winds.'

'Thank you,' said Steven. 'I'll pass on your good wishes, shall I?'

'Please do. I like Nick.'

'Unlike some others, eh?' smiled Steven. Sometimes he hated himself for doing it but if he sensed he might be able to get more information out of anyone he often did it just for the hell of it. You could never have too much, he reckoned.

'You could say,' smiled the woman. 'Nick's all right and the Professor was a real gentleman but some of them...' She shook her head and Steven smiled.

'I've nothing against foreigners; don't get me wrong but some of them treat me like I was invisible and it gets my back up. I suppose it's their culture but that doesn't excuse bad manners, my mother always said. It costs nothing to be polite and she was right, don't you think?'

'I couldn't agree more,' said Steven. 'Do you have many foreigners on the staff?'

'Let's see,' said the woman, looking upwards for inspiration. 'There's Pierre – Dr Bruel – he's French. Then there's Dr Martin and Dr Muller and Dr Sanchez. Four.'

'And the others are all English?'

'Apart from Paddy – Dr O'Brien – he's Irish. You might have guessed!' The woman laughed and Steven joined her. 'Just one big happy family, eh?'

'I wouldn't say that exactly but it's all right really, I suppose.'

'Good,' said Steven. 'I'll tell Dr Cleary you were asking after him.'

Four Winds proved to be an attractive detached house near the shore with black mock Tudor beams spanning a whitewashed exterior. It had leaded windows – or rather the modern double-glazed version of leaded windows and a black-painted, wood-panelled front door incorporating a thick circular pane of glass. Various children's toys were strewn about the garden and a rope ladder leading to a tree house hung from the lower branches of a sycamore tree, denuded by winter. Steven rang the bell and a pretty woman wearing denim jeans and a close-fitting black top answered.

'Mrs Cleary?'

'If you're selling kitchens or bathrooms, forget it.'

Steven shook his head.

'Monobloc driveways or roof linings?'

Steven smiled and showed her his warrant card. 'I spoke to your husband the other day,' he explained, 'but there are still some things I have to ask him. I travelled all the way up from London so when the institute told me he was ill I hoped I might still have a word with him...if he's not too ill, that is?'

'Just an upset stomach,' said the woman. 'Probably the sausages we had last night, although I'm all right and the kids are fine. Come in; I'll tell him you're here. I'm Shirley Cleary by the way.'

'Steven Dunbar; pleased to meet you.'

While he waited, Steven thought about the much loved and used British euphemism, "upset stomach". In Cleary's case that might well have been caused by being in a blue funk about what he had found out in Devon's office. He suspected that being handed a Sci-Med warrant card by his wife wasn't going to do his "upset stomach" much good and might even bring on another bout. He smiled when he heard feet rush along the landing upstairs and a door bang shut.

Shirley Cleary re-appeared, wearing a smile. She directed her eyes back upstairs and said, 'He'll fit you in between...engagements.'

'Nice place,' said Steven, trying to fill the silence.

'We like it and the kids absolutely love it,' said Shirley. 'A bit cold in the winter but a lot going for it in the summer. We lived in London before.'

Steven nodded as the sound of a toilet being flushed upstairs reached them.

'Kids will be at school, I guess,' said Steven.

Shirley nodded. 'Ten and seven. Boy and a girl.'

The bathroom door opened upstairs and feet padded along the landing. 'Why don't we talk up here, Dr Dunbar,' came the voice at the head of the stairs and then, with a weak attempt at humour, 'Might be safer.'

Steven climbed the stairs and Cleary dressed in a plaid dressing gown and slippers led the way into what was obviously his study. 'Bloody hell,' he said as he slumped down into his desk chair. 'I'm all washed out.'

Steven could see that Cleary appeared drawn but he could also see that his eyes had a haunted look. It was a look he'd seen many times before: it was fear. Cleary was afraid of something.

'What can I do for you?' asked Cleary.

'You can tell me what Timothy Devon was working on and what the escaped animals were really carrying,' said Steven without the hint of a smile.

'I told you,' protested Cleary. 'Flu virus.'

'You're not shitting yourself over flu virus,' said Steven, pressing on with his offensive and keeping Cleary fixed with an unblinking stare.

'Oh, Jesus,' said Cleary holding his head in his hands and taking slow deliberate breaths.

Steven let him suffer in silence.

'I wasn't lying. Tim *was* working on flu virus and the

animals *were* inoculated with flu virus...'

'But?'

Cleary made the effort to pull himself together. He sat up straight in his chair and cleared his throat before asking, 'How much do you know about flu?'

'A viral infection,' replied Steven. 'Cyclical. People get in winter. More serious than a cold and can even be fatal in the old and infirm but as a general rule, it's something that confines you to bed for a week or so and then you get over it.'

Cleary nodded. 'That's the view held by most people and one which may work against us in the end.'

'How so?'

'The influenza virus appears every winter: that's why people are so familiar with it and, like the saying goes, familiarity breeds contempt. But every year it is in effect a different virus because of changes in its antigenic structure. As a consequence it's more dangerous in some years than in others. 1957 and 1968 were bad years for instance but nothing like what happened in 1918.'

'Not too many people remember that, I imagine,' said Steven.

'Another thing that works against us. The 1918 pandemic is history: only the facts and statistics remain in the history books. In 1918 the flu virus killed between 20 and 40 million people across the globe. Think about it. The 1918 strain killed more people in one year than the Black Death did in its four-year rampage across the known world in the fourteenth century and it wasn't the infirm and aged it went for. It was the twenty to forty age groups that suffered worst.'

'Go on.'

'In the past few years scientists have uncovered the structure of the 1918 virus in an effort to find out what made it different.'

'How could they do that?'

'They obtained nucleic acid remnants of the virus from the bodies of dead soldiers who succumbed to the virus in 1918.'

'They re-created the 1918 virus?' exclaimed Steven. 'What the hell for?'

'I think the truthful answer to that might well be, because they could,' replied Cleary.

'But of course, they wouldn't admit to that,' said Steven.

Cleary shrugged and said, 'The rationale was that by re-creating the deadly 1918 strain they could design a vaccine against it.'

Steven looked incredulous. He said, 'They created a virus in order to design a vaccine to fight against it?'

'Does sound a bit suspect when you put it like that,' agreed Cleary.

'Jesus,' said Steven. 'Isn't science wonderful?'

'Science did learn from the study though,' said Cleary. 'They learned just how similar the 1918 strain was to some of the avian strains of flu virus we've seen emerge over the past few years. So much so, that many workers believe that the 1918 strain actually arose from a bird strain. A small mutation is all it would require for bird flu to turn into the pandemic strain.'

'Where does Devon's work come in to all this?' asked Steven.

'The World Health Organisation have been aware of the situation for some time. Almost every year avian flu breaks out in the Far East. The WHO swings into action and tries to keep the lid on the situation through mass culls of birds and the like. 'You've probably seen pictures on television of hens being carted off in cages to be slaughtered in Hong Kong.'

Steven nodded.

'The big fear has been that someone suffering from the early stages of human influenza would also come into contact with an avian strain and there would be a genetic cross-over between the viruses.'

'And we'd end up with the 1918 virus.'

'Just so. Well, this year there was an outbreak in Cambodia of an avian flu strain that resembled the 1918 virus more closely than ever before. This has convinced the WHO and major western governments that it's only a matter of time before we have a 1918 situation all over again, a world-wide pandemic. I'm sorry.' Cleary got up from his chair and made to go the door.

'Just before you dash off,' said Steven. 'Are you about to tell me that that's the strain Timothy Devon was working on?'

'More or less,' said Cleary, breaking off to make a run for the bathroom.

When he returned, Cleary plonked himself down in his chair with a sigh and said, 'Some lab work was carried out on the Cambodian strain in the lab before it was sent to Tim.'

'The last step in the mutation?' asked Steven.

'From what I could determine from his notes, that's what it looked like,' said Cleary. 'To all intents and purposes, Tim's strain is the 1918 virus.'

'I can understand why you are spending so much time in the lavatory,' said Steven. 'How much did you already know about this?'

'Nothing,' replied Cleary. 'I swear it. I found this out when I was going through Tim's papers. I recognised the strain designations from having read about them in the scientific literature and there was a letter from a university in the USA listing induced base mutations in the viral genome.'

'Is anyone else aware of what you know?'

'I didn't tell anyone, not even my wife.'

Steven thought for a moment before saying, 'Well, at least this explains why the man, Lees, from the Department of Health turned up so quickly on the day of the murder. DOH must know all about this. Did you have any contact with him? Did he say anything to you?'

Cleary shook his head. 'I met him and he knows I went through Tim's desk and reached the conclusion that he had been working on flu virus. I didn't say anything more than that but he may suspect that I know more than I let on.'

'Just like I did,' said Steven, 'But no one from DOH has questioned you since?'

'No.'

'I thought you told me that the Crick didn't have BSL-4 labs for handling high-risk pathogens?' said Steven.

'We don't. BSL-3 is the best we have.

'So Devon and whoever asked him to carry out the work – probably DOH – were in breach of regulations?'

'Strictly speaking, no,' replied Cleary. 'Flu virus is not on the list of high grade pathogens requiring BSL-4 labs.'

'But this wasn't ordinary flu virus.'

'The rule book wouldn't know that.'

'And common sense didn't come into it?'

'That's what it looks like in view of what happened,' agreed

Cleary. 'The strain Tim was working on wasn't actually the 1918 virus itself, which would have been covered by the regulations as a special case; it was a genetically altered avian virus... It's called Cambodia 5.'

'But it's identical to the 1918 strain,' said Steven.

'To all intents and purposes,' said Cleary.

'And now we have a monkey infected with Cambodia 5 virus running around the Norfolk countryside.'

Cleary shrugged uncomfortably.

'You say Devon was working on a vaccine against this strain?'

'Yes, that was quite clear,' said Cleary.

'Could you make out if he was having any success?'

'There was no indication of that.'

'Jesus.'

CHAPTER SEVEN

'I'm afraid he's not back from the Department of Health,' said Jean Roberts when Steven arrived to see John Macmillan. 'He shouldn't be long: he's been away three hours.'

Steven took a seat facing Jean and she said, 'How's Jenny? I hear you spent your leave with her.'

'She was in good form,' said Steven. 'It was good to see her for a decent amount of time. It's usually just every third weekend.'

'Must be difficult,' agreed Jean. 'What's she getting for Christmas?'

'A bike,' replied Steven. 'She was quite sure about that. A mountain bike with plenty of gears and lights back and front.'

'For coming down mountains in the dark?' said Jean.

'That sort of thing and oh yes, it should be pink.'

'Pink?' exclaimed Jean.

'Took me a while to find one but I managed.'

The door opened and John Macmillan passed through the office with a face like thunder. 'Brains in their backsides,' he muttered to no one in particular before closing his office door.

'Life's rich pattern,' murmured Jean.

'Sci-Med...an everyday story of scientific folk...' said Steven. 'Do you think he noticed me?'

Jean shrugged and showed the palms of her hands. She pressed the intercom button and said in her business voice, 'Steven Dunbar is here, sir.'

'Send him in.'

'Idiots,' said Macmillan as Steven closed the door behind him. 'They open Pandora's Box and then show me a piece of paper to demonstrate it was all perfectly legal and they've done no wrong. It's not on the list,' he mimicked in mincing tones. 'Not on the list! They should be on the list of the certifiably insane. Whatever happened to common sense in this country?'

'I have this theory that says it was wiped out and replaced by political correctness some time in the early nineties,' replied Steven. 'Sounds as if you've found out just what kind of flu virus Devon was really working with.'

'Unbelievable!'

'Was this solely a DOH initiative?' asked Steven.

'Hard to say. They're passing the buck like the parcel at a kids' party,' said Macmillan. 'But, reading between the lines, I think getting Devon to work on a vaccine against the 1918 strain was seen as being "far sighted" and "imaginative". Your man, Nigel Lees, apparently had a conversation with some chap from the World Health Organisation who convinced him he might get brownie points for initiative if he commissioned work on a new vaccine against bird flu.'

'I suppose he might have done if the work hadn't been assigned to a small institute in Norfolk without the proper lab facilities; one which was vulnerable to outside attack by animal rights extremists,' said Steven.

'According to Lees, thought *was* given to the need for heightened security surrounding the storage of such a virus on the premises. Cambodia 5 virus wasn't kept with the other viruses in the deep freeze. It was stored separately in a safe similar to the sort used on nuclear submarines to store launch codes: two keys were required to open it. Of course, in this case, it also had to be kept at low temperature.'

'Who was the other key-holder?'

'It had to be someone outside the institute to guard against the risk of terrorist attack so DOH held the second key. When Devon needed access to the live virus he would call DOH and the second key holder would come out to the institute accompanied by security people.'

'But when it came to testing the new vaccine it had to be done in live animals rather than locked safes,' said Steven.

'And that's when it all went tragically wrong.'

'Presumably the virus itself is still in that safe?'

'I've never been keen on presumption. Maybe you could check that out?' said Macmillan.

'Will do,' said Steven. 'Did you manage to get anything out of them about the Elwoods?'

Macmillan nodded. 'It's pretty much as you suspected. Harry Elwood didn't feel well so they are keeping both him and his wife under surveillance for the time being.'

'And the escaped animal?'

'The army are still hunting it.'

'And tonight's lucky winner in the police computer draw of the week for red-headed suspects is...could I have drum roll please?'

'Get on with it,' said Morley to his friend and fellow sergeant, Keith Barnes in the criminal records section.

'Kevin Shanks, aged twenty-four, drop-out from Liverpool University, two illegal substance convictions and three for breach of the peace at hunt meetings. A member of the animal rights movement since 1999. Lives in Norwich...and has long red hair.'

'Address?

'Last known address at time of arrest seven months ago was a shared flat in Elton Road, number sixteen.'

'You're a star Barnesy. Giles will be well pleased.'

'Anything to help a pal...who'll be buying me a beer at his earliest convenience?' said Barnes.

'Don't hold your breath mate; I'm beginning to think I'll never see the inside of a pub again.'

Morley relayed the information to Giles.

'We're off then,' said Giles looking at his watch. 'It's just about our time anyway.'

'Our time, sir?'

'Three a.m. It's the time when policemen knock on doors in all the best books; something to do with disorientation of the mind in the wee small hours. It makes it more difficult for the villains to lie to us.'

'Yes, sir,' said Morley. He didn't sound convinced.

After the third heavy knock, a youth wearing a grubby T-shirt and boxer shorts opened the door to the flat in Elton Road. He blinked against the light, scratched his crotch and mumbled, 'What the fuck do you want?'

'Police,' said Morley, holding up his warrant card. 'We'd like to talk to Kevin Shanks.

'He aint here.'

'I think we'll just check on that sir,' said Morley, brushing past the youth.

'Pigs, everybody! Pig attack!' the boy cried out.

'Shut it!' warned Giles, taking the boy by the scruff of the neck and pinning him against the wall.

There was a general scuffling in the flat: doors opened and shut and there was the sound of a toilet being flushed. 'They're flushing away drugs, sir,' said Morley.

'I know,' smiled Giles. 'Reward enough, don't you think? Let's hope it cost them a bundle.' He was watching bodies emerge from sleeping bags on the floor of the living room, hands held up to shield their eyes from the light he'd switched on. One of the girls had no clothes on. 'What the fuck are you looking at, you fucking pervert?' she demanded.

'A young woman with no brains, no class, no sense and no manners,' replied Giles. 'How am I doing?'

'Here, have you got a fucking warrant?' demanded a spotty youth with what looked like dried vomit on his T-shirt. He tried to come towards Giles but found it difficult to make a path through the empty bottles on the floor.

Giles ignored all questions as he continued his search for someone with long red hair. He moved through to the first of the bedrooms where a good looking boy was in bed with two girls. 'What are you looking at, tosser?' the boy demanded.

'An arsehole?' suggested Giles calmly. '...and that was without phoning a friend.'

'You've got no fucking right...'

'So sue me. Get up.'

'Fucking pig, you've no right to burst in here and...'

'Shut the fuck up!' snapped Giles as he returned to the

living room and silence descended on the flat. 'We're looking for Kevin Shanks...

'You're still looking.'

'In connection with a murder inquiry,' completed Giles.

'He aint here, pigs.'

'I can see that,' said Giles quietly. 'Where is he?'

'Think we'd tell you?'

'No,' said Giles matter of factly, 'I don't, but I am obliged to ask you officially so that I can come back and charge the lot of you later with being accessories to murder.'

'You can't do that!' protested the spotty youth.

'Are you really going to bet your pimply arse on that, sonny?' said Giles in measured tones.

The boy looked uncertain.

'Kevin's staying the night with his girlfriend,' said one of the others, 'Her folks are away.'

This attracted the disapproval of the others.

'Fuck this, I aint getting into any murder rap,' the boy retorted.

'Girlfriend's name? Address?'

Morley wrote down the details and the two policemen left. 'If anyone lifts that phone to warn Shanks, we'll come back and charge all of you,' was Giles' parting shot.

Giles paused before getting into the car and Morley asked, 'Everything all right, sir?'

'I was just thinking about the parade at the Cenotaph a couple of weeks ago,' he replied. He inclined his head in the direction of the flat they'd just left. 'That lot make you wonder why these blokes bothered.'

* * *

Morley turned into a pleasant suburban crescent of 1930s bungalows and brought the car to a halt outside number 27.

Giles read, 'Hellvellyn,' on the house name plate by the side of the door. 'Must have more imagination than me...'

Giles stopped half way up the garden path and said, 'Something tells me Shanks is going to do a runner when the door bell goes. You go round the back.' He waited for half a minute to give Morley time to get into position then rang the bell. After the second ring a light clicked on and a girl's voice asked, 'Who is it?'

'Police, open the door please.'

'My God, do you know what time it is? Give me a moment to get some clothes on.'

Giles sighed. 'No thoughts of mummy and daddy and the terrible accident they might have been involved in?' he murmured.

Time passed and the door did not open but Giles did not bother to ring or knock again. He felt he had read the situation correctly. 'Any second now...' he said under his breath. The sound of shouting and a short struggle came from the back garden. Seconds later Morley appeared with a red haired man held bent over in an arm-lock in front of him.

'Mr Shanks was just on his way out for an early morning run, sir.'

'Nice of you to postpone it, sir,' said Giles pleasantly, then with a change of demeanour, 'Kevin Shanks, I'm arresting you in connection with the murders of Robert Lyndon and Timothy Devon. You need not say...'

A girl appeared at the front door, protesting loudly. 'Leave him! Leave him alone! He hasn't done anything!'

'Mr Shanks is being arrested in connection with a murder inquiry, Madam. Step back please.'

'Murder?' exclaimed the girl. 'Don't be ridiculous. Kevin wouldn't hurt a fly. He wouldn't say boo to a goose.'

'Then he's got nothing to worry about,' said Giles.

'Tell him, Kevin,' pleaded the girl. 'Don't let them walk all over you. Don't let them fit you up.'

'Fit you up? You watch too much television, Madam,' said Giles.

'Tell them about the skinheads, Kevin,' pleaded the girl.

The red headed man looked like a deer caught in headlights. Giles noticed that he'd put his T-shirt on inside out in his haste. His allegiance to Nirvana had to be read backwards. 'I'm sorry, Mandy,' he stammered. 'I never meant to...honest to God, I never meant to hurt Stig but he wouldn't see reason. I did it for us. I told him no one would ever believe the truth.'

The girl looked at him in horror and took a step backwards, holding her hands to her face. 'You killed Stig?... It was you? How could you? You said it was skinheads...'

Giles lowered himself into his chair in the interview room and Morley switched on the tape and initialled it. Giles looked at Shanks and said, 'It's been a long night, son. Let's not make it any longer. You killed Robert Lyndon. You killed him because he was planning to come to us and confess to the murder of Timothy Devon at the Crick Institute.'

'Christ no!' said Shanks, almost leaping out his chair. 'We had nothing to do with the old guy's murder. Sure, Stig was threatening to tell you about us doing the institute. He thought you'd believe him when he told you we had nothing to do with the old guy's death. I kept telling him you would stitch us up anyway but he wouldn't listen. I tried reasoning with him, honest to God I did, but he was shitting himself. We had a bit of a fight after we left the pub and Stig ended up getting stabbed. I never meant for it to happen...it just did. Christ, I'm really sorry...' Shanks broke down in tears and Giles looked at Morley.

Giles scratched his neck: it was itching because he needed a shave. Three hours had passed, the dawn had come up on a frosty, misty morning and Shanks still refused to admit to the torture and murder of Timothy Devon.

'You do realise what your defence amounts to, don't you?' he said. 'A big boy done it and ran away... How believable is that? The Prosecution will be in danger of dying laughing. Why don't you just come clean and get it off your chest? You're already going down for the murder of Robert Lyndon so what odds does it make?'

'I didn't do it!' insisted Shanks. 'I keep telling you that. Stig and I were there and we sprayed the walls and messed up the furniture but the old guy was alive when we left.'

Giles pushed the photographs of Devon across the desk.

'Jesus!' exclaimed Shanks and turned away with his hand to his mouth.

'I don't think Jesus is going to listen to you either,' said Giles.

'It must have been Ally,' said Shanks, shaking his head. 'He must have gone back.'

'Ah,' said Giles flatly. 'The big boy.'

'It was his idea in the first place.'

'Of course,' said Giles. 'Well, it would be, wouldn't it?'

'It bloody was!' protested Shanks.

'Does the big boy have a last name?'

Shanks shook his head.

'Let me guess,' said Giles. 'You have no idea where he lives either?'

Shanks shook his head.

'I seem to have known that big boy all my life,' said Giles. 'The things he's got up to in his time... Take him away.'

'What do you think, sir?' asked Morley when they had both returned to Giles' office.

Giles shook his head. 'I'm sorely tempted to charge the bastard with both murders and be done with it but there's something not quite right...'

'He's not the type, you mean?'

'Exactly that, Sergeant, he's not the type.'

'He could have been on drugs at the time.' suggested Morley.

'That's a thought,' said Giles. 'And one I didn't consider... Do you know why not?'

Morley shook his head.

'Because I'm bloody knackered. Let's get some sleep.'

'I hear congratulations are in order,' said Chief Superintendent James Rydell.

'I think that might be a bit premature, sir,' replied Giles, wishing he could say otherwise.

Rydell's brow furrowed. 'I'm not with you. 'You've got the villain who broke into the Crick and you've charged him with a double murder. What's the problem?'

'Shanks was one of those who broke into the institute and he certainly murdered Robert Lyndon who was also concerned in the break-in but I don't think Shanks murdered the professor...'

'Are you trying to tell me the professor was already dead when these two broke in?' exclaimed Rydell.

'No, of course not, sir, but Shanks claims a third man was involved and that he was responsible for torturing and murdering Timothy Devon.'

'A big boy done it...'

'That was my first thought too, sir, but...'

'So the other two just stood and watched while this third man put Devon through a living hell?'

'No sir, Shanks claims that he and Lyndon weren't present. The third man went back to the institute on his own.'

Rydell looked incredulous. 'And you believe this rubbish?' he exclaimed.

Giles felt uncomfortable in pursuing a line he had no real wish to. 'I just can't see Shanks as the sort who would...'

'Commit murder?' exclaimed Rydell. 'He stuck a knife into his best friend for God's sake. What more do you want?'

'It's the systematic torture thing, sir. It just doesn't fit. Shanks isn't the type in my view.'

'He's known to take drugs, isn't he?'

'Yes sir.'

'Well, Inspector, people change 'type' when they get into that sort of business. I'm surprised you didn't realise that.'

'Yes sir, but...'

'But what?'

'I'd like another go at breaking him down before we charge

him with both murders. He may know more about this third man than he's letting on.'

Rydell looked at Giles in silence for a long moment before saying, 'Have your go but then you charge him with both murders whether he breaks down or not. Understood?'

'Yes sir.'

Giles returned to his office where Morley was waiting. 'I take it he didn't wear it?' said Morley, interpreting the expression on Giles' face.

''Fraid not,' said Giles. 'What do you think, Morley? Honestly.'

'I think I'm with the Chief Super, sir. I think Shanks and Lyndon did it.'

'Set up the interview room, will you?'

Shanks and his appointed legal representative were seated at one side of the table when Giles entered and Morley prepared to start the tape. Giles nodded and Morley initialled it.

'So, tell us about Ally,' said Giles.

'Not much I can tell you,' replied Shanks.

'C'mon, you've had a whole night to make something up. I take it you didn't sleep too well?'

'I'm not making it up,' said Shanks.

'So tell us about him.'

'I can't. I don't know anything.'

'You mean he was a stranger who turned up in the pub on the day of the raid and asked if he could come along for the fun of it and you said, yeah, why not.'

'Of course not.'

'Then don't waste my time! There was no Ally, was there?'

'Yeah, I swear on my mother's life. He set up the whole thing.'

'If you think for one second that a jury is going to swallow that, you probably still write letters to Santa. But maybe you think it doesn't matter as you're going down anyway but it does... Being in denial of a crime you're convicted of will stop you even being considered for parole. There will be no review board. You will go down for ever and ever, amen.'

'I did not kill the old guy.'

'So Ally did it; why?'

'Ally was really intense about things. He really hated what they were doing to animals in these places.'

'So did you.'

'Yeah, but...not like Ally. He was...'

'A nutter?'

'Fanatical, I suppose. He sort of despised the rest of us for being so soft. He said that nothing would change unless we took some real action that would make people sit up and pay attention.'

'Well, you certainly did that, son,' said Giles quietly. Once more he pushed the photograph of Devon's body across the table.

Shanks shied away from it as he had done before. He said, 'I didn't think he would do anything like that... Christ!'

'Where did you first meet him?'

'We were sabbing a hunt near Leicester.'

'He just turned up?'

'Yeah, he turned up on the day and really pissed some people off by telling them they'd be as well waving their dicks in the air as waving the placards they were carrying. No one read them. No one gave a shit.'

'What did he do himself?'

'He pulled one of the huntsmen off his horse and gave him a bit of a kicking. He said that's what they really understood.'

'Was he arrested?'

Shanks shook his head. 'Ally was too smart for the pi...police. He said that anyone who was with him should meet him in the Black Flag that night then he pissed off smartish.'

'But you met up with him later?'

'Stig and I went along to the pub to hear what he had to say. None of the others did because of the way he'd made fun of them. He told them they were nothing more than a bunch of middle class tossers having a laugh. He said they would never do anything effective to help the animals in case it upset mummy or daddy.'

'So, what did he have to say later?' asked Giles.

'More of the same, really. If we really cared about the animals we'd do something about it, something that hit the bastards where it hurt. He said he was going to carry out a raid on a research lab and wreck it so they couldn't hurt the animals any more. He asked if we were with him and we said yes. He gave us the time and place to be and he picked us up in his van. He supplied the paint and everything. We tied up the old boy and wrecked the place; then we pissed off.'

'All three of you?'

'God's honest truth. Ally dropped Stig and me off in Swaffham where we went for a drink. Ally didn't want to come: he didn't drink. That's the last we saw of him.'

'Description?'

'Older than us, early thirties, black hair, six one, medium build.'

'What was the name of the hunt you met him at?'

'The Thorne; bunch of wankers.'

Giles nodded to Morley who said, 'Interview suspended 11.27 a.m. Inspector Giles leaving the room.'

'Still feel the same?' Giles asked Morley when he joined him.

'I think we have to check this guy out, see if he exists,' said Morley.

'Good. Get over to the pub he mentioned, the Black Flag; take along some pictures of Shanks and Lyndon; see if the landlord remembers them. In particular, does he remember a third guy?'

'Yes, sir. You're not going to charge him with Devon's murder?'

'Not just yet.'

'Rydell won't be pleased.'

Giles shrugged and tried out a bad John Wayne impression. 'Sometimes, Morley, a man has to do what a man has to do.'

'Yes sir, and what do you have to do exactly?'

'Talk to the master of the Thorne Hunt.'

CHAPTER EIGHT

Steven phoned to make sure that Nick Cleary was back at work before driving up to the Crick Institute in the morning. He was. Thinking about Cleary and his behaviour on the journey up made him think about the uneasy relationship between science and society. Cleary's first reaction on finding out what Devon had been doing had not been to blow the whistle and issue a warning, it had been to keep quiet and say nothing. Why? What was behind that? Did loyalty to a dead colleague come before duty to the public in trying to prevent a possible national disaster? Was the public school ethos still that strong in the UK? There was certainly more secrecy around than in the USA where public scrutiny of government was accepted if not encouraged. Trying to get information from UK government departments was often like trying to get blood from the proverbial stone. It seemed as if low level clerks were trained to say, 'I am not at liberty to divulge that information,' on their first day while their masters hid behind, 'I'm afraid I can't comment on individual cases,' or 'It would be inappropriate of me to comment at this moment in time.'

A plague on all their houses, thought Steven as he gunned the MG past a slow moving tractor. There was without doubt a place for secrecy in government but all too often it was being used as a smokescreen for incompetence.

'Just one of these things, I suppose,' replied Cleary when Steven inquired about his health. 'Right as rain now.'

Steven wondered briefly about confession being as good for 'upset stomachs' as it was reputed to be for the soul; before asking Cleary if he was aware that a special safe had been installed for Devon to keep the Cambodia 5 virus in.

Cleary shook his head. 'News to me but I suppose Tim couldn't have told us anyway.'

'You'd think it would be difficult to install something like that without anyone being aware of what was going on,' said Steven.

'Perhaps it was done over the weekend or in the middle of the night,' suggested Cleary.

'I suppose,' said Steven. 'This may seem like a daft question but any idea where it might be?'

Cleary looked perplexed. 'I'm ashamed to say that I haven't,' he said. 'I haven't noticed anything new appearing in any of the labs and there's certainly nothing like that down in any of the animal rooms. I can't understand why the Department of Health man didn't say anything about this when he was here at the weekend. You'd think he would at least have mentioned the presence of a secret virus store!'

Steven snorted. 'DOH obviously thought that they could keep everything secret at that time. They hoped they might get away with everyone thinking that the animals were infected with "just flu" – although you going through Devon's desk must have given them a bad moment.'

'It didn't do me a lot of good either,' said Cleary. 'It was a bit of a shock, I can tell you.'

'But the fact that you didn't let on what you'd discovered must have encouraged them to push their luck,' said Steven.

Cleary picked up on the accusation. 'I had no idea what was going on,' he said. 'I didn't know what to do. I take it DOH has now come clean about their involvement?'

Steven nodded. 'Most people confess immediately after they're found out and break open a bottle of regret.'

'Why don't you just call DOH and ask where the virus safe is,' suggested Cleary.

'Call it inter-departmental rivalry but I'd rather hoped to find it without having to ask them. Could it be in the professor's office?'

'I don't recall Tim having any work carried out in there in recent weeks,' said Cleary. 'Although, in view of what we said about the weekend or middle of the night, maybe that's not surprising. I did notice that he had a couple of new filing cabinets when I was going through his papers...'

Steven smiled. 'Shall we take a look?'

Cleary got out the key for Devon's office, which he'd been keeping in his own desk drawer, and they went along the corridor to Devon's room, slaloming between workmen's ladders and equipment, trying to talk above the noise of drills.

It went quiet again as Cleary closed the office door behind them. 'These two in the corner,' he said, indicating two metal, three-drawer units in civil service green. 'They're new.'

Steven pulled out the top drawer of the first cabinet and found nothing more sinister than alphabetical file holders holding general information files about safety and fire regulations. There was also a thick folder on Home Office rules regarding the housing and use of experimental animals.

Much the same applied to the next drawer and the next: routine paperwork. Steven was beginning to think that they were just everyday office filing cabinets when he pulled out the bottom drawer of the second cabinet and was left with a false drawer front in his hand. 'Well, this is different,' he said, pulling back a secondary inner leaf to expose the door of a small safe with a red LED blinking on and off at one second intervals. It looked heavy and secure and had been cemented into the floor, its electrical connections enclosed in armoured sheathing.

'Bloody hell, this was built to last,' said Cleary when he bent down to take a look. 'You'd need a small nuclear device to open it.'

'I suppose that was the general idea,' said Steven. 'Unless of course, you had the keys...' He pointed to the two key-card slots in the front door. One of the cards had been left in its slot. 'That was careless.'

'That's not like Tim to do something like that,' said Cleary. 'But I suppose it didn't matter too much when you have to have the second one present before you can open it. Maybe he just kept the card there.'

'No,' said Steven, shaking his head emphatically. 'He would have been instructed never to do that. Leaving one card in place destroys the whole point of the thing. As it is, it's just an ordinary safe that anyone can open if he can get his hands on the other card. Leaving one key there is a big no no. Devon would have been told that.'

'I take your point, said Cleary.

Steven thought for a moment before saying, 'But it is interesting to hear you say that doing something like that would be out of character for the professor...'

'Tim was an absolute stickler for protocol and detail,' said Cleary.

'Do you have a plastic bag?' Steven asked

'Sure, I'll just get one.'

'And forceps too,' said Steven.

Cleary returned a few moments later with a roll of small plastic bags and a pair of forceps, still in their sterile wrapping, the black stripes on the special sealing tape indicating that they had been through autoclave sterilisation. He handed both to Steven who'd put on surgical gloves – there was a box of them at the side of the small hand-basin in the office. 'Just in case it wasn't the professor who left the card in the slot...' he said. He extracted the key-card with the forceps and dropped it into a plastic bag.

'I take it, this means you are going to take this key away with you?' said Cleary, watching Steven seal the bag.

'Yes,' said Steven.

'What if DOH should come to call, wanting to reclaim their virus?'

'You can tell them Sci-Med has the other key.'

'They *will* be pleased,' said Cleary.

'It was more embarrassment I was hoping for,' said Steven. 'This was a crazy operation from the outset.'

Two days later, Steven was requested to attend a meeting of high level officials from the Department of Health, the Ministry of Defence and the Security Service. Just before they went in, Steven asked Macmillan why he thought Sci-Med had been invited to attend.

'Maybe it's the cynicism of my years,' said Macmillan. 'But intuition tells me that we are about to be asked to cooperate.'

'In what?'

'In keeping our mouths shut,' replied Macmillan.

Nigel Lees from DOH, who had obviously been detailed to clear up his own mess, convened the meeting. He opened by 'regretting' what had happened at the Crick Institute. They had had a difficult decision to make and in the light of unforeseen events it had turned out to be 'ill-advised.'

Steven noted that he had avoided using the word 'wrong'. 'When I offer you an explanation for our actions, I hope you will accept that what we did was for the best of motives and very much in the long-term interests of the public.'

Steven noted that 'he' had also become 'we'. He and Macmillan exchanged cynical glances.

'When Dr Malcolm, our man on the World Health Organisation vaccines committee, approached us and stressed the immediacy of the problem regarding bird flu we felt that we should act rather than just table it for consideration in the future. We approached Professor Devon and I suppose it was our hope,' Lees cleared his throat and continued, 'that he would be successful in designing a vaccine against avian strains of influenza in time for incorporation into the vaccine schedule for next year. As you are probably aware, the decision as to what flu strains to use in vaccine preparation has to be made as early as possible. In view of the warning from the WHO about the imminent high risk of an outbreak of a form of the disease to rival the 1918 pandemic, we thought it imperative to pursue this course of action with vigour.'

'Without reference to cabinet?'

'It was…our…my own initiative,' admitted Lees.

'That doesn't explain why you commissioned the work to be carried out at the Crick Institute without proper security or facilities' said Macmillan.

'We quite understand your concern,' said Lees, who gave the impression of a man used to handling hostile questioning. 'But it was a logistical thing and time wasn't on our side. We thought Professor Devon the right man for the job but when we approached him it was clear that he had no desire to move to Porton Down, which was our first suggestion. Apart from his reluctance to move, he pointed out that there wouldn't be time to set up a new lab there anyway and still make the deadline so, in spite of our misgivings and in view of the anomaly surrounding the regulations for work on flu virus, we agreed that the work could take place at the Crick.'

Steven took note of how neatly Lees had moved the blame on to the dead man and it irked him. 'Exploiting that "anomaly" could have wiped out half the country,' he said. 'You must have realised the dangerous nature of the virus whatever the "rule book" happens to say about influenza virus.'

For the first time, Lees lost his suave self assurance. 'Well, luckily it didn't,' he said sharply.

'One animal is still missing,' said Steven.

'And that is regrettable. However, I'm sure that the army are on top of things. The main thing is that no member of the public has yet come into contact with the escaped animal and therefore there can be no risk to the public at large. It may well be that the animal is already dead.'

'Or on its way to London in a taxi,' said Steven, attracting an angry glance from Lees but it was only there for a moment before the urbane air of calm reasonableness returned. 'We at DOH would, of course, prefer if this whole unfortunate affair were to end here and without repercussion. In a nutshell, this is why you were asked here this morning, ladies and gentlemen – to request your understanding and forbearance. We sincerely regret what happened but we do hope that you accept the well-intentioned motivation behind it. Her Majesty's Government, at the highest level, has decreed that it is of the utmost importance that we prepare ourselves for any likely outbreak of disease in our country and not only from natural causes, as I'm sure our Defence colleagues will agree – the threat of biological attack is ever present. I do hope you will let matters end here but of course, if your conscience should insist that questions be raised in the house and that the matter should be taken into the public domain then of course, we will understand...we were at fault.'

Nice finish, thought Steven. Not a dry eye in the house.

The senior man from the Ministry of Defence was first to respond. 'I'm sure none of us here wants a scandal,' he began. 'There's little to be gained by trying to score cheap political points off each other.'

'And a scandal is precisely what we'll have if this hits the papers,' said a woman from the Security Services. 'There will be demands for resignations and calls for public inquiries from all varieties of *homo politicus* jostling for position and their place in the limelight.'

'Not to mention ambulance-chasing lawyers submitting claims for compensation for imagined trauma from half the population of Norfolk,' said the Home Office minister.

'Then I am delighted that we all seem to be agreed, ladies and gentlemen,' said Lees. 'We let the matter end here?'

There were no dissenting voices but when the hubbub died down Macmillan said quietly, 'If the design of a vaccine against the imminent threat from an..."altered avian strain" was an absolute imperative for DOH, what's happening about it now?'

'Ah,' said Lees. He smiled like a naughty schoolboy caught scrumping apples. 'I was just about to bring that up... Although we don't have the results of Professor Devon's last experiments due to his untimely death, we do know from a report he submitted three weeks ago that he had been successful in constructing several attenuated forms of the...er...virus and had high hopes for one of these strains being useful as the seed strain for an effective vaccine. Ideally...we would like work to continue on it at full speed, still with a view to incorporating it in the vaccine schedule for February...'

My God, he means at the Crick, thought Steven. He's got balls; I'll give him that. He could see that others were exchanging surprised glances.

'As this strain is – and I can't stress this too highly – a much attenuated form of the...er...Cambodian virus, we were rather hoping that you might all agree to work being allowed to continue at the Crick. There simply would not be time to move the project elsewhere... Naturally there would be a thorough overhaul of security measures...'

'Just how attenuated is "much attenuated"?' asked the Security Services woman.

'The BSL-3 labs at the Crick would be more than adequate for its containment,' replied Lees.

'Who would do the work?' asked Macmillan.

'At the outset, when we asked Professor Devon about a possible collaborator on his staff at the Crick should one be necessary, he suggested Dr Leila Martin in view of her past experience with flu vaccine both with WHO and in her own lab in Washington. We believe that Dr Martin is more than capable of carrying on the work.'

'As long as there's no danger to the public,' said the Home Office minister. 'It makes sense.'

'None at all,' said Lees.

'But is there going to be time?' asked Macmillan.

Lees made an ambivalent gesture with his shoulders. 'You're right to question that,' he said. 'It's going to be touch and go but Dr Martin has agreed to give it her best shot and work all the hours that God sends. We, for our part, have made arrangements with the vaccine manufacturers to delay things until the very last moment in order to incorporate any new seed strain should it arrive late. Red tape will be cut to an absolute minimum. No one wants a repeat of this year's debacle when the USA was 50 million doses short of winter vaccine and we were twenty percent down on requirements ourselves.'

'So you've already asked her?' said Steven.

'I'm sorry?' said Lees.

'Dr Martin, you've already asked her.'

Lees suddenly saw what Steven was getting at and smiled disarmingly. 'I'm sorry if you thought that presumptuous but I felt that we had to put the idea to her before I approached you people on the subject...otherwise...there wouldn't have been any point...'

Nicely done, thought Steven. Lees was doing the little boy lost act to perfection and it got murmurs of understanding all around the table.

As the meeting broke up and people started to leave, Lees caught up with Steven and Macmillan in the corridor. 'I believe you chaps are in possession of a certain key-card that belongs to DOH? I think you will agree that the sooner we remove all traces of the Cambodia 5 virus from the institute the better?'

Steven said, 'The card should be back from the lab tomorrow.'

'The lab?' exclaimed Lees, unable to keep the surprise out of his voice.

'We asked for some tests on it,' said Macmillan unhelpfully.

'I see. Perhaps you'd be so good as to call me and I can make arrangements for its collection,' said Lees.

'No,' said Macmillan.

Lees was taken aback again. 'I'm sorry; I don't think I quite understand...'

'The virus in that safe is one of the most dangerous pathogens on the face of the Earth,' said Macmillan, 'whatever the anomalies of the regulations.'

Nice one, thought Steven.

'Absolutely, I have no argument with that,' agreed Lees. 'That is exactly why I want it removed.'

'Then until that time we should observe security precautions to match the danger. If we hand over the card you will be in possession of both keys – not good practice.'

'I hardly think…' began Lees.

'Professor Devon hardly thought that animal rights extremists were going to attack his institute,' said Macmillan. 'I think Dr Dunbar should retain possession of the one we hold until such times as secure arrangements are in place for the opening of the safe.'

'Very well,' said Lees with a sigh of resignation.

'I'll call you when the card comes back and we can arrange for myself and the other key-holder to be present at the Crick at an agreed time,' said Steven. 'I'll leave it to you to arrange suitable secure transport?'

'Of course,' said Lees. 'Might I ask why the card was sent to a lab?'

'Just a precaution, Mr Lees. We wanted to be sure that Professor Devon was the last person to touch it.'

'But he was the only person at the institute who even knew of its existence,' said Lees. 'Who else did you have in mind?'

'We didn't,' said Steven. 'Call it routine Sci-Med procedure. Who is the second card holder by the way?'

'As a matter of fact, I am,' said Lees.

'Then I'll see you up at the institute in the next few days,' said Steven.

Frank Giles drove through the black iron gates of Stratton House and slowly round the semi-circular drive, taking comfort from the crunch of his tyres on the gravel. 'Hi honey, I'm home,' he murmured in admiration of the solid stone-built building with its tall Georgian windows and Virginia creeper clambering over the walls. There was a black Volvo 4 x 4 sitting to the right of the steps leading up to the front door so he parked beside it and got out to the sound of dogs barking and a power saw operating somewhere in the woods which surrounded the property on three sides. His tug at the brass bell-pull was rewarded with a distant ringing and a fresh outbreak of dog barking. A tall, blonde woman appeared at the door, holding back two black Labradors on their leads.

'Yes?

Giles showed his warrant card. 'DI Giles, madam. I wonder if I might have a word with Mr Hugo Blackmore?'

'Hugo's not in at the moment. I'm Ingrid, Hugo's wife. Can I help?'

'I'm afraid not, madam. Any idea when your husband will be back?'

'He went into Nottingham early this morning but he did say he'd be back for lunch. What time is it now?'

'Ten to twelve,' replied Giles.

'Then perhaps you'd like to wait?'

'That's very kind,' said Giles. 'You've got quite a handful there,' he said, eyeing the dogs straining at the leash.

'They haven't had their walk yet,' said Ingrid. 'Come through: the kitchen's warmer.'

Giles followed the tall slim woman into the kitchen and saw what she meant. The Aga had done its job.

'Tea? Coffee?'

'Coffee would be good.'

'I hope Hugo's not in any trouble.'

'No trouble, madam, just a few questions about the Hunt I believe he's involved with.'

'Involved with?' laughed Ingrid. 'It's his whole *raison d'etre*. God knows what's going to happen when this legislation to ban hunting goes through.'

'You don't sound terribly upset by the prospect,' said Giles.

'I'm Swedish,' replied Ingrid. 'Many English customs are a complete mystery to me and always will be, I fear. Milk? Sugar?'

'White, no sugar,' replied Giles. 'You speak perfect English.'

'I know the words,' smiled Ingrid. 'I don't always know all the nuances. I constantly get into trouble.'

'So do I,' laughed Giles. 'Although with me it's the words not the nuances that get me into bother.'

'You probably just say what you think,' said Ingrid, 'just like people in Sweden. It's much harder to find out what people really think in this country. They say one thing but mean another.'

'Have you been married long, madam?'

'Six years and please stop calling me "madam". I met Hugo when he came to Sweden with a trade mission. I was working for a biotech company.'

'So this will be quite a change for you,' said Giles.

Ingrid's reply was cut short by the sound of a car horn outside. 'You're in luck,' she said. 'Hugo's back early.'

Ingrid excused herself and went off to meet her husband. No doubt she would warn him of the police presence in the house, thought Giles.

'What can I do for you, Inspector?' asked the tall, handsome man who came into the kitchen. Giles disliked him on sight but admitted to himself that this might have something to do with the fact that he was tall, handsome, rich and had a beautiful Swedish wife. Silverspoonaphobia had always been a problem for him. 'Just a few questions about your involvement with the Thorne Hunt, sir.'

'Tony's not made it illegal already has he?'

'Tony, sir?'

'Tony Blair and his merry band of yobbos, trots and social workers who wouldn't know the country if you stuck an oak tree up their arse with directions pinned to it.'

'Well, I'll leave you boys together,' smiled Ingrid, as she backed out the door.

'I understand you had a bit of trouble a couple of months back,' said Giles. 'With hunt saboteurs?'

'We have trouble with them all the time. There's a type of person who becomes a hunt saboteur, you know, Inspector. Feckless bastards, the lot of them.'

Giles had noticed this. He had also noticed there was a type of person who appeared on horseback at hunt meetings but didn't say so. 'I understand there was one occasion recently when you were pulled from your horse by one of these saboteurs, sir?'

'Him?' exclaimed Blackmore. 'The wog? Whoops, shouldn't say that I suppose; I could end up in the dock these days. Mustn't upset our Muslim brothers, must we eh? Oh no. They can come over here and yank me off my bloody horse and kick shit out of me but say anything about it and you're in trouble. Crazy!'

'Are you saying the man who pulled you from your horse was coloured, sir?'

'You bet he was.'

'Did he say anything to you, sir?'

'No, he was enjoying kicking me while I was down too much.'

'Did anyone say anything to him?'

'One of the great unwashed called out, 'Leave him be, Ali, he's had enough.'

'You're sure he was called, Ali, sir?'

'Aren't they all?'

Giles remained silent.

'Yes, Inspector, I'm sure.'

CHAPTER NINE

'Are you seriously telling me that you want to start looking for someone called Ali among the Asian community across Norfolk and the Midlands?' exclaimed Chief Superintendent Rydell. 'Please tell me this is some kind of seasonal joke.'

'I know it seems somewhat daunting, sir' said Giles.

'Somewhat daunting?' mocked Rydell. 'Christ! Half of bloody Leicester is called Ali!'

Giles remained silent, knowing that Rydell would realise what he'd just said and hoping this might strengthen his own position.

Rydell interpreted the silence correctly. 'You know damn well what I mean Inspector and you also know I'm no racist.'

'Of course not, sir.'

'But facts are facts. It would be like looking for someone called Wu in China.'

'Or a Freemason in the police force; spoilt for choice.' Giles received a black look. 'I know what you mean sir, but if we don't follow this up we could be accused of allowing a psychopath to continue wandering the streets.'

'If we were to even contemplate such an investigation with so little to go on, it would swallow up our budget for the next ten years,' said Rydell.

'I wasn't suggesting we do that, sir.' He had a mountain to climb here. 'But I tend to believe Shanks when he says it was this Ali character who tortured and murdered Prof Devon. I think some more enquiries – confined to the animal rights people and known hunt saboteurs – might well yield more information about the man in question.'

Rydell shook his head. 'No,' he said. 'Draw a line under this one. I want you to charge Shanks with both murders. Even if there were three people involved, we got two out of three and let's settle for that. If at any time in the future someone with that name and a connection to the animal rights mob should come to our attention, we'll consider reopening proceedings and certainly interview him about the Devon killing.'

'Yes sir,' said Giles, with an air of resigned acceptance.

'Any word of the missing monkey?'

'Still out there somewhere,' said Giles.

The key card appeared on Steven's desk just after eleven next morning. It arrived by special delivery along with a note suggesting that he call the lab.

'Good news and bad news,' said Dr Mac Davidson, the chief of Biosciences, the lab that Sci-Med used for independent analyses. 'We did find evidence of someone other than Timothy Devon having touched the card recently. We got two DNA profiles from it. One was Devon's.'

'You did?' exclaimed Steven.

'The bad news is that we can't tell you who the second person was. It wasn't anyone connected with the case so far and there was no match for the profile on the police computer.'

'So it was someone without a police record?' said Steven.

'That's about the size of it,' agreed Davidson. 'Could be perfectly innocent. Your call. You decide.'

Steven thanked him and put down the phone. He let out his breath in a long exasperated sigh. Why was life continually like this, he wondered. A simple yes or no answer to a question would be a welcome change instead of being continually presented with what politicians would call, 'a range of possibilities' – twin brother of a 'raft of opportunities' and equally ill-defined. Had someone other than Devon really tried to use that card or was there an entirely innocent explanation for the second profile? It could even have been his own DNA when he thought about it. Although he had tried to avoid touching the card when he'd removed it from the safe – had worn gloves for the procedure – it was still just possible that he had contaminated it. The act of putting surgical gloves might have involved touching the outside surface of one or other of them at some point, causing the transfer of a few epithelial cells which could in turn have been transferred to the card. The PCR reaction used by the lab to amplify tiny amounts of DNA on any surface was incredibly sensitive. He could of course, ask the lab to analyse his own profile for elimination purposes but that led on to thoughts of asking everyone at the institute to do the same. He called Lees to tell him of the card's return.

'Then I suggest that we meet tomorrow morning at the Crick and move this damned virus before it causes any more trouble,' said Lees. 'I take it your "routine" tests revealed nothing to worry about?'

Once again, Steven noticed Lees distance himself from

responsibility. He really was establishing himself as one of Whitehall's finest when it came to moving his arse out of the firing line. 'Nothing to keep us awake at night,' replied Steven, not wanting to say anything more.

'Good. How about eleven?'

'Fine. Where's it going?' asked Steven.

'Porton Down,' replied Lees. 'Best place for it. Bomb proof container in an armoured van with armed police escort. We'd hate to further incur the wrath of Sci-Med.'

Steven ignored the snipe. 'Good,' he said. 'See you at eleven.'

At three in the morning Steven saw the irony in telling Lees there had been nothing to keep them awake at night when he found himself lying awake wondering about the unknown DNA profile on the card. It was, strictly speaking, none of Sci-Med's concern. Their interest lay in what the escaped animals had been carrying – and a right can of worms that had turned out to be and one that wasn't quite over yet with one animal still at large – but that was no excuse for adopting blinkered vision and rushing for the finish line. Sci-Med investigators were given a great deal of latitude in how they went about their business and they had been hand-picked for the way they thought. They didn't miss much. Going off at a tangent was actively encouraged by John Macmillan in people who had demonstrated the value of doing so in the past. 'Pick away at it' was one of his favourite expressions. Steven was one of those who recognised that problems were seldom circles; they were more often spheres. Trying to get an overall picture which would embrace all dimensions could rival mapping the dark side of the moon at times but it could also be a seductive challenge. He gave up on sleep and got out of bed to make some coffee. It took him an hour's consideration but he did come up with a couple of things he might do the following day. The first involved him leaving early and getting up to the Crick Institute in time to have a talk with Nick Cleary before Lees arrived with the virus removal crew.

'Hello, what brings you back?' asked Cleary when Steven knocked and entered his office.

'DOH are removing the Cambodia 5 Virus and moving it to Porton today.'

'Can't say I'm sorry about that.'

'The place is looking much better,' said Steven. He'd noticed that there were fewer workmen about and very little mess left in the corridors, although the outside of the building was still badly scarred.

'We're getting there. What can I do for you?'

'It's a small point but I was wondering if telephone calls were logged individually in the institute?'

'This is the civil service,' smiled Cleary. 'All calls are timed and itemised.'

'So it would be possible for me to see the log for the Sunday on which Professor Devon was murdered?'

'I should think so. With a bit of luck I can do it for you right now on the computer. We have an internet link to the BT billing operation.'

'Great.' Steven glanced at his watch: it was ten thirty. He sat in silence while Cleary retrieved the information.

Cleary pushed his glasses up on his head and leaned his elbows on the desk while he waited for the screen to fill. 'Here we are,' he said. 'Two calls were made on that Sunday, a three minute call in the morning to a number I recognise as Tim's home and a ten second call made to a London number I don't recognise at one-thirty in the afternoon. Not many but it was a Sunday. Tim was the only person here that day.'

Steven wrote down both numbers and thanked Cleary for his help. 'How's the race for a vaccine going?' he asked.

'Leila Martin is hard at it,' said Cleary. 'We've all got our fingers crossed.'

'I was wondering...' began Steven. 'How you and the staff would feel about having a swab taken for DNA analysis, purely for elimination purposes?'

Cleary shrugged and said, 'No problem as far as I'm concerned and I'm sure the others will be happy to cooperate too. Anything that helps catch Tim's killer.'

'I thought you'd feel that way,' said Steven. 'I'll make arrangements and let you know.'

Nigel Lees arrived at eleven in a small convoy which included himself in a DOH Rover with official driver, a black armoured van with two crew members wearing crash helmets and neck protectors and two unmarked police cars, each with two occupants.

'Got your key?' asked Lees.

Steven took out his card and held it up.

Lees smiled and said, 'Let's get started then.'

Some people were just born to take charge, thought Steven as he followed Lees inside. Nothing dents their confidence, not even coming up with the cretinous idea of working with Cambodia 5 virus at the Crick.

Lees knelt down in front of the safe and Steven did likewise,

Lees to the left, Steven to the right. Behind them the two
security men stood ready with a steel canister full of dry ice.
The fog from it was spilling over the side and tumbling down
to the floor, creating a stage mist effect worthy of a rock
concert.

'What's the virus held in?' asked Steven.

'Sealed glass ampoules maintained at -70 degrees.'

Steven held his card over the right hand slot. 'Ready when
you are.'

'After three. One, two, three.'

Both men entered their cards and the flashing LED turned
to green. The safe handle now turned with ease and a waft of
icy cold air drifted out from the thick-walled chamber as Lees
paused to put on a heavy glove to protect his skin against low
temperature burns. He reached in to remove a metal rack
containing eight glass vials and transferred them slowly and
carefully to the metal flask the guards were holding. One of
them then screwed the top back on.

'All over,' said Lees.

'It will be when you recapture the last monkey,' said Steven.

Lees smiled wanly and nodded to the guards who left the
room with the flask.

'The army have been asked to step up the hunt,' said Lees.
'It can't possibly survive out there in December.'

'Let us know when you have the body,' said Steven.

Lees removed the key cards from the safe. 'I'll make
arrangements for removing this,' he said.

'Nobody knew it was there,' said Steven, unable to resist
highlighting the secret nature of its installation. 'No one's
going to trip over it.'

Lees smiled wanly again.

'Just as a matter of interest,' said Steven. 'What *was* the procedure for opening the safe?'

'Professor Devon would phone me at the ministry and I would drive up with the second key at an arranged time.'

'Can I ask the number at the ministry he would call?'

Lees reeled off the number. 'It's my direct line. Why do you ask?'

'So you wouldn't be there at weekends?'

'No,' replied Lees, 'unless pressure of work demanded it...' he added lamely. 'What's this all about?'

Steven thought Lees' first response the more likely. 'I was just interested in how these security measures work in practice,' he said. 'Supposing Professor Devon had needed access to the virus at the weekend and you weren't there...did he have another number to contact you? Home number, mobile?'

'No, there was no need for access at the weekend. That was agreed at the outset.'

'I see.'

'Now, if you'll excuse me.'

Steven watched as the convoy drove off. Lees looked directly at him from the back seat of the Rover as it passed but didn't smile, neither did Steven. It wasn't rudeness: he was thinking about the number that Lees had given him. It was the same as the one Cleary had found on the call list for the day Devon died. Someone had tried to obtain the second key.

As he stood there outside the institute in the cold of a grey December day with a bitter wind whipping across the empty courtyard, making his eyes narrow, Steven experienced what his friend and fellow Sci-Med investigator, Scott Jamieson, would have called an 'Oh fuck moment'. The little puddle he had stepped in was actually six feet deep.

So the animal rights intruders had found the safe that none of the staff bar Devon had known about and had tried to gain access to it. They must have forced Devon to make the call to Lees in an attempt to get the second card but that didn't necessarily mean that they had any idea about what was inside…did it? It was a safe and would therefore be of interest to thieves…but these people weren't thieves, they were idealists…but also misfits, losers and probably opportunists went the counter argument. 'Shit,' murmured Steven under his breath. There was no way to be sure. He tried telling himself that he should concentrate on the positives. The safe had not been breached. The Cambodia 5 virus was now on its way to secure storage at Porton Down. All was right with the world, wasn't it?

Steven's first idea, born at 3 a.m. that morning, had been to ask Cleary about the phone register – and it had come up trumps. His second was to have a chat with Frank Giles, the policeman in charge of the case, about the arrest he had made. He drove over to police headquarters and found Giles about to go out for lunch.

'Join me?' Giles suggested. 'I've got to get out of here for a while.'

Steven smiled and agreed. He liked people who wore their hearts on their sleeves – probably a reaction to dealing so much with the denizens of Whitehall.

'Still looking for your monkey?' asked Giles as they sat down in the lounge bar of The Green Man and were handed two menus that had seen a lot of service.

'The army are,' replied Steven. 'I understand you've made an arrest over the Crick case?'

'We fingered two but one's dead,' said Giles. 'Robert Lyndon and Kevin Shanks. Shanks stabbed Lyndon when he showed signs of blabbing to us. He's now going down for both murders. Scampi please, love,' he added when a waitress started to hover round the table.

'Same for me,' said Steven. 'Did they both have form?'

'Breach of the peace, possession of Mary Jane, low grade stuff for a pair of low grade losers,' said Giles. 'Why?'

'Do low grade losers usually move up to torture and murder?' asked Steven.

'What's on your mind, exactly?'

'Was there any chance at all that a third person was involved in the crime?'

'Bloody hell,' exclaimed Giles. 'Every chance. What have you got that I don't know about?'

'There was a secret safe in the institute. Someone tried to gain access to it on the day Prof. Devon was murdered. That someone left a DNA fingerprint but didn't have a record. You've just told me that Lyndon and Shanks did.'

'Shanks maintains there was a third man on the raid – as he insists on calling it. His name was Ali and according to Shanks, he organised the whole thing. He claims that the professor was alive when the three of them left the institute but that this bloke Ali must have gone back later and murdered him.'

Steven looked doubtful.

'That's what I thought at first,' said Giles. 'It sounds pretty weak but after talking to Shanks at length I think I believe him.'

'Presumably you're looking for this guy, Ally?'

Giles shook his head. 'The Chief Super has pulled the plug on that. Too many Alis to interview.'

'Wait a minute,' said Steven, realising that they were talking at cross purposes. 'You're talking about Ali as in Mohammed not Ally as in Allan or Alistair?' he said.

Giles nodded. 'That threw me at first because Shanks didn't mention that Ali was Indian or Pakistani or whatever. I only found out later when I was talking to somebody else. When I asked Shanks about it he said it hadn't occurred to him because Ali spoke better English than he did.'

'And the name Ali is all you have to go on?'

'Afraid so.'

'Then I see the problem.'

Their scampi arrived so they paused until the waitress had put the plates down and enquired, 'Any sauces for you gentlemen?'

'Tartare,' said Steven.

'Same,' said Giles.

'My inclination was to pursue him through the connection with hunt saboteurs and animal rights groups. Somebody must know something about him but big white boss say no...unless of course he got into this safe you mentioned and something valuable is missing? That might alter things,' said Giles.

'No, he failed.'

'Pity,' said Giles. 'I'd have liked to put this psycho away. What was in it anyway?'

'A virus.'

'Dare I ask?'

'I'd rather you didn't.'

'So the suit who turned up from DOH wasn't being quite honest with his assurances?'

'Now, there's a surprise,' said Steven.

'I've a good mind to…'

'Don't,' said Steven. 'It's already been decided at high level that no action will be taken against DOH.'

Giles shook his head. 'You couldn't make it up, could you?'

'Good intentions count for a lot apparently,' said Steven.

'They also pave the road to hell,' added Giles. His phone rang. 'Thanks for letting me know,' he said after listening for a few seconds. 'Dr Dunbar will be pleased.'

Steven looked up from his food, wondering if Giles was being sarcastic or not. There was no sign of it.

'The army have found your monkey. It was found dead near Burnham Market. They're taking the body back to the institute for incineration.

'Thank God for that,' said Steven, surprised at the relief he felt flood through him. 'Nothing left lurking in the woods.'

'What was it really carrying?' asked Giles.

'Flu,' replied Steven, feeling more than a little guilty for bending the truth.

'So that's it then,' said John Macmillan when Steven told him.

'I think so,' agreed Steven. 'It was a messy business but it could have been so much worse. It's probably the wrong man going down for Professor Devon's murder but he was going down anyway...'

'And it's not a perfect world,' said Macmillan.

'Frank Giles of the Norfolk police has alerted neighbouring forces and they'll keep an eye out for this Ali character in the future. It's odds on he's going to get into more trouble sooner or later.'

'Remembering these photographs of Devon, I really hope it's sooner,' said Macmillan.

'What next?' asked Steven.

'There's a hospital in Newcastle the computer thinks we should take an interest in,' said Macmillan. 'The Victoria Hospital for Children. Its paediatric heart surgery results are giving cause for concern. Pick away at it, will you?'

CHAPTER TEN

Steven completed his investigation into suspicious surgical death patterns at the Victoria Hospital during the second week of January. The inquiry had straddled Christmas, which he had spent with his daughter Jenny and Richard and Susan and their children – a happy time although quickly overshadowed by the *tsunami* that hit the Far East on Boxing Day. Jenny had wanted to send her new bicycle to Thailand to make a child there happier.

The investigation had proved quite straightforward in the end and although the surgical death rates were undoubtedly higher than in other comparable hospitals, examination of the dead children's notes had revealed the reason why. The head of paediatric surgery at the Victoria had real courage. Unlike so many of his contemporaries who always kept one eye on the statistical returns, Mr Cecil Digby FRCS, had taken on challenges that many other surgeons would have turned down and often agreed to operate on cases which were generally regarded as being too difficult or just plain hopeless. As a direct result of this, the death rate in his unit was much higher than the norm. Common sense dictated that it would be, but common sense didn't show up in hospital returns; only numbers. On paper – the government's preferred method for assessing so much, particularly in education and health – Digby's figures looked worrying but the numbers weren't telling the whole truth. The babies who died would have died anywhere else. The babies who lived however, had special reason to be grateful – or rather, their parents had – because anywhere else, they would probably have died too.

Steven had been able to determine this without ever confronting Digby personally. It was Sci-Med's policy to keep their inquiries as discreet as possible and in this case, confidential arrangements had been made with the hospital records people in order to grant Steven access to patients' notes. He managed to leave the hospital without Cecil Digby ever knowing he'd been investigated...or why. Steven was pleased and relieved at the outcome. At the outset, he'd been afraid that he had been sent to investigate the not uncommon problem of a surgeon continuing to operate after his or her abilities had started to decline.

The facts of the case however, made him reflect on the government obsession with auditing and target setting – well intentioned, no doubt, but disastrous in practice and the cause of much figure manipulating. Surgeons avoided high risk operations in favour of routine ones with a much higher success rate. Short operations were preferred to longer ones simply because you could get through more and therefore make the figures look better on paper – fine for those patients who needed a short, routine operation, not so good for those who needed complex surgery. Another example of the road to hell being paved with good intentions, he thought and then puzzled over who had said that to him recently...

* * *

It was after ten on Saturday evening when Steven got back to London after driving down from Newcastle – too late to start writing up his report for Sci-Med he reckoned: that could wait until Sunday. A hot bath, a large gin and tonic and a film on TV sounded a better option, but first he wanted to catch up on what had been happening in the world. He tuned to the Sky News channel and stuck with a discussion about the upcoming Iraqi elections until the headlines came up. The first item made his blood run cold. 'Animal rights extremists carry out a second murder at English research institute,' intoned the presenter over filmed footage of the Crick Institute and a dramatic musical score.

The substance of the report was that fifty-seven year old Robert Smith, a lab assistant employed to look after animals at the institute, had been attacked in his car as he drove down for his morning newspaper. Three men, reportedly driving a Land Rover, had forced him off the road, locked him inside his vehicle and set fire to it. He had been burned alive. Leaflets found near the scene had proclaimed his attackers' allegiance to the animal rights movement.

Nick Cleary, appearing deeply upset, was interviewed on the steps of the institute. He pointed out the bitter irony of murdering someone who had been involved in animal welfare rather than experimentation – Smith had been employed to clean and feed the animals, he pointed out. Frank Giles, ill at ease in front of camera and sounding stilted, appealed for witnesses to come forward after stressing the horrific nature of Smith's death and just how important it was that such vicious killers be caught. The head of a recognised animal rights movement was also interviewed – somewhat reluctantly, thought Steven. He condemned the murder while doing his best to distance himself and his organisation from the perpetrators, just as he had had to do only a couple of months before.

Steven phoned Giles. 'I just saw it on the news.'

'If ever there was a stupid, pointless crime, this is it,' said Giles. 'It doesn't make sense on any level. They get huge adverse publicity after last time and then they go back and hit the same place all over again! What's more, they pick on the one guy in the place who looks after animals. Talk about shit for brains!'

'Does this put the mysterious Ali back in the frame?' asked Steven.

'In the worst possible way,' said Giles. 'There's something I haven't told you yet. Between you and me, I've got one good witness and I really wish I hadn't.'

'You don't hear that too often from the police,' said Steven.

'Ever since his arrest, Kevin Shanks's relatives have been doing their level best to drum up press interest in his claim that there was a third man involved in the attack on the Crick Institute. They've been telling the papers that a man named Ali was the real murderer and stressing the fact that he's a Pakistani. Up 'til now the Press have refused to run with it. Even they can see the danger of fuelling racial tension by suggesting that Devon's torturer and murderer was a bit duskier than a whiter shade of pale.'

'But?'

'My witness is a woman who says she passed the Land Rover a few minutes before the attack on Smith. She says the three men in it were, to use her words, "the people you see in corner shops these days".'

'Oh dear,' said Steven.

'Oh dear indeed,' said Giles. 'We could be talking Christmas riots when this particular crock of shit hits the fan.'

'It never rains...'

'How true,' sighed Giles.

'I don't suppose they could have had another reason for picking on Smith, could they?' asked Steven.

'Like what?'

'Like maybe he caught sight of the mysterious Ali the first time around and could identify him.'

'Smith didn't strike me as someone holding something back,' said Giles. 'I saw him a few minutes after he'd found that the institute had been broken into and the intruders had long gone by that time.'

'Just a thought,' said Steven.

'Keep 'em coming,' said Giles. 'We're going to need all the help we can get on this one.'

Steven put the phone down and considered for a moment. All desire to watch a film had evaporated. Giles was right; another attack on the Crick seemed all wrong, ludicrously wrong from the point of view of an animal rights activist. And to pick on Smith, a low level employee who had looked after the animals' welfare beggared belief. He was the wrong man in the wrong job working in definitely the wrong place to attack again. What else could you get wrong...from the point of view of an animal rights activist? But suppose there was another view, Steven wondered as he refilled his glass. The leaflets found near the burned out car had naturally been construed as a responsibility claim and a declaration of motive but could there have been another agenda hiding behind the obvious? Giles had discounted the one alternative possibility he had come up with – that Smith had known more about the first attack than he'd let on – so what did that leave? Maybe he should talk to Smith's widow just in case. He would drive up there in the morning.

The Smiths' house was a small white-painted cottage sitting just outside the entrance to the Crick Institute and surrounded by neatly clipped privet hedges and cherry trees. There were two cars parked outside, one on the road and one in the short drive-in in front of the garage. Steven had been prepared for relatives to be present but was surprised to find a woman PC at the door. He showed her his ID and asked how things were.

'The Press have been pretty merciless in their attempts to talk to Mrs Smith. I wouldn't have believed it if I hadn't seen them myself,' she said. 'Hyenas don't come close.'

'How is she bearing up?'

'Pretty well, I'd say, all things considered. Her GP was here again this morning so I guess she's getting something to help her through it. Her main concern seems to be the house: it came with the job.'

'Bad luck,' said Steven. It seemed inadequate but at least he hadn't said it to Amy Smith who agreed to see him after the WPC had gone inside to ask her. She had however, requested that her sister, Ethel, who had stayed overnight with her, be allowed to remain in the room. 'Of course,' said Steven and he was shown inside.

The cottage was gloomy despite the brightness of the day outside, a direct result of its age. Its walls were solid stone, more than two feet thick so the windows were deeply recessed

– good for providing nice deep windowsills to stand vases and books on but bad for letting in light. The standard lamp beside the chair Amy Smith was sitting on was switched on, lighting her below like a small, pale porcelain figurine. Steven was introduced to both women and offered his sympathy.

'I hate disturbing you at a time like this, Mrs Smith,' he said. 'But I'm sure you, more than anyone, appreciate the need for us to catch these monstrous people.'

'Smithy loved animals,' said Amy. 'Why pick on him?' She held a handkerchief up to her face while her sister put a protective arm round her shoulder.

'It doesn't make sense, I agree,' said Steven. 'This may seem like a very strange question Mrs Smith, but can you think of any reason at all why someone might have wanted to harm your husband?'

Amy bristled. 'No, of course not,' she said. 'Smithy got on with everybody. Everyone liked him.'

Steven noticed the look that appeared briefly on her sister's face and figured that this might not be an entirely accurate answer. Amy looked up at her sister as if seeking reassurance and, suspecting that it was less than solid, she added, 'He always said what he thought but no one blamed him for that... He told the truth. They respected him for it.'

'I'm sure they did,' said Steven, trying to think of an alternative angle to approach the subject from. 'Did you notice anything troubling Smithy in recent weeks?' he asked. 'Any change in his behaviour? Had he become worried, irritable?'

Once again, Steven read the look on Ethel's face. It suggested that Smithy had always been irritable.

'He was very upset over what these people did to the professor,' said Amy. 'We all were. Smithy said they should bring back hanging for them and even that would be too good for them.'

'Apart from that.'

'I don't think so...apart from that silly business with the monkey but that was just Smithy...'

Steven felt the hairs on his neck start to rise. 'What business was that?' he asked.

'Oh, it was daft,' said Amy. 'Nothing really. Something and nothing you could say. When the soldiers finally found the body of the last monkey who'd escaped – they'd been searching for it for weeks – and brought it back to the institute for burning, Smithy went up to see it. He said it was a different animal... They'd got the wrong monkey.'

'A different animal,' repeated Steven, feeling his blood turn to ice.

'Smithy said he knew his Chloe and it wasn't her; it was a different monkey,' said Amy. 'I think the soldiers thought he was having a laugh, telling them they'd got the wrong monkey after all the trouble they'd been to, but he wasn't. He was quite serious.'

'Can't be too many monkeys out there...in Norfolk,' said Amy's sister, suppressing a jaundiced little smile.

'That's what the soldiers said,' said Amy. 'Silly old fool. But once he got an idea into his head... You see, Smithy prided himself on knowing all the monkeys by name. He said they were as different from each other as human beings once you got to know them. They all look the same to me mind you.'

Steven smiled in order to encourage her. 'Me too.'

'Six of them escaped. Five were brought back to the institute. Smithy said that Chloe was the missing one but then, when they brought the last one in, he said it wasn't her.'

'Typical Smithy, if you ask me,' said Ethel. 'If you said black, he'd say white on principle.'

This attracted a hurt look from Amy and her sister gave her shoulder an affectionate squeeze and said, 'You know what I mean, Ames. He'd cross the street to find an argument.'

'I suppose,' said Amy. 'The soldiers pointed out the monkey had been out in the wilds of Norfolk for weeks in the middle of winter and that Smithy'd look a bloomin' sight different as well if he tried that, but he wouldn't change his mind. Said it was another monkey. Nothing like Chloe, he said.'

With the words 'nothing like Chloe' reverberating inside his head, Steven thanked Amy for agreeing to talk to him and was shown to the door by Ethel who whispered to him as he left, 'He was an old bugger really.'

Steven gave a conspiratorial nod.

'Learn much, sir?' asked the WPC on the door.

'A little more than I bargained for,' said Steven cryptically before continuing to his car where he sat for a moment with both hands clasping the top of the steering wheel tightly. If Smith was right and it was the wrong monkey that the soldiers had brought in, it opened up a whole new can of worms. Please God, he was wrong. Please God, it had been the animal's suffering in the wild that had altered its appearance. He started the engine and nodded to the WPC before driving off.

Back in London, Steven wrote up his report on paediatric surgery at the Victoria Hospital although he was continually distracted by doubts arising from what he'd learned in Norfolk. Why couldn't every investigation be as straightforward as the Newcastle one with clearly defined questions attracting clearly defined answers and everything ending in unequivocal conclusions? He answered his own petulant question with the unpalatable – but inescapable – rejoinder that there would be no need to employ him if that were the case.

'So what's your feeling?' asked Macmillan when Steven told him next morning about his talk with Amy Smith.

'The soldiers might well be right about the animal looking significantly different after weeks in the wild...' said Steven, 'and Smith was a contrary old sod by all accounts...'

'That's the explanation I would prefer to go with,' said Macmillan. 'But not you?'

'I just feel uncertain,' said Steven. "Uncertain" seemed such a prissy little word to describe what was going on inside his head.

'Call me unimaginative but I can't see an alternative explanation,' said Macmillan, 'unless global warming is more advanced than we thought and monkeys are to be found swinging from the Norfolk trees these days...'

'Chloe was the virus control animal in Devon's experiment,' said Steven. 'She was infected with live Cambodia 5 virus: she hadn't been given the vaccine he was testing.'

'Another reason perhaps for her change in appearance,' said Macmillan. 'Not only was she living rough in winter, she was also very ill. Chances are she'd been born and bred in captivity so she wouldn't know what to do out there anyway.'

'That animal was a genuine threat to the health of the nation,' said Steven.

'Dramatic...but true I suppose,' said Macmillan. 'But it strikes me that any alternative explanation cannot be a simple one. If the monkey the soldiers found really wasn't Chloe it implies that someone must have deliberately carried out a substitution with intent to deceive and all that goes with that can of worms.'

'I know,' nodded Steven. 'It might also suggest that Robert Smith was murdered to keep his mouth shut about the monkey.'

'Something that nearly worked,' said Macmillan. 'If you hadn't decided to go talk to his widow we would never have known about his doubts.'

Steven thought for a moment before saying, 'All things considered...it makes more sense than his murder being another animal rights hit. They just couldn't be that stupid.'

Adopting an air of resignation, Macmillan said, 'Unfortunately, I have to agree with you...which leaves us with potentially a very big problem.'

'What happened to the real Chloe; where is she; who has her and what do they intend doing with her?'

'That just about covers everything,' said Macmillan. 'How is Dr Martin coming along with the vaccine?'

'She's optimistic, I understand.'

'Thank God for that,' said Macmillan. It sounded heartfelt.

'Have you heard how the Elwoods are?' asked Steven.

Macmillan looked thoughtful. He said, 'Actually no. Lees was supposed to phone me last week about their condition.

Strikes me, the way things are going, no news could be bad news.' He pressed the intercom button and asked Jean Roberts to get him Nigel Lees at the Department of Health. Sitting back in his chair he crossed his legs and said, 'So where do we go from here?'

Steven sighed and said, 'Frank Giles of the Norfolk Police is faced with looking for someone named Ali in the Asian community and I'm left looking for a monkey that's disappeared into thin air.'

The phone rang and Macmillan asked Lees about the Elwoods. Steven watched his face as he listened to the reply. It was not encouraging.

Macmillan replaced the receiver with deliberate slowness. 'David Elwood is dead,' he said. 'Officially, bronchial complications setting in after treatment for animal bites...can happen in the elderly.'

'And unofficially?'

'Cambodia 5.'

'And his wife?'

'Not at all well. Could go either way.'

Steven shook his head and said, 'What a mess. And all to be swept under the official carpet.'

'Right now, we have other things to worry about,' said Macmillan. 'There's a meeting of the *Earlybird* committee tomorrow. I'm going to voice your concerns about the virus.'

'The monkey that attacked the Elwoods,' said Steven. 'It was one of the test animals which *had* received Devon's experimental vaccine.'

'Your point being?'

'The vaccine didn't work,' said Steven. 'The animal was

infectious. I want to call Code Red status on this.'

Macmillan got up from his desk and walked slowly over to the window. Snow had just started to fall. 'At times like this, Steven...retirement and the south of France seem very attractive...but you're right. Code red status is granted.' Almost as an afterthought he added, 'You don't suppose Dr Martin is using the same seed strain for her vaccine, do you?'

'Maybe I'll ask her,' said Steven.

Requesting Code Red status meant that the investigator on the ground had decided that preliminary investigations were over and that there was a serious Sci Med investigation to be made. If granted, all the stops would be pulled out to support that investigator and he would no longer be reliant on voluntary cooperation from police and other authorities. He would have full Home Office backing in making any requests he saw fit. He would have access to a wide range of auxiliary services ranging from lab support to the supply of weapons. Three admin staff in the Home Office would operate twenty four hour cover on a special telephone line for requests and inquiries coming in at any time of the day or night and special finance arrangements would be set up through the supply of two credit cards.

'Jean will make arrangements and let you know in the usual way,' said Macmillan.

When he got back to the flat, Steven wondered if he should phone Frank Giles and tell him of his suspicions surrounding the death of Robert Smith. He recognised that his reluctance had more than a little to do with the fact that he hadn't been totally honest with Giles about the virus carried by the escaped animals. What made him even more uncomfortable was that he had used the same ruse as Nigel Lees in telling Giles that it was influenza without elaborating any further on the strain. He convinced himself that their motivation in doing so had been different. Lees had been trying to cover up a serious mistake in judgement while he had been...what exactly had his intentions been? He supposed after a moment's thought that he had been afraid that Giles might have felt obliged to tell his superiors about the true identity of the virus and they in turn would have made the matter public, not out of concern but in order to protect themselves – the prime motivation for any form of warning being issued these days. He felt strongly that 'Beware of Falling Rocks' should be subtitled 'Just so you can't sue us'.

The real question he had to ask himself was, would the police investigation take a different course if he gave them a possible alternative motive for Robert Smith's death? At the moment, they would be mounting a major offensive to tackle the animal rights brigade over the identity of Ali, hoping it might lead not only to him but also to the three Asian men in the Land Rover who had murdered Smith. He couldn't see that changing even if he told Giles about his suspicions. For the moment he would let things take their course. It might be Machiavellian, but media pressure was on the police right now to hunt down Smith's murderers and that was fine by him: he didn't want to ease it any by throwing them a ready-made diversion concerning a monkey's identity and a possible health hazard.

Steven's mobile announced an incoming message. It said, 'Dunbar: Code Green', indicating that his Code Red status had been activated. It also listed a telephone number. Steven called it and made his first request to the duty officer. 'I need to know something about how you buy monkeys in this country,' he said. 'How you go about it, who does it and who has been doing it over the past three months?'

CHAPTER ELEVEN

Steven called the Crick Institute and asked to speak to Leila Martin, telling the operator who he was and stressing that it was important. He still had to wait for over a minute but smiled when he heard the French sounding, ''Allo.'

'Dr Martin? This is Steven Dunbar of Sci-Med.'

'I remember, the science policeman.'

'If you insist,' said Steven. 'Look, I know you must be terribly busy working on the vaccine but I'd really like to speak to you. There's something I have to clear up and the sooner the better.'

'I'm sure I'll be here in the lab whenever you care to call,' said Leila. 'My social life seems to be a thing of the past.'

'I'm sorry,' said Steven. 'I know you're in a race against the clock but it is important or I wouldn't have bothered you.'

'If you say so.'

'It shouldn't take long,' said Steven. 'How about tomorrow morning around eleven?'

'I'll be here.'

The first thing that struck Steven next morning when he saw Leila Martin walk towards him was that she managed to look sexy even in a loose-fitting lab coat. Not too many women managed that.

'Nice to see you again,' he said.

'As you're a policeman, I'm not sure I can say the same for you,' said Leila, but she was smiling when she said it. 'We can talk in my office.'

Leila took off her lab coat and hung it on the back of the door before smoothing her skirt and choosing to sit down and face Steven in front of her desk rather than from behind it. He couldn't help thinking about the old Hollywood ruse of making beautiful actresses wear glasses when they wanted to suggest intelligence. Leila wore glasses. He couldn't help but notice the sound her stockings made when she crossed her legs.

'How can I help?' she asked.

'You probably remember that one of Professor Devon's escaped experimental animals bit a member of the public?'

'I remember well enough but the animals didn't escape,' corrected Leila. 'They were deliberately set loose by the unspeakable people who murdered Tim Devon.'

Steven conceded the point. 'The man who was bitten died a couple of nights ago in a private clinic. His wife is now also very ill.'

'Are you going to tell me that they were infected with the Cambodia 5 virus?' asked Leila.

'Yes, I am.'

'Oh my God, that is awful.'

'I take it you knew nothing about Professor Devon working with Cambodia 5?'

Leila shook her head. 'I knew of course, that he was running some experiments that he couldn't talk about – we all knew that – but not that he was working with Cambodia 5 here in the institute. I didn't know about that until the people from your Department of Health approached me after Tim's death and asked me if I would continue development of the vaccine.'

'That's what I thought,' said Steven. 'The thing is, the animal that bit the dead man had been vaccinated before being challenged with Cambodia 5 and yet it still proved to be infectious… We were wondering if you were using the same seed strain for your vaccine?'

'Because if I was, it would be no good?' said Leila.

Steven nodded.

'Relax, Dr Dunbar. Professor Devon left notes on three possible seed strains he had constructed and hoped could be used against the Cambodia 5 strain. I found a slight flaw in the one he chose to try first so I rejected that in favour of one of the others when I took over.'

'A slight flaw?' said Steven, unable to keep the surprise from his voice.

'No criticism of the professor intended,' said Leila reading his mind. 'Tim didn't have the results of some tests available to him when he had to make the decision. Certain aspects of the haemaglutinin structure made the strain unsuitable for vaccine production.'

'I see,' said Steven. 'Can I ask how your work is going?'

'Perhaps you would like to come down to the lab and see for yourself?'

'I'd love to.'

'You'll have to gown up.'

Steven was shown to a cloakroom outside the lab suite where he changed into green surgical scrubs and put plastic covers over his shoes. He covered his hair with a surgical hood and adjusted his mask so that his mouth and nose were properly covered. He met Leila outside.

'We will not be going into the virus lab itself,' she explained, 'but even so, I don't want to risk introducing any contaminants from the outside world. As you know, if bacteria were to get into the egg culture room we would lose everything and there would be no time to start again. We all gown up, even for the outer rooms.'

Leila placed her key in the electronic lock outside the lab and entered a five digit code: the mechanism buzzed and the door clicked open. Leila nodded to the technicians who were working inside and led the way over to a long, rectangular window in the far wall. 'That's where the race is being run,' she said.

Steven looked through the glass into an adjoining lab where row upon row of hens' eggs were incubating under dull red lights.

'The seed virus for a vaccine against the Cambodia 5 strain,' said Leila. 'It's now just a question as to whether enough will grow up in time to make the schedule for commercial production.'

They both watched as a technician working inside the egg lab examined the eggs one at a time by holding them over a simple box with a light source inside it. The Technician, who was wearing a full biohazard suit, acknowledged Leila's presence at the window and angled the box so that she and Steven could see what he could see. The light shining through the thin shell showed up the developing embryo inside. The extra heat from the light bulb made it move. Steven thought it looked like an ultra sound scan of a human foetus.

'We inject the virus into the amniotic cavity,' said Leila.

'And let nature take its course.'

'Can you monitor viral growth?' asked Steven.

'We occasionally withdraw amniotic fluid from a single egg to check the titre,' said Leila. 'One egg will yield about two millilitres of amniotic fluid containing several billion virus particles if the conditions are right.'

'But of course, there's no way of knowing whether the seed strain you've chosen will be effective against the Cambodia virus until you try it?' said Steven.

'That's true,' said Leila. 'But we can do certain lab tests,' said Leila, 'Of course, animal tests are out of the question after what happened.'

'Quite so,' said Steven.

'Tests on monkeys – the only real way to be sure if the vaccine would be effective or not – would have to be carried out at a secure facility such as Porton Down or Fort Dietrich in the USA and there won't be time for that.'

'So it'll be lab tests or nothing if the strain is to make this year's vaccine?'

'*Oui.*'

'Will that really be good enough?' asked Steven. He saw the smile reflected in Leila's eyes above her mask.

'Depends on how great the risk of a pandemic is perceived as being,' she said. 'And how badly governments want to protect their citizens.'

'What's the worst that can happen?'

'The seed strain won't work and the vaccine won't provide any protection at all against the Cambodia strain.'

'Then it sounds like there's nothing to lose by giving it a try if it's ready on time,' said Steven.

'That would be my view too,' agreed Leila. 'But the American FDA and the British MHPRA may have different ideas. They may want a different third strain incorporated in the vaccine – one that has been tried and tested.'

'And which would be no good at all against an outbreak of the Cambodian virus?' said Steven.

Leila nodded ruefully and added, 'But no one would sue them for having taken a risk with public safety.'

Beware of falling rocks, thought Steven.

'How much do you know about flu virus?' asked Leila.

'I'm no expert.'

'Come, I'll show you what we've been doing with it.' She led Steven into her small office in the lab suite and spread an illustration of the virus particle on the desk. 'You see, it is these spike-like molecules – the haemaglutinins – that bind to receptors on the surface of the cell that we have been concentrating on. If we can stimulate antibodies in the human body to attack them we will prevent the virus entering the cell and if it can't get into the cell...'

'It can't replicate,' said Steven.

'Exactly.'

'Then I wish you all the luck in the world, Doctor.'

'Leila, please.'

'And I'm Steven.' He seized the moment. 'Perhaps I could repay you for the tour by offering you dinner?'

Leila smiled. 'Perhaps when this is all over,' she said. 'And we all have more time.'

'I'll hold you to that.'

'It was only a perhaps.'

*　*　*

'I thought you would be staying up there,' said Macmillan when Steven appeared in his office next morning.

'Not much I can do at the moment,' said Steven. He told Macmillan of his meeting with Leila Martin and what he'd learned of the seed strain she was using. 'Definitely different from the one Devon used.'

'Thank God for that,' said Macmillan. 'I told the *Earlybird* committee yesterday about your misgivings over the monkey the army recovered. You've started quite a furore. The thought that Cambodia 5 virus might have fallen into the wrong hands seemed to concentrate minds wonderfully.'

'What are they going to do?'

'It was agreed that priority must be given to the new vaccine that Dr Martin is working on. The Health minister will speak to the Prime Minister about approaching the Americans with a view to relaxing FDA regulations for US vaccines and fast-tracking it through. He's already warned the MHPRA not to throw unnecessary red tape at this one. They weren't exactly flavour of the month with HMG last year when they pulled the plug on Auroragen and to top it off, this year's an election year for us.'

'We mustn't forget that,' said Steven sourly.

'So what do I tell the papers?' demanded James Rydell.

Frank Giles sighed and held up his palms. 'I'm sorry, sir, I simply don't know. We have questioned everyone with even the remotest connection to animal rights organisations and drawn a complete blank. No one knows this Ali and no one has ever heard of him save for the few who saw him at the

Thorne Hunt on one occasion – the time when he pulled Hugo Blackmore off his horse and allegedly recruited Lyndon and Shanks that same evening.'

'What about the three men who murdered Smith?'

'Same story. No one has any idea who they are and I don't think anyone's protecting them. The animal rights brigade seems as shocked by the killings as everyone else.'

'What about the car they used? Someone saw that and gave a description.'

'But she didn't get the number and Land Rover Defenders are part of the landscape in this part of the country.'

There was a long pause before Rydell said, 'You do realise where you're going with this, don't you?'

Giles' throat had gone dry. He had to swallow before saying, 'Yes sir, I think I do... It pains me to say it but it's beginning to look as if the killings had nothing at all to do with the animal rights movement... That was a blind. Devon and Smith were murdered for a different reason.'

Rydell nodded. 'Unfortunately by people with names like *Ali*. Makes things awkward, wouldn't you say?'

'It does but I'm certain this wasn't a racial thing.'

Rydell nodded. 'What we need is an alternative motive and quickly. Others may not be so circumspect.'

'Unfortunately, I don't have one at the moment, sir,' said Giles. 'But hitting the same organisation twice suggests a definite motive. I don't think we're talking random killings either.'

'So that's what I should tell the media, Inspector, is it? We don't know who carried out the killings or why but we're pretty sure they weren't random? Bloody hell, I'm going to look a right prick!'

'With respect sir, we are not particularly well equipped to see the motive behind these killings and that's a major problem.'

'We're policemen for Christ's sake. It's our job!'

Once more Giles held up his palms against the onslaught of his superior. 'Of course we are, sir, and yes, you're right, it is our job but the very nature of the organisation involved here, a research institute engaged in work we know nothing at all about, may be what is actually stopping us from seeing the motive – and if we can't see the motive...'

'We are working blind,' said Rydell, finally accepting what Giles was saying.

'Precisely, sir.'

'But isn't that what Sci-Med is for? A sort of interface between science and us? You told me one of their people came to see you.'

'Yes sir, Dr Steven Dunbar, but Sci-Med were interested in the animals that had escaped or, more correctly, what they might be carrying in case it was a threat to public safety. Of course, at that time, we all thought that the crime had been carried out by animal rights extremists so Sci-Med would have seen that as a police matter and left it alone.'

'But now...'

'You're right, sir. Things have changed. If there was some other reason behind the killings, we're going to need help in finding it. Dr Dunbar left me his card. With your approval, I'll get in touch with him and suggest we talk.'

'Do it.'

* * *

Sergeant Morley found Giles rinsing out his mouth in the men's room. 'Sore throat?' he asked.

'No,' said Giles. 'I've been kissing arse all morning. I'm just trying to get the taste out my mouth.'

'The word is that the papers have got hold of the fact that Smith's killers were Asian.'

'Christ,' said Giles, wiping his mouth with a paper towel. 'It never rains but it pours. That's all we need. If they combine that with the Shanks family's claim that "Ali" was a Pakistani they'll start a bloody race war.'

Morley held the door open for Giles. 'Can't we do something to stop them?' he asked.

'Appeal to their better nature, you mean?' said Giles, leading the way along the corridor.

Morley sensed that no reply was necessary.

'Journalism is an equal opportunity occupation, Morley. Being a half-arsed fuckwit is no impediment to employment.'

Steven knocked on Macmillan's door.

'I'm going back to Norfolk. This time I'm going to stay up there for a bit.'

'A change of heart?'

'I've just spoken to Frank Giles of the Norfolk Police. He's good. He already suspects that someone other than the animal rights brigade might be behind the killings at the Crick but he's having trouble coming up with an alternative motive. He thinks there might be some scientific reason involved so he's asking for our help. What do you think?'

'The fact that the police have more or less eliminated the animal rights theory through their inquiries makes your explanation all the more plausible,' said Macmillan. 'Maybe the time has come to share a little more information. Play it by ear.'

'There's going to be an added complication,' said Steven.

Macmillan arched his eyebrows.

'Giles says the papers are about to suggest that the killings were racially motivated.'

'Oh, happy day,' sighed Macmillan. 'I'd better get the Home Secretary up to speed on this. I'll tell him it's beginning to look more than ever likely that animal rights involvement at the Crick was a red herring and then I'll throw in what the Press are about to do. Poor chap, he's only been in the job a few weeks and he's already got the judiciary on his back.'

'My God, don't you ever go home?' asked Steven when Giles answered the phone at 9 p.m.

'Not tonight I don't,' replied Giles. 'One of the evening papers ran with the story. All leave's been cancelled. Where are you?'

'In your neck of the woods. I decided to drive up tonight. I've booked into a hotel for a couple of nights. When do you want to talk?'

'As soon as possible,' said Giles.

'How about socially over a pint right now?'

'Nipping out to a pub in the line of duty sounds just fine to me,' said Giles.

'I'm staying at the Pear Tree.'

'See you in ten minutes.'

Steven's suggestion had not entirely been made for social reasons. He was hoping that if he and Giles met on their own he could perhaps persuade the policeman that certain things he might tell him should remain confidential. He smiled as Giles came into the bar and shook his hand. 'What are you having?'

'My favourite question,' said Giles. 'Pint of best.'

The two men sat down at a table in a corner where the nearest people were three tables away – an elderly foursome drinking sherry before going in to dinner. *VERY LATE DINNER!*

'So you've run out of animal rights extremists?' said Steven.

'I think we've interviewed every bugger who ever patted a dog in the street,' said Giles, 'and drawn a complete blank. I think we've been taken for a ride. The animal rights stuff was a blind.'

'I think so too,' said Steven.

Giles's glass which had been on its way to his mouth was replaced on the table. 'Now we're getting somewhere. It sounds like you know something I don't,' he said.

'I *suspect* something,' corrected Steven, 'and because it's just a suspicion at the moment I would appreciate if we could keep it between ourselves?'

Giles sipped his beer and appeared to consider. 'Depends,' he said.

'On what?'

'On whether keeping things between ourselves impedes a murder inquiry in any way.'

'A legitimate concern,' said Steven. 'Supposing I were to tell you that what we are dealing with here is a determined attempt by person or persons unknown to get their hands on a biological weapon.'

'Jesus,' said Giles. 'You're serious?'

'It's beginning to look that way.'

'What weapon exactly?'

'It's a virus known as Cambodia 5,' said Steven. 'It's a kind of influenza.'

'Influenza?' exclaimed Giles. 'You mean we're all going to get flu?' He managed to sound both relieved and puzzled at the same time.

'No, I don't,' said Steven flatly. 'If the mortality rate of the virus transfers directly from its original avian host we are talking about a 90% death rate.'

'Bloody hell.'

'It's a variant of the strain of flu that killed more than 20 million people back in 1918.'

'Shit,' said Giles as if he'd just realised something. 'That's what your escaped monkey was carrying, wasn't it?'

Steven nodded.

'And you just said, flu.'

'Sorry.'

'Well, thank God they found the bloody thing,' said Giles...before he noticed the look on Steven's face. 'They didn't?' he asked.

'I don't think so,' admitted Steven. He told Giles about his interview with Robert Smith's wife and what she'd told him about her husband's insistence that the animal the army had recovered had not been the one which had escaped.

'So Shanks's story about Ali could be true. This Ali character could have gone back to the institute on his own.'

'And tortured Devon into telling him what he wanted to know about the location of the Cambodia 5 virus but, when he found he couldn't get his hands on it because of the double key lock on the safe, he did the next best thing and took one of the infected monkeys. He let the rest go to make it look as if he'd liberated them in the cause of animal rights.'

Giles's shoulders sagged and he shook his head. 'So we're not only looking for Ali,' he said. 'We're looking for Ali...and a monkey.'

'It's my guess you'll be joined soon,' said Steven.

'Who?'

'Just about every intelligence agency in the country.'

'That'll be nice,' said Giles. 'Maybe I'll get a day off.' His phone rang, attracting black looks from the would-be diners at the nearest table and stage whispers of 'I'm in a bar, on a bus, on a train...absolutely bloody awful, isn't it...'

'Giles...right, on my way.'

'Indian restaurant,' said Giles in answer to Steven's look. 'Windows smashed, owner and two waiters given a kicking. It's started. I'll have to go.'

'And our agreement?'

'If Whitehall are sending in the cavalry, I presume *they'll* have the courtesy to inform the relevant police authorities... No need for me to spoil the surprise.'

'Thanks,' said Steven.

CHAPTER TWELVE

Steven bought a selection of morning papers and read them over breakfast. They did not make for happy reading. '*Police Consider Racial Motive in Crick Killings*' in one was rivalled by '*Animal Activists Not To Blame?*' in another. He read each story carefully to make sure that they did not contain any information other than Kevin Shanks's claim that a third man, 'Ali', had been responsible for the murder of Timothy Devon and that a woman witness had described the three men involved in the immolation of Robert Smith as being of possibly Asian origin.

He understood that the main concern of the police would now be an outbreak of racial violence but he himself had other things to consider. He tried to put himself in the shoes of Ali and his companions. They would know that their animal rights cover had been blown but would that panic them into changing their plans or could they be past the stage when that mattered?

Steven was pondering this over his third cup of coffee when his phone rang. He was surprised to hear Leila Martin's voice.

'I need someone to tell me what's going on,' she said.

'I'm sorry?'

'I have had four separate telephone calls from different

government departments over the last twenty-four hours asking when my vaccine strain is going to be ready and now I've just read in the papers that it wasn't animal rights extremists who attacked the institute and killed Tim. When is someone going to tell me what's happening?'

Steven felt surprised that Leila should think it his job to tell her but recognised that she did have a right to feel concerned, maybe even aggrieved that no one had seen fit to keep her abreast of what was going on. He silently blamed Nigel Lees but then, as he admitted to himself, he was only too happy to blame Nigel Lees for anything.

'I'm not sure there's anything I can really tell you, Leila...' he said, stalling for time.

There seemed to be a long pause before Leila said, 'You're right, I'm sorry, I don't know why I called you...it was just that you left your card the other day and I was so angry I suppose I just wanted to talk to someone who might know something. I'm sorry I bothered you.'

'You didn't. Feel free to call me any time you like.'

'Look...about your dinner invitation...' said Leila.

'It still stands,' said Steven, hoping to sound casual but feeling an undeniable frisson of excitement at the prospect of spending an evening with Leila Martin.

'There's nothing I can do here to make the seed virus grow any faster. It just might do me good to have an evening away from here. I feel under so much pressure to succeed...'

'Pick you up at seven thirty?'

'Thank you Steven.'

'At the institute?'

'No, I'll have to change. I'm renting a cottage outside Guist. Come there. It's called Lion Cottage.'

'Lion?'

'There are ornamental iron lions on the eaves.' Leila gave him directions on how to find it.

'Sounds very old,' said Steven.

'The plumbing certainly is.'

'Well, well, every cloud has a silver lining,' murmured Steven as he put away his phone. Just when he thought life was on a downward spiral, fate had taken a hand and decided to cheer him up. Leila Martin was the most exciting woman he had met in ages. As he tried to get his thoughts back into order, he considered calling Giles to ask how bad the night had been but then decided against it. If Giles had been up all night he might well be sleeping. He would wait until the policeman called him. He thought it might be him when his phone rang thirty minutes later but it was John Macmillan.

'Word has come from on high that someone wants the Crick affair cleared up before it has any chance of interfering with the election. All the stops are to be pulled out.'

'Nice to know our leaders have a sense of priority,' said Steven. 'What exactly does pulling out all the stops mean in this case?'

'I'm not sure I know myself,' confessed Macmillan. 'But it sounds good..."and that's what's important,"' they both intoned.

'Seriously, there's going to be a high level meeting tomorrow at 11.30 to decide on a course of action and just how we should deal with an outbreak of Cambodia 5 should the worst come to the worst. Your presence has been requested.'

'I don't suppose I could get away with washing my hair?'

'Damned right you couldn't. You started all this.'

'I'm not sure I'll have anything to contribute,' said Steven. 'Don't they have plans for just such emergencies? They seem to practice enough with people in Casper-the-friendly-ghost outfits running around the underground and others playing doctors and nurses in the streets.'

'Sometimes Steven, I find your lack of reverence for authority a little hard to take,' said Macmillan.

'Sorry. Call it gallows humour.'

'In this instance I'd rather not. Be here at 11 a.m.'

Frank Giles called at 2.30p.m. 'I thought I wouldn't disturb you,' said Steven. 'Rough night?'

'No worse than we expected, I suppose,' said Giles. 'But you're right; I did have a kip this morning when I got in. It was mainly drunks having a go at Asian premises – nothing like chucking a brick through the corner shop window to gain the moral high ground – but it could be worse tonight after the coverage in this morning's papers. I take it you saw?'

Steven nodded. 'Any word from your bosses about spooks moving in?'

'Not a thing. Of course, they could be keeping it a secret.' Giles chuckled as he saw the irony in such a situation. 'Little do they know that I know that they know that I know... So, apart from keeping a look out for people called, "Ali" and following up reports of monkeys being seen on the streets, is there anything else we should be doing in our spare time?'

'Reports of people falling ill,' said Steven.

'With flu, you mean?'

'Exactly that.'

'And if we should hear?'

'Let me know and we'll take it from there.'

Steven arrived at Lion Cottage just before 7.30p.m., having given himself plenty of time to find it – he only missed the turn-off once. He was invited in by a vivacious looking Leila Martin. 'Not quite ready,' she said. 'Take a seat or better still, run around and keep warm otherwise you might freeze to death.'

Steven had noticed that the cottage was cold. 'Heating problems?' he asked.

'I think the "problem" is that there isn't any,' said Leila. 'The radiators seem to be full of cold bricks as far as I can tell.'

'Ah, storage heaters,' said Steven. 'Specially designed to heat the house while you're out and maintain fridge-like conditions while you're at home. It's a British tradition. Builds character... Quaint cottage though.'

'Right now, I would happily swap 'quaint' for a nice warm apartment,' said Leila. 'Where are we going?'

'I thought we'd try a restaurant over in King's Lynn. Someone at the hotel recommended it.'

'As long as it's warm,' said Leila, coming back into the room and picking up her handbag from a chair. 'Will I do?'

'You look stunning,' said Steven. And he meant it. He'd heard that most women had a 'little black number' in their wardrobe but was prepared to bet that most women wouldn't look like Leila in it.

'I'm tempted to put a sweater on top,' she said.

'Oh, don't,' said Steven and their eyes met for a moment.

'Let's go,' smiled Leila, wrapping a leather blouson round her shoulders.

To Steven's relief, the restaurant was warm and welcoming and neither too crowded nor too empty. He immediately felt comfortable and saw that Leila was beginning to relax too.

'God, it's so nice to get away from the lab for a while,' she said. 'I was beginning to feel as if I was in prison. So tell me, what is all the panic about?'

'You saw the papers this morning. The police have changed their minds. They no longer think that animal rights extremists were behind the attack on the institute or the murders of Professor Devon and Robert Smith and that of course, has certain implications...'

'But the mess...the slogans everywhere...the leaflets...'

'Red herrings,' said Steven, watching to see if Leila was familiar with the expression. She was.

'And you? What do you think?'

'I agree,' said Steven.

'But what other reason could there be?'

'The worst scenario would be that the attackers knew about the Cambodia 5 virus and wanted to get their hands on it.'

'Oh, my God,' said Leila. 'But Smithy, the animal man, why kill him? He didn't know anything about viruses, poor man.'

Steven told her about the doubts raised by Smith over the last monkey brought in by the army.

'But this is terrible!' exclaimed Leila.

'But it does explain why so many people have been asking you about the progress of your vaccine strain,' said Steven.

'Of course,' said Leila. 'They think someone is going to use the Cambodia 5 strain as a weapon and they need the vaccine.'

'We know that they didn't manage to get their hands on the concentrated, pure virus, which Devon had in the special safe in his room, but there is a very real chance that they will be able to recover it from the infected monkey if that's really what all this is about. I say "if" because this is still all conjecture.'

'It doesn't bear thinking about,' said Leila.

'I'm afraid it does,' said Steven. 'A great deal of thinking about, but not necessarily by us and certainly not tonight. What d'you say we have an evening without talk of labs and viruses and "what-if"s?'

Leila appeared to relax. She smiled and said, 'Agreed, but thank you for telling me, Steven.'

It was just after midnight when they got back to the cottage. 'Would you like to come in for coffee…if you don't freeze before it's ready?' asked Leila.

Steven walked her up the path to the door with his arm round her shoulder. 'Brr, you're right,' he said as they got inside and didn't notice any perceptible change in temperature. 'Don't you have any other form of heating?'

'There is an old electric fire in the bedroom,' said Leila. 'It keeps me alive while I'm dressing. Why don't you bring it through while I make the coffee?' She pointed to an arched wooden door. 'Through there.'

Steven ducked his head and walked through. The whole house seemed to smell of cold and damp although it was mixed with a hint of *Anais anais* perfume in Leila's bedroom. He smiled as the thought occurred to him that he had made it into Leila Martin's bedroom and he couldn't resist a sideways glance at the bed where an old fashioned patchwork quilt sat on top of what appeared to be a mountain of blankets in front of a dark mahogany headboard. He unplugged the ancient, one bar electric fire that sat in the middle of the floor: it had rust patches all over its reflective back plate and a badly frayed flex. He brought it through to the living room and plugged it into the wall. The smell of burning dust started to compete with the smell of damp.

'Thank you so much for tonight,' said Leila as she came through from the kitchen with two steaming mugs of coffee. 'It was so nice to escape for a while.'

'Then we must do it again,' said Steven.

'That would be nice,' agreed Leila. 'But I have a vaccine to make and so many people seem to be depending on it... Excuse me... I'll just have to put on a sweater.' Leila shivered and rubbed her arms before disappearing into the bedroom and coming back a few moments later wearing a heavy knit sweater over her 'little black number'. She hugged herself with crossed arms and Steven smiled as she re-joined him on the couch. 'You have an open fireplace,' he said. 'It's just a question of getting something to burn in it, logs, coal...'

'Maybe start with the furniture,' said Leila, looking about her.

Steven conceded that she had a point. The cottage appeared to have been furnished from jumble sales of long ago.

They finished their coffee and Leila said, 'Well, I should really get some sleep now.'

'Me too,' agreed Steven. 'I've got an early start. I have to drive to London for a meeting at the Home Office.'

'About the virus?' asked Leila.

'And what they intend doing about it should it get free,' said Steven, getting to his feet.

'Thank you again,' said Leila, getting up too.

'Don't mention it.' Steven leaned towards her and kissed her gently on the lips, hoping she wouldn't pull away but giving her the opportunity. When she didn't, he put his arms round her and brought her closer. She seemed to melt into him easily enough and the surprise he felt when she parted lips brought on such a feeling of excitement that he moved his hands down her back, over the hem of the long sweater and on to her bottom. He felt a resistance begin in Leila's body and relaxed his grip. 'Not tonight,' she murmured in his ear.

'I'd like to see you again,' Steven said.

'You will,' said Leila. 'Now go before we both freeze to death.'

The hubbub in the room died down as the Home Office minister brought the meeting to order. 'I need hardly remind you why we are here, ladies and gentlemen,' he said. 'Sci-Med have identified and reported to the *Earlybird* committee what might well be a serious threat to the security of our country and we are here to consider our response. For once, we know what the threat is rather than having to deal with a vague notion. It's the Cambodia 5 virus and you have all been briefed on its capabilities.'

'There was no mention in the briefing notes of a mortality rate for Cambodia 5,' interrupted one of the intelligence services people.

Nigel Lees accepted the nod from the Home Office minister and answered. 'That's because we simply don't know,' he said. 'There has never been an outbreak of Cambodia 5 to provide us with precedent. If it should turn out to be similar to the 1918 flu virus, we can expect something around 30 percent fatality. If the very worst should happen and the avian mortality rate should prove transferable to humans then we could be looking at...90 percent?'

There were gasps around the table. 'Nine out of ten will die?'

'If the very worst comes to the very worst.'

'The key to dealing with the problem is isolation,' said Lees. 'And the key to that is preparation. We must be on the look-out at all times. The merest suspicion of people going down with flu must be acted upon and the victims kept in isolation to contain spread of the disease. There's no treatment for the virus and as yet – although we are hopeful – no vaccine against it, so the only way to stop it is to prevent people getting it in the first place. Warnings are being sent out to all hospitals, clinics and doctors' surgeries. Vigilance is the key.'

Vigilance is the key, thought Steven. Another bloody sound bite. Did the whole world speak in them these days?

'How much time do we have?' asked a woman from the General Nursing Council.

The question was passed to a man identified as a microbiologist attached to Defence Intelligence Services. 'That rather depends on who the opposition are and how well they are organised.'

'So you don't know for sure that it's al-Qaeda?'

'Far from it, all we have to go on is that one is named "Ali" and they all look Indian or Pakistani. Even that's not reliable as the witness wasn't capable of that degree of identification.'

'Ye gods,' said someone and there were sighs of agreement.

'The fact that they would need decent lab facilities and the wherewithal to isolate and grow up pure virus from the escaped monkey tends to work in our favour,' said the microbiologist. 'Even if they've got suitable premises, it will still take some time to obtain enough pure virus to mount an attack of sufficient magnitude to ensure an epidemic. It has to be grown up in fertile hens' eggs.'

'Strikes me that not too many people order up fertile hens' eggs,' said Steven. 'That might be a way of getting to them.'

'DIS are on that as we speak,' smiled the microbiologist.

'You don't think they'll just infect a few people and let nature take its course?' suggested someone else. 'It is highly infectious.'

'We think not. The newspaper stories will have alerted them to the fact that we didn't fall for the animal rights motive at the Crick so they know that all GPs and hospitals will have been warned to be on the look-out for flu in the coming months. We think they'll hold off and go for the big hit – always assuming that they have the lab facilities.'

'If they do go for the big one, any idea what form it might take?'

'Aerosol attack in a crowded place, rail station, department store, something along those lines.'

'And if things should get that far?'

'If things should get that far and no vaccine protection has been made available...an epidemic would be unavoidable.'

'Supposing a vaccine was available, how long does it take to become effective in preventing infection?'

'Thankfully, not long at all, two or three days should be sufficient.'

'Nothing more has been mentioned about a 9/11 style attack on Canary Wharf,' said the officer from the Metropolitan Police. 'Can we assume that this has now been discredited?'

'I rather think we can,' said the Home Office Minister. 'It seems as if the scepticism of DIS expressed at our last meeting was justified. It was a diversion.'

'To divert attention from an attempted Cambodia 5 virus attack?'

'That may well be the case.'

'It didn't stop certain government sources claiming success for smashing a planned attack on Canary Wharf though, did it?' said someone.

The Home Office minister looked uncomfortable. He said, 'Sometimes those at the interface between government and the media interpret things differently...'

'Spin doctors,' said the same person with obvious distaste.

'I think such an interpretation is called lying in your own interests,' added the London Fire Brigades officer.

'I think internal explanations and apologies, where seen fit, have already been made,' said the Home Office minister. 'Although it would be fair to say that no deliberate intent to deceive was involved.'

Perish the thought, thought Steven.

'When the first reports from DIS came in they had to be treated as a genuine al-Qaeda threat. It was only after interrogation that DIS started to suspect they were being fed erroneous information.'

'Perhaps Colonel Rose would care to give us an update on what DIS obtained from the suspects under interrogation?' suggested John Macmillan.

'Not a great deal,' admitted Rose. 'The truth is they didn't know much to begin with – that's why we were led to them in the first place. They were low level people, sacrificed by al Qaeda in order to send us on a wild goose chase. The best we've managed to get out of them is a few more names, which we're checking out, but it's odds on they'll be low level operatives too.'

'Thank you, Colonel.'

'Well, ladies and gentlemen,' said the Home Office minister, 'if there are no more questions or comments, I think I'll call this meeting to a close. Perhaps the Sci-Med people would stay behind for a few minutes.'

Steven and Macmillan looked at each other. Macmillan's shrug told Steven that he didn't know either why they'd been asked to stay.

'No need to look so worried,' said the Home Office minister when he rejoined Steven and Macmillan after seeing the others out. 'Sherry?'

The two Sci-Med men sat sipping what Steven expected Macmillan to call 'a decent amontillado' although he didn't, while the Home Office minister took a phone call. 'Nothing I couldn't handle, Home Secretary... Absolutely, Home

Secretary... Nice of you to say so, sir... I certainly will, they're with me now.'

'The Home Secretary sends his regards and his congratulations to you Dr Dunbar for seeing through the animal rights ruse.'

Steven gave an 'all in a day's work' nod.

'I thought it only right to keep you chaps abreast of our efforts to clear the decks for Dr Martin's vaccine if and when it becomes available. We have reached agreement with the FDA in the USA and with our own people at MHRA. They have both agreed to give her vaccine their seal of approval subject only to routine tests for bacterial contamination before distribution – understandable I think in the circumstances, when that's what caused all the problems last year at Auroragen.'

'So it's all coming down to a simple race between Dr Martin and al-Qaeda,' said Macmillan.

'I saw her yesterday,' said Steven. 'The vaccine seed strain has been constructed. It's growing up in fertile eggs as we speak. It's just a question of whether it grows up in time to be handed over to Auroragen.'

'Latest possible date is February 21st,' said the Home Office Minister. 'Any later than that and the company will revert to using the three strains recommended by the World Health Organisation.'

'Has WHO been made aware of the situation?' asked Macmillan.

'Of course, but they can't recommend incorporation of a vaccine seed strain that doesn't as yet exist. They say they'll have to advocate use of the best three known strains for the preparation of next year's vaccine.'

'And if Leila's strain *is* ready in time?' asked Steven, immediately wishing he hadn't used Leila's first name.

'Then, like the FDA and MHPRA, they are prepared to nod it through with the minimum of paperwork.'

'Good.'

CHAPTER THIRTEEN

'A patrol car has just radioed in with some information, sir,' said Sergeant Mark Morley. 'They've been called to a flat in Sefton Road. Neighbours have been complaining about a smell...'

Frank Giles got to his feet. 'I take it we're talking about a particular smell if the officers have called in?'

'Yes sir, PC Robson's a twenty year man: he knows the smell of death well enough and in view of your alert about reports of illness...'

'Do we know who the flat's registered to?'

'The lease holder is one Abu Zahid. The neighbours say three young Asian men live there.'

'Better organise a biohazard team and I'll call Dunbar. This could be what he was looking for.'

Forty minutes later Steven, Giles and the biohazard team met up in Sefton Street which had already been sealed off by uniformed officers.

'Do we know what we're dealing with here?' asked the leader of the biohazard team when he'd been introduced by Giles to Steven.

'Not for sure, but possibly a highly infectious virus,' said Steven. 'We'll need full containment protocol set up before entering the flat and full wash-down facilities for those coming out. The smell from inside says we'll also need hermetic-seal body bags but we don't know how many yet.' Steven turned to Giles and asked, 'I take it you have a forensic team standing by?'

'They're here, just waiting for the nod.'

'They'll need respirators.'

'I'll tell them. I take it you're going in with the team?'

'If they can give me a suit,' said Steven.

The team leader detailed one of his men to fetch one. The man took a few seconds to appraise Steven's size before heading off.

'We're going to look a right bunch of clowns if it turns out to be a dead rat in the drains,' said Giles.

'I could live with that,' said Steven, considering the alternative. He took the suit that was handed to him and started getting into it. The other waited for him and then they all checked the seals on each other's suits and hoods before setting off towards the entrance to the flat where two of the team had already set up a secondary entrance out of plastic sheeting. This amounted to a porch which would prevent any organism escaping from within the flat when the door was opened. Once they were all inside the plastic bubble, the sheeting was sealed behind them before the door was forced open and they moved inside.

There were three dead bodies in the flat, all of Middle Eastern appearance and all three found in the one bedroom where they lay on separate single beds. There was no obvious sign of violence and the abundance of tissue boxes and bottles of cough remedies and aspirin suggested illness rather than violence. There were bowls of congealed, blood-flecked sputum lying next to the beds and blood-stained tissues scattered across the floor. After making sure that all three were dead, Steven signalled to the team leader that they should leave things as they were and gestured towards the door. They trooped out in single file and were washed down with disinfectant sprays before removing their hoods.

'Good call from your men,' said Steven to Giles. 'Three dead and they all look like virus victims. We should let forensics do their business before we touch anything. When they're finished, the biohazard boys can wrap the bodies for removal and clear and disinfect the site. You'll have to warn the police pathologist about the danger at post-mortem.'

'I'll tell Marge,' said Giles.

When he heard the name, Steven remembered that he'd met her before and that she'd been right – they were all a long way from Walton's Mountain.

By three in the afternoon, the dead men had all been identified from ID found in the flat. They were Abu Zahid (24), Nasser Qatada (23) and Ahmed Mohammed (23). A preliminary investigation established that they appeared to have no connection with anyone else in the city but all three had relations living in Leicester.

'How did you get on?' Giles asked Morley when he came back from leading the team interviewing the neighbours. 'Let me guess. Quiet, respectable chaps who kept themselves very much to themselves?'

'Incredible. You could give Paul Daniels a run for his money, sir,' said Morley.

'The point is,' said Giles, 'Was one of them "Ali"?'

'Maybe we could try out Shanks with a photograph of the bodies?' suggested Morley.

'A good thought; do that, will you?'

'I didn't draw a complete blank with the neighbours,' said Morley. 'One of them told me that the dead men had a vehicle, an old Land Rover, he said. The kind farmers use. He thinks they kept it in a lock-up round the back in Granary Lane. Uniform are on it right now.'

'Well done. Warn forensics and tell them to give it a right going over. They're looking for anything that will connect the vehicle to the Robert Smith murder.'

Steven returned to his hotel and called Macmillan to tell him of the day's events.

'God, it's like a nightmare unfolding before our eyes,' said Macmillan. 'Did you find any indication of what they were up to in the flat?'

'No,' said Steven. 'But it wasn't being used as a lab if that's what you were getting at.'

'It was,' agreed Macmillan. 'So on the face of it we have three dead men of possibly Middle Eastern origin with Cambodia 5 being the likely cause of death but with no indication as to how they got it?'

'That's about it at the moment but stay tuned, as they say,' said Steven.

'Wild horses, etc,' said Macmillan.

Three hours later, as Steven was preparing to drive over to the city mortuary to check on progress of the post-mortem examinations of the men, he got a call from Colonel Rose at the Defence Intelligence Service.

'They're on our list,' said Rose. 'All three of them.'

'You have the better of me, Colonel,' said Steven. 'What list?'

'Suspected al-Qaeda associates. The three dead men are all English, born in Leicester, but they got sucked into the Muslim fundamentalist movement by persuasive clerics working the Midlands. All three have recently been 'on holiday' to Pakistan but it's odds on they spent time at what we like to call, "Butlin's, Kabul" – Mujahadeen training camps in Afghanistan.'

'So now we have a definite al-Qaeda connection.'

"Fraid so,' said Rose. 'Albeit a low level one as far as these three were concerned. They're puppets. It's who's pulling the strings we have to worry about.'

'And what kind of show they're planning to put on,' murmured Steven. 'Thanks Colonel.'

'Well, John Boy, weren't we lucky it was only flu that you and Sci-Med were worried about?' said Marjorie Ryman sarcastically as Steven, gowned and masked, entered the post mortem room. Frank Giles was already there.

'Just doing my job, Elizabeth,' said Steven although he was stung by the comment. Ryman was another of the people he had had to be circumspect with at the outset.

Ryman continued to work without saying anything for fully a minute although the sound of instruments she tossed into the metal tray beside her acted as punctuation marks in a silence that spoke eloquently of her displeasure. Eventually, she looked up at Steven and said, 'This man's airways were so full of bloody mucous that he actually drowned in it. That's how he died...'

The stare continued and Steven was prompted to say, 'Thank you, Doctor.'

'Thank you, Doctor?' exclaimed Ryman. 'Is that all you have to say?'

'What would you like me to say?' said Steven evenly.

'I would like you to tell me *why* his airways are so full of bloody mucous, Doctor,' said Ryman.

'Influenza,' said Steven. 'I wasn't lying. It really is flu.'

'But not as we know it, Captain?' suggested Ryman acidly.

'It's a strain called Cambodia 5,' said Steven. 'It's a genetically engineered variant of an avian flu virus found in Cambodia last year and is very similar to the pandemic strain of 1918. Professor Devon of the Crick Institute was asked by government to design a vaccine against it because the World Health Organisation thinks that such a strain will evolve naturally in the very near future.'

'Well, thank *you* for that, Doctor,' said Ryman. She turned to Giles. 'Now I can tell *you*, Inspector, that this man almost certainly died of Cambodia 5 virus infection although lab tests – which I suspect will not be performed in the circumstances – would be needed to confirm that conclusion.'

'And the other two as well?' asked Giles.

'No,' said Ryman. 'They were murdered.'

Giles and Steven looked at each other, stunned and equally taken aback. 'Murdered?'

'Both were suffering from the same disease as the man who drowned in his own mucosal secretions and probably would have died anyway judging by the state of their lungs and airways, but this obviously wasn't quick enough for the person who decided to help them on their way. They were both asphyxiated.'

'Shit,' murmured Giles.

'I guess they became surplus to requirements,' said Steven.

'Whose requirements?' asked Ryman.

'We don't know that yet,' said Steven. It drew a doubting look from Ryman but she carried on with her work.

Steven and Giles left the mortuary together. It was already dark and frost was making the pavements sparkle under the street lights. 'Anything back from forensics?' Steven asked.

Giles shook his head. 'They're still working on the Land Rover although they did find three empty petrol cans in the back. It's almost certainly the vehicle used in the murder of Robert Smith.'

'So the three dead men were the murderers?' said Steven. 'It was three men your witness saw, wasn't it?'

'Yep, three, the woman was absolutely certain about that.'

'Which now leaves us looking for at least a fourth,' said Steven.

'What was all this John Boy – Elizabeth stuff about?' asked Giles.

'Just an ongoing joke about real life versus Waltons' Mountain,' said Steven. 'Dr Ryman has noted significant differences.'

'She's not alone,' said Giles. 'So how come these guys got infected with Cambodia 5?'

'That's something I'd like to know too,' said Steven. 'They

must have come into contact with the missing monkey or with biological material obtained from it.'

'Now there's an unhappy thought,' murmured Giles. His phone rang: it was Mark Morley. After a brief conversation he snapped it shut and said to Steven, 'Shanks didn't recognise any of the three men as being Ali.'

'So Ali could be their killer,' said Steven.

'Strikes me that Ali is running the show,' said Giles. His phone rang again. 'Yes sir,... I think you can... Well, the neighbours saw what was going on anyway...yes sir, as you say, best to quash any wild rumours in the bud...no sir, no harm at all in suggesting that... Good bye, sir.

'That was the Chief Super. He's about to brief the Press about the three dead men. Wanted to know what I thought about letting it be known that they were prime suspects in the murder of Robert Smith. Thinks it would be good for public relations.'

'Not to mention his career,' said Steven.

'Way of the world, Steven,' said Giles. 'Way of the world.'

The story was carried by the morning papers and came out exactly the way the police wanted it to: the murderers of Robert Smith had been traced to and found dead in a flat in Sefton Street. The police had got their men. The public had been spared the expense of a trial. There were no loose ends. End of story. Steven was reading it over breakfast when Giles rang.

'I thought I'd give you an update on forensics,' he said. 'The lab has identified hair found in the back of the Land Rover as belonging to a monkey.'

'Well done,' murmured Steven. 'Now we know how they were infected.'

'Maybe Shanks was telling the truth about Ali going back to the institute after the initial raid, only he wasn't on his own; he had these guys with him.'

'And they stole the infected monkey directly from the institute using the Land Rover,' said Steven. 'That would make more sense. That monkey was never out in the wild at all. That's why the army couldn't find any trace of it.'

'Then later, someone planted another monkey out there for them to find just to get rid of them,' said Giles. His phone rang. 'Shit...hang on... What is it, Morley?'

Steven waited while Giles spoke to Morley. He heard Giles say he would be 'right with him' before he came back on the line.

'That was Morley with the final forensics report on the Land Rover. It was pretty clean apart from the petrol cans I told you about earlier and of course, the monkey hair but they did find a petrol receipt under one of the front seats. We're off to check with the filling station. It's a bit of a long shot but the cashiers might remember something.'

'Good luck,' said Steven.

'Oh, and the Chief Super has just told me officially that the Intelligence Services are now operating on our patch. I've been instructed to give them every assistance should they request it. I hear they've already muscled in on our forensic people and taken away some of their samples.'

'Well, we're all going to the same party,' said Steven.

'I'll try to remember that,' said Giles.

*　*　*

Steven felt at a loose end. He tried to think of something constructive he could be doing to help but the game, as Sherlock Holmes might have put it, was afoot, and now he could only wait. The fact that the prospects of success did not seem to be good wasn't helping. The police and security services had no leads at all as far as the man, Ali, was concerned and the only hope of finding out more about what the three dead men had been up to seemed to lie in a single petrol receipt and with the memory of a filling station attendant. Steven checked on his laptop for any messages from Sci-Med. There was one: it was the list of animal suppliers he had asked for when he'd first heard about Robert Smith's doubts regarding the identity of the dead monkey brought in by the army. This was now largely redundant: Smith had been proved all too right. The real Chloe had been stolen by terrorists.

Wondering if there was anything else he could be doing, Steven remembered that DIS was investigating suppliers of fertile hens' eggs. He called Colonel Rose.

'We drew a complete blank, I'm afraid. No orders for fertile white leghorn eggs have been received by any of the suppliers from anyone other than accredited laboratories in the past six months. I suppose the opposition could be experimenting with cell culture instead of using eggs?'

'I doubt it,' said Steven. 'That's what everyone in the business would like to be doing but there are so many problems that they've always had to come back to hens' eggs in the end. I can't see terrorists succeeding in makeshift premises where the big boys of the pharmaceutical industry have failed.'

'I can't see them having their own chicken farm either,' said Rose.

'Fair point,' agreed Steven.

Steven was pondering on what Rose had said when his phone went. It was Leila.

'Just thought I'd see how you were,' she said.

'It's nice to hear a friendly voice.'

'I read that the police caught the men who murdered Smithy,' said Leila.

'Unfortunately they were already dead when the police got to them but they did well to find them so quickly,' said Steven.

'The papers didn't say how they died...'

'Cambodia 5,' said Steven.

'Oh my God,' said Leila. 'But how?'

'That's what everyone's working on at the moment. How are things at your end? How's the vaccine strain coming along?'

'Still touch and go but I'm confident we could be ready on time if we keep up the sub-culture schedule and the Department of Health did something to keep the damned bureaucrats off my back.'

'Is that a problem?'

'I'll say. They seem to be reneging on their original agreement. I'm getting continual requests from both the FDA and MHPRA for inspection visits to be made to the institute and quality testing to be done. I really don't have time for all this nonsense right now.'

'I thought that the powers-that-be had dealt with all that?' said Steven.

'The latest people to get in on the act are Auroragen. It

seems like they've changed their minds about relaxing their own company regulations. They want to send people to take samples for testing and there isn't time.'

'I suppose they're a bit sensitive about what happened last year when MHPRA pulled the plug on them,' said Steven.

'Maybe, but I wish they'd stop trying to make their problems mine.'

'They lost a lot of money over contaminated vaccine last year.'

'But it was their own staff who contaminated the vaccine,' exclaimed Leila. 'They should concentrate on putting their own house in order and let me take care of things at the institute.'

'I take your point,' agreed Steven. 'I think everyone is getting a bit jumpy at the moment. Nerves are strung to breaking point.'

'Well, I have turned all requests for visits down,' said Leila. 'The technicians and I have been working our butts off to get this vaccine strain ready in time and I refuse to let a bunch of bureaucrats with clipboards make us miss the deadline. If they don't like it I have a good mind to pull out of the whole thing and hand in my resignation. I feel that strongly.'

'I'll have a word with John Macmillan,' said Steven. 'If anyone can cut through red tape, he can.'

Leila's voice softened, 'Thank you, Steven,' she said. 'I'm sorry for sounding off at you. I suppose I'm just tired. Everything seems to be getting to me these days.'

'I could offer you dinner and conversation...?'

'I'd love to but I'm going to be at the lab until well after ten tonight.'

'I understand.'

'But you could come round after? We could have a nightcap perhaps?'

'Wonderful,' said Steven, 'I'll see you at the cottage about eleven?'

'Quarter past.'

Steven had been feeling depressed before getting Leila's call but now he was whistling softly as he dialled John Macmillan's number.

'I thought Lees at DOH had seen to all that,' said Macmillan when Steven told him about the red tape problems that Leila was having. 'I'll get on to him. Not much I can do about Auroragen though,' he added. 'They're a commercial enterprise.'

'Maybe I should go see them?' suggested Steven. 'The personal touch might succeed where officialdom has failed.'

'Wouldn't do any harm,' agreed Macmillan. 'I'll have Jean contact them and set something up. She'll get back to you.'

'God, I'm so sorry I'm late,' said Leila as she got out of her car and came over to where Steven was sitting in his.

'Nonsense,' he said, smiling and getting out. 'You're a busy lady.'

'It's still very rude,' said Leila. 'And I'm sorry.' She stood there looking up at Steven and he leaned forward and kissed her on the forehead.

'I wasn't happy with the virus titre after the last sub-culture so I repeated it on a new batch of eggs.'

'No need to explain, really,' said Steven. 'I'm just happy to see you at all under the circumstances.'

'Come, let's set fire to the furniture and get warm,' said Leila leading the way indoors.

'It will be a close-run thing – red tape or hypothermia to drive me mad first,' said Leila. 'You get the fire from the bedroom; I'll put the kettle on.'

'I had a word with John Macmillan,' called Steven as he plugged in the electric fire in the living room. 'He's going to do what he can to get the pen-pushers off your back and I'm going up to see the people at Auroragen to see if I can talk some sense into them.'

'Thanks, Steven, I really appreciate it,' Leila said from the kitchen.

'Well, it's a fair bet the opposition don't have red tape to contend with.'

'Are the police making any progress with their investigation?' asked Leila as she put down two mugs of coffee on the table in front of the couch and then went over to a cupboard to return with a bottle of brandy and two balloon glasses. 'I promised you a nightcap,' she said.

'All they've got to go on is a receipt from a petrol station. It's not much.'

'I suppose there's a chance that the three men who died got the disease before they could do anything about growing up the virus.'

'I'd like to think so but two of them were murdered so we know there's a fourth person involved – maybe more – and there was no indication of what happened to the monkey.'

'Murdered?' exclaimed Leila and Steven explained.

Leila took a gulp of her brandy. 'My God.'

'You look done in.'

'Another couple of weeks and it will all be done,' sighed Leila. 'Then I can sleep and sleep...and sleep.'

Steven wrapped his arm round her shoulders and Leila snuggled into him. 'Thank you, Steven,' she murmured.

'For what?'

'For being there and putting up with my bad temper. It's good to know I have someone to call on. The people in London tell me nothing.'

'It's a way of life for them. Silence born of insecurity.'

'Well, I'm grateful; I really am.'

Steven kissed her gently.

'God, I am just so tired... I'm sorry. I'm such awful company.'

Steven kissed her again and put a finger to her lips. 'There will be time enough for us when this is all over.'

'Yes please,' said Leila.

CHAPTER FOURTEEN

'God has turned over a new leaf,' said Giles on the phone to Steven. 'He's been kind to us. The attendant at the filling station remembers three Asian men in a Land Rover. Apparently they'd been in before and she got the impression that they were living or working locally. We've investigated and they weren't employed anywhere within a ten mile radius of the garage but with the aid of the lab and an analysis of the muck that was in the tyres we think we know where they've been hanging out.'

'Brilliant,' said Steven. 'Where?'

'It's an old mill property between Docking and Heacham called, Jessop's Mill. We've checked with the agents and it's under a six months lease agreement to a Mr Zahid.'

'Who was one of the three men in the flat,' said Steven. 'Great work. I take it you haven't approached the place?'

'Fat chance,' said Giles. 'DIS, MI5, Special Branch and the SAS are all tooling up to go in mob handed as we speak.'

'Let's hope they don't get in each other's way,' said Steven.

'They've graciously agreed that the police can come along for the ride,' said Giles. 'As long as we don't interfere with the professionals...'

'I'd like to join you.'

'Be here in fifteen for the briefing.'

Steven was the last to arrive and was introduced to the others in the squad briefing room. There were about twenty men, all in civilian clothes apart from the SAS soldiers whose leader came over to Steven and offered his hand. 'I understand you were regiment?'

'Some years ago.'

'You're still well thought of at Hereford.'

'Good to know,' said Steven. 'I take it you're carrying out the initial assault on the mill?'

'That's our brief...with particular emphasis on the fact that no one and nothing must escape from the building.'

'And if it should turn out to be heavily defended?'

'We torch the lot with incendiaries until it and everything in it is a pile of ash.'

Nice clear mandate, thought Steven as the officer walked to the front of the room. There never had been much room for Rupert Brooke in the SAS.

The officer briefed the room on what would be the unfolding chain of events. The SAS already had a recce team in position near the mill: they had been watching the building from before dawn. So far, they had reported no comings or goings. The SAS would carry out the initial assault on the building and make it secure. The biohazard team would then enter and report back. Anyone captured inside the building would be handed over immediately to the security services to be taken away for interrogation. When the situation inside the building was considered safe and stable, Steven and the police teams would be free to carry out inspection and forensic examination of the mill and its contents.

'Any questions?'

There were none.

Shortly after 11 a.m., with everyone in position, the SAS troop went into action. Steven watched as camouflaged figures flitted across and around the building, crouching and running, pressing themselves to the walls as they came close to windows. It was like watching a silent film, as he saw the soldiers communicate by hand signal alone. He had expected them to use stun grenades before breaking in through the front door but he could see from his position in the undergrowth that there had been an impromptu change of plan: they must have concluded that the ground floor was unoccupied. Their leader obviously felt that the element of surprise was still with them and should be exploited. A window at the side of the mill was forced open and two gas-masked soldiers disappeared inside.

Steven held his breath, steeling himself for the sound of an explosion or a burst of automatic fire coming from the upstairs rooms but the silence continued until the minutes started to pass like hours. It seemed such an anticlimax when the front door was opened by the two soldiers who had climbed inside. They were stripping off their masks and loosening their protective gear.

The biohazard team went inside after a brief discussion with the soldiers' leader and Steven walked over to have a word with him.

'Nobody home,' said the soldier. 'Is that good or bad?'

'Could be either,' said Steven. 'Did it look like an orderly withdrawal or a drop-everything-and-run job?'

'I'd guess at the former,' said the soldier. 'Nothing Mary Celeste about it, no personal possessions lying about, in fact, not much of anything lying around.'

'Any room that looked like it was used as a lab?

'There's a tiled room downstairs in the basement with a large fridge in it and a few bits of glassware. There's a little room off it which I thought was a sauna at first but maybe not. It was certainly warm but not that warm if you know what I mean and there were some empty boxes in it.'

'What kind of empty boxes?' asked Steven.

'The sort you get eggs in. You know, *papier mache* trays.'

'Their incubator room,' said Steven.

The soldier gave Steven a blank look.

'Where they were growing the virus. It's grown in fertile hens' eggs kept at body temperature.'

The biohazard team didn't take long to declare the building free from any overt biological or chemical danger and Steven and Giles took a look at the 'lab' for themselves when the forensic team had finished their work.

'The whole place was probably cleared out when the three of them fell sick,' said Giles, running his fingers along a smooth, plastic-topped table. 'So it's back to square one.'

Steven took a look inside the incubator room where the egg boxes had been found. He counted the number of tray spaces and did a rough calculation in his head. 'Not a big operation,' he said. 'They'll need to culture a lot more virus if they're going for a big hit.'

'Excuse me, sir,' said one of the forensic team who'd been

going through the upstairs rooms and had just appeared in the doorway. 'We found this in one of the drawers.'

Giles took what looked like a folded map from the man and opened it out on the table. Steven thought it was going to be a road map of the surrounding area but it turned out to be something quite different. It was a map of the UK. On it, six major cities including London and Edinburgh had been circled in red.

'Even my cat, Tiddles, could work this one out,' murmured Giles.

'They *are* going for the big one,' said Steven, feeling a sense of desolation come over him. Although the spectre of nuclear and biological weapons had been around for long enough, many people including himself had been clinging to the hope that they wouldn't be used in their lifetime and hopefully never – in the way that tomorrow always seems very near but never actually comes. Now the red circles on the map were painting pictures of people falling down in the streets of major cities, struggling for breath as bloody mucous choked their airways and fever sent them into delirium. Schools and offices would close, transport would grind to a halt, electricity and water supplies would fail, food would run out and the law of the jungle would rule the streets.

'You OK?' asked Giles as they climbed the stairs.

'Fine,' said Steven.

As they reached the front door, Steven stopped and said, 'I wonder if they took their rubbish with them...'

'We can check,' said Giles. 'If they were any good, they would have...'

They walked round the sides and back of the building looking for rubbish bins and found three plastic wheelie bins lined up beside the old mill wheel enclosure. One contained mouldy grass clippings, probably left over from the summer and probably by a previous tenant, thought Steven as the sour smell of partially fermented grass assaulted his nostrils: the other two bins were empty.

'Guess they were smart enough to take it with them,' said Giles.

'Guess God stopped being kind,' said Steven.

'What were you looking for anyway?'

'I don't know...' said Steven, giving an uneasy shrug. 'Eggshells...syringes...dead chick embryos...general lab detritus...' He spread his hands and looked about him. 'A dead monkey even...'

'You know, getting rid of a large monkey would be almost as difficult as getting rid of a human body,' said Giles after a moment's thought. 'Not easy at the best of times but I can't honestly see them carting it round the country with them. Maybe I should put some of the guys on to searching the grounds for shallow graves?'

'Or the site of a recent bonfire,' said Steven. 'They may have burned it but the bones should still be around.'

When Giles returned from setting up the search he found Steven taking another look at the wheelie bins.

'Dry,' he said. 'They didn't use these bins at all.'

'Maybe they put the waste in plastic bags?' said Giles.

'Maybe,' agreed Steven. 'But they didn't store the bags in the bins either. The dirt on the bottom hasn't been disturbed for many months. You could write your name in it.'

'Strikes me this Ali is a real pro,' said Giles. 'He leaves nothing to chance.'

Steven nodded thoughtfully. Any reply was cut short by a shout from one of the policemen searching the grounds. Steven and Giles headed off in that direction.

'Ground's been disturbed here,' said the Constable, pointing to an area of bare earth that seemed loosely packed compared to the surrounding area.

'Well done,' said Giles. He turned to Steven and asked, 'What do you think: forensics or biohazard?'

'Definitely biohazard,' said Steven. 'We can't take chances. The virus will die quickly when it doesn't have living cells to grow inside but we don't know how long the monkey's been dead – if it's the monkey. The virus will certainly survive for a few days after death. Maybe longer if the temperature and the conditions are right.'

Steven joined the biohazard team for the disinterment. A plastic tent was erected over the site and a body bag was laid out nearby. Disinfectant spray operators stood by upwind of the site. Inside the tent, Steven watched as two men, using trowels, started to remove the loose earth gingerly and pile it up on one side. They had excavated the site to a depth of some eighteen inches when one of them held up his hand and pointed to something in the trench. Steven took a closer look and saw that it was a hairy hand. Chloe, the missing monkey.

The body of the animal had been buried face down in the grave. It seemed complete and fairly well preserved, thought Steven. The cold temperatures had delayed decomposition but this also meant that there was a danger that the virus might still be alive in its tissues. Steven asked the team to turn the animal over slowly, causing a general recoiling among the team when it became apparent that the animal's torso had been sliced open from neck to crotch.

Steven knelt down by the grave to take a closer look. He could see that the trachea and lungs had been removed from the animal and not by someone boasting any great medical skills. The surgery looked as if it had been carried out using a Swiss Army knife. He got to his feet and signalled that the body could be bagged.

Outside the tent, Steven was first in line to be decontaminated by the men operating the disinfectant sprays. Finally he removed his visor and went over to join Giles.

'The right monkey this time?' asked Giles.

'The right monkey,' confirmed Steven. 'They cut the lungs and trachea from it. That's where they would get the initial virus to start off the egg cultures with.'

'At least the bloody thing's not running round the country,' said Giles.

Steven reported back to Macmillan and was told in turn that a meeting had been arranged for him with Auroragen next day at 2p.m. 'Do your best to smooth things over with them. From what you've said, it's beginning to look more and more like that vaccine is going to be our only chance,' said Macmillan.

'The trouble is,' said Steven, 'I can't tell Auroragen just why the new vaccine has become so important. I have to stick to the WHO story that a mutated avian strain of flu is likely to appear in the near future.'

'You're right,' said Macmillan. 'It lacks impact but any suggestion of an imminent al-Qaeda strike using Cambodia 5 leaking out into the public domain and we'll have mass panic on our hands. Do your best.'

Steven drove up to Liverpool through rain and wind. The weather matched his dark mood as did the Gregorian chant he had playing on the car's CD player. He sought escapism in a sound that had come down through the centuries in celebration of a belief which, although he did not share, represented some kind of calming continuum in an ever changing landscape of doubt. He found it hard to analyse what he was feeling. There was fear and tension and frustration but there was something else as well and he couldn't quite put his finger on it and that was adding annoyance to the mix.

He clicked off the CD as he came to the gates of the Auroragen building and wound down the window to show his ID to the white-haired security man who came towards him. The man limped as though he had an arthritic hip and resented being obliged to move it.

'Visitors car park on the left,' he snapped. 'Stay between the white lines. If you want to stay longer than two hours, you'll need a pass.'

Steven parked the MG between the white lines and walked towards the building pausing briefly at the base of a large abstract sculpture to read the plaque below. He felt sure that it would have a pretentious title and was proved right when he read, 'The Quality of Mercy'.

'Shit,' he murmured. 'And here was me thinking it was a

pile of scrap metal… Sorry, Eduardo.'

He entered the building through smoked glass doors which led to a modern reception area with tiled floors and mosaics of virus particles along the walls. Three young women in corporate navy blue uniform were seated behind the desk, apparently mesmerised by computer screens. He showed his ID to the one who finally looked up and affected an air stewardess smile; he told her that he was expected.

The woman – Melissa from her lapel badge – lifted a blue phone and said into it after a moment's wait, 'Dr Dunbar is here.'

'If you'd like to come with me,' smiled Melissa, coming out from behind the desk and leading the way to a bank of three lifts. She pressed the button and spoke about the weather while they waited. She concluded with, 'Still, we're into February now; it'll soon be spring.'

Steven smiled and hoped it didn't look as contrived as it felt. Being 'into February' meant that they were now counting down the days to the deadline for Leila's vaccine strain to be ready.

Steven was shown into a boardroom where he was introduced in turn to five senior executives of the company. The man doing the introductions was a well-preserved man in his sixties who said curtly that he was, 'John Lamont, in charge of UK operations'.

'Well, Dr Dunbar, how can we help?'

Steven found it difficult to gauge the mood of those present because of the smiling corporate face being presented. He thought due deference might be the way ahead. 'Ladies and gentlemen, it would be ridiculous of me to lecture you on the seriousness of our position should we have to face an outbreak of the type of flu that WHO has issued a warning about recently: so I won't. I am simply here to try and allay some of the fears you have expressed about the new seed strain being prepared and advocated for inclusion in this year's vaccine schedule. I understand that you are having second thoughts about it and have asked for certain safety conditions to be complied with?'

'Dr Dunbar,' said Lamont, pausing to turn a chunky gold pen end over end a few times on the table, 'when we agreed to government requests that certain procedures be...streamlined, for want of a better word, we did not know that the institute providing the new seed strain would be the Crick. In view of recent events and publicity surrounding that particular establishment, it has to be said that we at Auroragen have become, understandably I think you will agree, nervous. In these circumstances it would be difficult for us to agree to anything other than the full letter of the law being applied to the inclusion of any seed strain for the vaccine.'

'You mean, you'll insist on all normal inspections and tests being carried out?'

'I do.'

'But the time factor involved in carrying out these tests would automatically preclude the Crick strain from being used.'

'I fear it would,' agreed Lamont. 'Frankly, we are of a mind to use the three strains currently recommended by WHO.'

'And ignore the threat of an avian strain outbreak?'

'We are a commercial organisation, Doctor. We are not in the business of taking risks we do not have to take, however laudable the cause. We lost a great deal of money last year through failing to meet inspection and regulation conditions set down by government bodies, we are not about to do the same thing again through failing to implement such standards ourselves.'

Ah, thought Steven, this is what it's all about, money, and the company was clearly in the driving seat. 'Frankly, I find that quite understandable,' he said pleasantly. 'You really can't afford to compromise... But supposing government were to perceive the risk of an epidemic as being great enough for them to offer you certain assurances should you agree to the inclusion of the new seed strain...'

'Then that might be a different matter,' said Lamont.

'We would of course, have to know exactly what these assurances were,' added the woman who had been introduced earlier as Lilian Morrison, the company's financial controller.

'Of course,' said Steven.

'And I think that these assurances might well have to extend to...guarantees,' added Lamont.

Well, here we are, thought Steven. That wasn't too difficult. Auroragen wanted government to shoulder all responsibility for including an untested seed strain in their vaccine and to guarantee that they wouldn't lose money over it. 'And if you were to receive such assurances and guarantees...?'

'We would be happy to comply with government wishes.'

'Then I feel optimistic,' said Steven.

The meeting broke up with Steven being asked if he would like to see round the production facilities, an invitation which he readily accepted. The man detailed to do the honours was one of those who had been at the meeting, David Nettles, head of quality control. They had coffee first in his office.

'Last year must have been a bit of a nightmare for you,' said Steven.

'I'll say,' said Nettles.

'What exactly happened?'

'We're still not sure to be honest. It seemed to start off as a simple case of bacterial contamination – which happens from time to time in all virus labs – and we responded accordingly and expected that to be an end to the matter and then it broke out again. We carried out a second massive clean-up operation, which we felt sure would see an end to the problem, although we didn't manage to identify the source of the contamination and blow me, if it didn't break out again. The regulations of course prevent us treating vaccine to get rid of any contaminating bacteria – even harmless ones – so our license was withdrawn and we had to destroy the lot. Forty-eight million doses down the tubes and no flu vaccine for half the USA.'

'Did you ever identify the source of the contamination?'

Nettles shook his head.

'Was it caused by the same organism throughout?'

'It was. A harmless everyday strain of *Serratia,* which you find all over the place but which kept getting into our virus cultures whatever we did to stop it. It ended up costing us millions.'

'Strange,' said Steven. 'No sign of it since?'

'No, touch wood,' replied Nettles. 'We stripped out and

refitted the entire culture suite. Everything that could be changed was changed – including the staff. We replaced all the lab equipment and implemented strict new aseptic measures whereby staff wear coverall suits and visors all the time – and there's been no sign of a problem since.'

Steven was shown round the facilities and was greatly impressed by what he saw. He was left with no doubt in his mind that Auroragen was a thoroughly professional organisation being run by an excellent management team. He drove back to Norfolk and phoned in his report to Macmillan.

'HMG won't like this,' said Macmillan, 'but I don't see that they have any option. They'll just have to agree to the conditions.'

'I don't think they can expect the company to carry the risk,' said Steven.

'It was the bad publicity surrounding the Crick that started the FDA and MHPRA getting cold feet too,' confided Macmillan. Nigel Lees tells me that government is going to have to give them some assurances too if they want them to continue playing ball. No one wants to carry the can.'

'Everyone needs someone to blame,' murmured Steven, thinking of falling rocks.

'Be that as it may,' said Macmillan, 'I think you can tell Dr Martin – or is it, Leila? – that she will not be experiencing any more obstruction from either government or commercial sources.'

'I'll relay the message,' said Steven, noting again that there wasn't much that Macmillan missed.

* * *

'Leila, it's Steven. How are things?'

'I've just seen the result of the latest titration. By my calculations we're going to make the deadline with a day to spare.'

'Great. Have you told the Department of Health?'

'I spoke with Mr Lees this morning. He told me that he's sorted out the problems with the regulatory bodies. He's now going to make transport arrangements to move the virus from the institute to the companies for production. He'll make sure they're ready to receive it and get it growing up as quickly as possible. He wants them to have teams of technicians standing by to do the egg inoculations. Round the clock if necessary Dubois in Paris have already been in touch to say they're all ready to go but I haven't heard anything from Auroragen.'

'That problem has been resolved too,' said Steven. 'They're going to drop the conditions you were worried about. There will be no more demands for tests and inspections and form filling. I spoke to them yesterday: the government will reach agreement with them today.'

'Thank you so much, Steven, you've been such a help.'

'Things are finally starting to look good.'

'I am so looking forward to this being all over,' sighed Leila. 'I feel absolutely exhausted.'

'You must be,' sympathised Steven. 'You've done so well.'

'Have the police made any progress?'

'They found the place the three men were using as a lab,' said Steven. 'It was an old mill house.'

'So they were growing the virus?' exclaimed Leila.

'Yes, but the place had been cleared out by the time we got there.'

'So it might still be too late for the vaccine to be of any use?' said Leila, sounding alarmed.

'Maybe not. It looked like a pretty small scale operation at the mill and presumably the three men dying must have set their plans back. I'm hoping it will take time for al-Qaeda to set up a new lab.'

'Maybe they already had,' said Leila.

'What makes you say that?'

'If it was only a small scale operation at the mill, they must have already been planning a bigger one somewhere else.'

Steven found that he couldn't argue with Leila's logic...but he seriously wished he could.

CHAPTER FIFTEEN

'I thought we might have a beer?' said Frank Giles when Steven picked up the phone. He had been going through his notes with a view to having to write up a full report on what had gone on at the Crick Institute and the events of the aftermath. 'Anything that gets me out of doing this for a while,' he replied, telling Giles what he was up to.

'Paperwork,' intoned Giles, 'the scourge of our times and never to be done on a Saturday night. The Green Man in half an hour?'

Giles expanded on the theme when Steven met him and they sat down with their drinks. 'You know what really gets me,' he said. 'Written reports of events rarely describe what actually happened. They list what should have happened if everything had followed a logical course.'

Steven smiled indulgently.

'It's true,' Giles asserted, 'There's no place in a report written after the event for the role of instinct, intuition or even actions based on common sense – the things that really shape an investigation. You have to pretend. You have to alter things to make it appear as if you followed a logical series of actions, so what good is that, eh? What does anyone learn from that? What's the point of it?'

'I hope you're not looking to me to defend the filling of forms,' said Steven.

'No, I just like having a rant from time to time – I like a good rant.'

'So, how are things with Norfolk's finest when they're not ranting?' asked Steven.

'They've quietened down a lot,' said Giles. 'Finding Ali has been taken out of our hands by Her Majesty's public schoolboys and what happened at the Crick is now yesterday's news. The attention of the great British public has moved on: the Chief Super can sleep easy and I can get a night off. Dare I ask if the spooks have had any success?'

Steven shook his head.

'So we're still in trouble?'

'Could be,' agreed Steven. 'But Dr Martin at the Crick has succeeded in coming up with a vaccine strain that should protect against Cambodia 5. Her strain is due to be delivered to the pharmaceutical company tomorrow. They'll put it into production right away.'

'What does that involve?' asked Giles.

'Full scale growth of the vaccine virus in fertile hens' eggs in Auroragen's virus culture suite.'

'Sounds like what they were attempting at the mill house,' said Giles.

'It's the same technique only they were growing up the Cambodia 5 virus itself to be used as a weapon and thankfully, on a much smaller scale. Auroragen will get through 100,000 eggs a day with production at full swing and produce something over a hundred million doses of vaccine.'

'Mind you, the opposition have had a head start. They may

have caught up a bit by now,' said Giles.

'And I thought you were going to cheer me up,' said Steven.

'Look on the bright side,' said Giles. 'It gives us both an excuse to get pissed.'

'Same again?' asked Steven.

'So what happens once the vaccine has grown up in the eggs?' asked Giles when Steven returned with two more beers.

'They harvest the amniotic fluid from the eggs – that's the stuff which contains the virus – and then it's put into injection vials which will be used to vaccinate people in Europe and the USA.'

'So you're injecting people with one virus to protect them against another?'

'That's exactly it,' said Steven. 'The body will produce antibodies against the first virus – the harmless one – which will also work against the killer because they are so similar – one is an attenuated form of the other. It's called live-virus vaccination. They use the same technique for smallpox. They inject a virus similar to smallpox called *Vaccinia* into you and it stimulates antibodies which work against smallpox itself.'

'How do you know the flu one will work?'

'In this case we don't,' said Steven. 'Normally it would be tested on animals first but there hasn't been time. We'll just have to hope.'

'And if the worst comes to the worst and it doesn't work?'

'The public will be defenceless against a Cambodia 5 attack. If the intelligence services don't find Ali and his pals in time and destroy the virus stocks they've been growing up, they'll spray it around city centres up and down the country and we'll have a major epidemic on our hands and by the end of the first month, probably a pandemic across the globe.'

'But surely there must be drugs they can use?' said Giles.

Steven shook his head. 'There's a common misconception that you can use antibiotics to treat virus infections – but you can't. Antibiotics work against bacteria not viruses.'

'They're all the same to me,' said Giles.

'The bugs know the difference,' said Steven. 'There are a few anti-viral drugs coming on to the market but they tend to be of limited use. Prevention is still better than a cure when it comes to virus infection.'

Acting on the spur of the moment, Steven drove up to Norfolk's north coast next morning and went for a walk along the beach. He felt decidedly rough after the night before but the cool breeze coming in off the North Sea soon cleared his head and he took pleasure from being outdoors on a day when gulls were wheeling above the waves and the sun was sparkling on the water. He'd always liked beach walking, particularly on wide expanses of hard packed sand where the horizons seemed infinite and the sky fell into the ocean. Today was a special day: it was the day Leila's vaccine strain would be handed over to the drug company. He glanced at his watch and saw that it would already be on its way – she had opted to travel up to Liverpool with it and supervise the handover personally. After that, she would get her life back – a life he very much hoped to be part of in the coming weeks. He would call her this evening when he got home.

It had been a long time since he had felt so interested in a woman and despite the fact that he knew so little about her, he had even started considering how Jenny might take to there being a new woman in his life and when might be the right time to tell her. Of course, this might be a two-way problem, he recognised. There had been times in the past when the revelation that he had a daughter had cooled a relationship. Many intelligent career women did not automatically warm to the prospect of playing mother to a ready-made family. He picked up a pebble and threw it out into the sea, berating himself for even thinking about such things when he hardly even knew Leila Martin.

Normally he would have sought out a pub to have lunch after such a walk but the excesses of the previous night steered him instead to a harbour-side coffee shop where he ordered scrambled eggs on toast and a mug of black coffee. He examined water colours of local scenes, painted by local artists, while he waited but he'd never been a big fan of water colour; he found it too insipid for landscapes or seascapes. He ate his meal and had a second mug of coffee before heading back to his hotel to continue what he had been about to start last night. Once the report was done he reckoned he might be able to take some time off. With a bit of luck Leila might even be persuaded to do the same.

'You smell of fresh air,' said the receptionist at the hotel when he asked for his key.

Steven smiled. It was something his mother used to say to him as a child when he came back from a day in the hills in his native Cumbria. 'I've been for a walk on the beach,' he explained.

'Lucky you,' said the girl. 'I've been stuck here all day.'

Starting to note down the various steps he'd taken during the investigation made him think about what Giles had said the night before about writing up reports. He found himself trying to order events in a logical way rather than in the sequence they'd actually happened. Giles was right; official reports were no place for recording gut instinct – the real reason he'd gone to Nick Cleary's house after feeling that the man was holding something back after he'd first interviewed him. Reports were written after the event, when hindsight was on tap.

He could see now that some of the tests he had asked for were redundant almost before the results had come back from the lab. The DNA profiles he'd asked for at the Crick to eliminate the possibility of a member of staff having touched the key on the secret safe had failed to reveal a match because there really had been a third man involved in the attack on the institute – the Ali character who seemed to have cropped up so often without being identified. DIS had found his DNA in the flat where the three dead men had been found, adding more fuel to the suspicion that he had killed two of them. They couldn't identify him from any data file but they had confirmed that his DNA was a match for the profile that had been found on the safe key in the Crick.

'He certainly gets around,' murmured Steven. It was a thought that made him wonder, *why?* If al-Qaeda was engaged in a big operation, why should one man crop up so often? True, Ali was probably the leader but it tended to imply that the team he led was small. There again, a small team would be more secure than a large one where the risk of capture or failure increased with the appointing of every additional member, but there were certain things that a small team could not achieve and cultivating a lethal virus and using it to carry out a major biological attack on several cities simultaneously across the UK was one of them.

Ali seemed to have been involved in everything from hunt sabotage to recruiting animal rights activists for the raid on the Crick. Ali had organised the raid. Ali had tortured the information he needed out of Professor Devon. Ali had murdered Devon and facilitated the theft of the infected monkey. Ali had been at the flat where the dead men were discovered – he had almost certainly murdered two of them...so how much manpower was Ali left with?

Had Ali been at the mill house too? Steven wondered. Maybe the forensics people had the answer to that and perhaps to how many other people had been present at the mill. He phoned Frank Giles.

'God, I hope you're not going to suggest going out for a beer,' said Giles when he heard Steven's voice. 'I've had a head full of broken glass all day.'

Steven told him what he wanted to know.

'Just the four,' said Giles. 'The three dead men and the one unidentified male who was also at the flat in town.'

'Thanks,' said Steven and put the phone down. He was feeling nervous. There was something not quite right about all this and the questions were coming thick and fast. Why had the operation at the mill been so small when the amount of virus required for a Cambodia 5 virus attack would be much greater? Four people involved and three were dead. The working hypothesis had been that they had other facilities somewhere in the UK – maybe even up and running, as Leila had proposed – but they would need skilled technicians and a supply of fertile hens' eggs – lots of them. The security people who had been monitoring the egg suppliers had reported no unusual orders being placed, so where were they getting them from? Steven phoned Colonel Rose at DIS.

After an exchange of pleasantries, Steven told him what was on his mind. 'There is no alternative to fertile hens' eggs,' he said, 'and they need thousands of them. Can you check again with the suppliers and make absolutely sure that none were left off the list?'

'Will do,' said Rose. 'But I'm pretty sure none has.'

Steven noted the slight rebuke but this was no time to tip-toe around other people's sensibilities. He added, 'And maybe they could examine orders from all their usual customers to see if there has been any abnormal increase being ordered. It's absolutely vital. The eggs are their Achilles heel. We know their intent and we know their targets but they can't hit them if they don't have enough virus and for that they need lots of eggs.'

'I suppose ordering them through an accepted source like a large research institute would be the thing to do if they could manage it,' said Rose.

'Cutting out the lab supplier altogether would be even better if they were to come to an arrangement with one of the large poultry concerns,' said Steven.

'We'll check that too,' said Rose. 'I'll let you know as soon as I hear.'

Steven didn't like it when things didn't make sense and he had just started thinking about another puzzle from the mill – the way the monkey had been opened up. There had been little or no surgical expertise involved and that was probably why the three men had contracted the disease. They had known nothing about aseptic technique or what safety measures to adopt when dealing with dangerous biological material. Someone had instructed them to remove the lungs and windpipe from the animal – and then what? Unskilled workers would be incapable of extracting virus and setting up egg cultures so who had done this? Ali? The ubiquitous Ali? Something wasn't quite making sense. Al-Qaeda needed a large team but he kept seeing a small one.

Steven was wrestling with this when Leila called.

'I'm back,' she said. 'God, I'm so relieved.'

'Well done,' said Steven. 'Did everything go all right?'

'Like clockwork. The technicians were standing by and the initial egg cultures had all been prepared: I was most impressed. They have wonderful facilities.'

'The very best,' agreed Steven.

'I went there to impress upon them the need for great care – any bacterial contamination of the virus cultures and there won't be time to start over again. But there was no need; they are already taking every conceivable precaution.'

'Good,' said Steven. 'I think they're hypersensitive to bacterial contamination problems. So now you are a free woman?'

'I suppose I am,' agreed Leila.

'Dinner?'

'That would be lovely.'

The Bella Napoli Italian restaurant in Norwich was quiet on a Sunday evening – there was only one other couple there and they seemed to have fallen out with each other as they sat in silence, examining their place mats. Steven was glad when one of the staff put on some music in an attempt to create atmosphere, although Dean Martin singing *Volare* failed to conjure up images of warm Italian nights when Norfolk rain was battering noisily on all the windows.

'Sorry,' said Steven.

Leila reached across the table and put her hand on his. 'It's fine,' she said. 'I'm just so relieved that I got the strain to the company on time that tonight nothing else matters.'

'You did incredibly well,' said Steven.

'And now I am going to sleep for a week,' said Leila. 'How about you? Is Sci-Med still involved in the investigation?'

Steven shook his head. 'Our interest is officially over. The security services have taken over.'

'But?' prompted Leila, noting some reservation in his voice.

'I just have a bad feeling about the whole thing…'

'You think al-Qaeda will make their attack before the vaccine's ready?'

Steven shook his head. 'No, it's not that…It's hard to explain. There's something not quite right about the whole thing…'

'Tell me,' said Leila. 'Get it off your chest as you English say.'

'The operation at the mill house where we found an incubator room and egg boxes… I can't help feeling there was something wrong with that,' said Steven. 'It smacked of a very small operation when they would need a much bigger one for what they're planning.'

'But isn't that the way terrorists work,' said Leila.

'What do you mean?'

'I don't know too much about such things but I do seem to

remember reading that they like to operate in small independent cells rather than large units. I think it's a security thing. If one member gets caught the damage will be limited to one cell rather than the whole organisation. Each cell operates on…oh, I can't remember what they called it…'

'A need to know basis,' said Steven.

'That's it,' agreed Leila.

'Maybe you're right,' said Steven. 'I suppose the operation at the mill house could have been just one small stage in the process. It was their job to raid the institute and obtain the virus. They would then pass it on to the next cell who would grow it up. They in turn would pass it on to another cell who would distribute it to yet more cells who would make the attacks. Yes, that makes a lot of sense.'

'But obviously doesn't provide much comfort!' said Leila with a smile, noting Steven's lack of enthusiasm for the idea.

'True,' agreed Steven. 'I hate it when things don't make sense.'

'I suppose you'll be going back to London soon,' said Leila.

'It's not that far,' smiled Steven. 'And I'd like to see a lot more of you.'

'I'd like that too,' said Leila. 'But…'

'But what?'

'I think it only fair to warn you that I am thinking about going back to the States.'

'Ah,' sighed Steven. 'Your career…'

'It's important to me and with Professor Devon dead the reason for my being here has gone.'

Steven took her hands and said, 'Then I think my mission in life over the next few weeks will be to persuade you otherwise.'

Leila smiled and raised her glass. 'Here's to an interesting few weeks.'

'How's your spaghetti?'

'Terrible.'

'Mine too. Let's go home.'

It rained all night and all through the next day. Steven had returned to his hotel and was making yet another attempt at writing up his report when Colonel Rose rang.

'No joy, I'm afraid. No abnormally large orders have been placed with egg suppliers from their regular customers and no consignments have gone out to private individuals. We've checked all the large poultry firms and none of them has been approached directly to make supplies available.'

'Shit,' said Steven. 'What the hell are they using?'

'You don't think they could have brought them in from abroad?' asked Rose.

'The logistics would be all wrong.'

'Then I don't know what to suggest.'

'The only other alternative is that they managed to get the virus out of the country and are growing it up abroad.'

'We've already alerted all our allies,' said Rose, 'as well as being extra vigilant at ports and airports.'

'Have you had any luck with the people you arrested?'

'We've come up with various links to small people involved in the red herring alert over an attack on Canary Wharf but no one we've picked up knows anything at all about a virus operation. There are a few more we'd like to pick up and hold but we've been told to cool it. The judiciary are on their high horse over the use of prevention of terrorism legislation.'

'I saw that coming,' said Steven. 'How about the relatives of the three dead men in Leicester?'

'Usual story in all three cases. Disaffected Muslim youths feeling the world's against them get sucked in to fundamentalism in their late teens and begin to see freedom fighting as a better alternative to the dole office as they get older. A couple of weeks at training camp under the guise of a holiday in the 'old country' – which they'd never actually seen in their lives before – and they're ready to do whatever they're told. Their families were kept in the dark or maybe it just suited them to maintain that.'

'I suppose.'

'I hear the vaccine has entered production.'

'At least something's going right,' said Steven. 'Let's just hope it'll be ready in time.'

'Amen to that.'

Steven put down the phone and felt thoroughly depressed. It was just so easy to imagine large modern lab facilities somewhere abroad swinging into full Cambodia 5 production and being ready before the vaccine thanks to the head start they'd had. His mind however, kept straying back to the mill house. Why bother to set up a small operation up if the intention had always been to set up full scale production abroad? He was staring out of the window at the rain when Leila phoned. 'What time will you be round tonight?' she asked.

'Any time you like.'

'I'll be at the lab until six thirty but I should still be home by seven. You can come and talk to me while I make dinner.'

Steven smiled as he switched off the phone. Leila's plan to

sleep for a week had been short-lived. She had taken only one day off before going back to work at the Crick. He was looking forward to seeing her but had to admit – as he saw the rain turn to sleet – that the prospect of an evening in a house heated by only a one bar electric fire was less than appealing, let alone romantic. He resolved to do something about it. He would take along the makings of a fire. He would pick up logs and firelighters at one of the local filling stations where he'd seen them stacked by the door the last time he'd been in for petrol. Add a few rolled-up newspapers and some matches and they could have an evening in front of a roaring fire.

The sleet had stopped by the time Steven left to drive over to Leila's place but the temperature had dropped sharply in the last hour and the roads had started to ice up. The attendant at the filling station told him that the authorities had been warned earlier about the likelihood of this but had been reluctant to send out grit spreaders, fearing that the rain would wash it all away and road grit cost money. Steven's MGF might be a joy to drive on smooth, dry tarmac but could turn into a nightmare in adverse weather conditions. The fact that it sat so low on the road meant that the screen constantly had to be cleared of muck flung up by other vehicles and its quick response to brake and accelerator meant constant sideways twitching on slippery surfaces.

Steven was ultra cautious on the narrow roads leading over to Holt but it was still heart-in-mouth time on a number of occasions when black ice made its presence felt and a disagreement regarding direction of travel arose between driver and car. As he approached a narrow bridge spanning a river gorge, Steven slowed right down when he saw the flashing yellow lights of, presumably, a road gritting vehicle coming towards him. He pulled in to the side, as close to the verge as he dared, half tucked in behind the bridge parapet on his side of the road.

He was just beginning to take comfort from the fact that at least the road ahead would be freshly gritted when he saw that the snow-clearing blade on the front of the gritter had been lowered as it came on to the bridge: this made the vehicle so wide that it filled the entire width of the road: there wouldn't be enough room for it to pass without scraping the side of his car. Fearing that the driver hadn't seen him sitting there, Steven moved a little further over on to the verge, sounding his horn and flashing his lights. But to no avail. The vehicle kept coming.

Just as he made a fear-fuelled decision to get out of the car, the inside wheels of the MG slipped down into the unseen ditch they had been precariously perched over. The car pitched 45 degrees to the left and Steven fell back inside, his shoulders ending up on the passenger seat and his knees curled under the steering wheel. He had just started to elbow his way up into a position where he could see out again when the steel blade of the grit lorry hit the front of the MG, smashing its off-side headlight and scraping along the metal until it pushed the car completely over onto its side. The impact threw Steven violently back into the car.

Once again he fought in the confined space of the two-seater to get upright. The only way out of the car was through the driver's door window which was now an escape hatch edged with broken glass above his head. When he finally managed to clear enough and poke his head out through it, he could see that the gritter had stopped some twenty metres away.

'Stupid bastard!' Steven yelled. 'Are you blind?'

The gritter started to reverse slowly and Steven could see the driver looking back through the rear window of his cab. He was well wrapped up against the cold and was wearing noise-protector ear muffs. Steven continued to mutter abuse as he tried to clear the remainder of the broken glass away from the window frame before attempting to climb out. 'Just what the fuck were you thinking of... The council's insurance company is really going to love you...'

The words froze on Steven's lips when he suddenly realised that the gritter was not going to stop. Fear gripped him and he stammered, 'What the f...?' as the grit hopper grew ever nearer until, finally, its snow blade crunched into the MG. The impact appeared not to register with the JCB; it continued pushing the car backwards like a child's toy with Steven inside, still struggling to push himself out through the driver's window space but being thrown off balance at every attempt. He felt a sudden jerk as the car was forced up on to the bridge parapet. He had no idea what lay in the darkness below but he knew that he was just about to find out.

CHAPTER SIXTEEN

Steven parted company with the car as it rolled over the parapet and spilled him out of the window gap he'd been so desperately trying to escape through. So many things flashed across his mind as he went into a tumbling free fall, not least thoughts of his daughter. I'm so sorry, Jenny, was the only cogent one he could muster before he felt tree branches whip his face and pummel his body as he crashed down through them until one almighty blow to his midriff halted his fall, knocking the wind out of him and making him regurgitate the contents of his stomach. He was dimly aware of stomach acid burning his throat before feeling himself slide slowly off the branch, despite his best efforts to grab on to something. He fell again through the black void until an explosion of light inside his head consigned him to oblivion.

When he awoke, Steven found that he could not stop his teeth chattering and the one limb that he did seem to have any feeling in – his right arm – was almost numb with cold. He tried to think logically but the pain inside his head kept distracting him from doing anything other than shiver and struggle for breath. Although his ability to feel pain was telling him that he was still alive, the fact that he couldn't feel his legs and that a nuclear explosion seemed to have gone off inside his skull was stopping any celebration of this discovery. He tried moving his shoulders and found that he could, but he could only feel the right side of his body and then only above the waist. He felt about him with his right hand, trying to investigate his situation and discovered that most of his body was immersed in a shallow, slow moving river. The flow was sluggish because its surface was turning to ice. He was lying on his left side with his face resting on a slime covered boulder.

Despite the pain and apparent hopelessness of his situation, Steven knew that he hadn't yet reached the final stages of hypothermia where he could expect the pain to lessen and the prospect of a long comfortable sleep to beckon with open arms as his metabolism slowed to a halt. Furthermore, the discovery that he was lying in an icy river suggested to him that his failure to detect any feeling in his lower limbs might be due to cold rather than spinal injury, which had been his first terrifying thought. He had to get out of the river.

He reached out behind his head with his right hand but immediately had to stop when he felt an agonising pain in his chest. He explored the area gingerly and discovered that he had at least two broken ribs and possibly a third. The last thing he needed right now was for a broken rib to puncture his lungs. He rolled his upper body as far as he could to the left and reached out again with his right arm, this time in the other direction. He found a sharp ridge in a boulder and hooked his fingers over it to start dragging himself towards the bank.

The dead weight of his numb, lower body meant that he

could only manage a few inches at a time but at least he was moving. In the end, it took him more than ten minutes to get completely out of the water and start work on his unfeeling limbs, left arm first. By the time he had regained feeling in his arms and legs it seemed as if every muscle in his body had gone into involuntary spasm with the cold. He was shivering so much that he had difficulty breathing as he tried to check himself out for any injury that had been masked through numbness.

Amazingly, the damage he'd suffered seemed confined to the broken ribs which must have happened when the tree somewhere up on the side of the gorge had broken his fall. Apart from that he had multiple cuts and bruises, including a lump above his left temple – which could of course, be signalling a skull fracture, he cautioned himself – but nothing else seemed to be broken. His situation was however, desperate; and right now, cold was the thing that was going to kill him.

Although he had been in very good physical condition, the fact that he had been wet through and outdoors in freezing temperatures for some hours was something he could not possibly sustain for much longer. However bad he felt and however great the danger of puncturing his lungs with broken ribs he simply had to start moving and keep moving until he found help or it found him.

He was attempting to stand up for the third time when the moon came out from behind the clouds and lit up the gorge with pale light. The sight did little to gladden his heart as the rock walls on both sides seemed almost vertical and, high above him, he could see the damaged parapet where the MG had come over. Along to his right he could see the wreckage of his car strewn across the river. He reckoned that his best chance – maybe his only one – might be someone seeing the damage to the bridge parapet and reporting it but it was on a minor road and he had no idea of the time or how long he'd been unconscious. It might well be the middle of the night.

His phone! His mobile phone! The thought prompted a frantic search through his pockets with wet hands that resisted entrance and exit to every one of them but then he remembered that it would have been in the hands-free holder in the car. Subsidiary thoughts about the chances of it still working being slim and the unlikelihood of there being a signal at the foot of this gorge were pushed to the back of his mind as he clung instead to the possibility that it had been flung free of the car and had landed in a patch of soft moss somewhere near his feet. A quick look removed this possibility from the equation.

Steven made his way along the narrow, stony river bank to the wreckage and started searching. Glancing up at the sky, he could see that the moonlight was not going to last much longer – a thick bank of cloud was approaching. Doing his best to protect his ribs with one arm folded across his chest, he peered into what was left of the cabin and saw that the phone mounting was still above water – but was empty. 'Shit,' he murmured as he felt around the submerged floor pan without finding anything. His search was constantly impeded by the bag of logs he'd bought at the filling station floating around in front of him. He yanked them out of the car angrily and threw them on to the bank before continuing but it seemed clear: the phone was not in the car.

Another quick glance up at the sky told him that he couldn't have more than three or four minutes of moonlight left. Sheer frustration left him trying to curse everything at the top of his voice although the contractions in his throat and the violent shivering in his body made even that impossible in any satisfactory way.

He was into his third chorus of, 'Bastard...bastard... bastard,' accompanied by thumping his fist on the grassy bank, when a glint caught his eye. There was something metallic lying on the bank about ten yards away... He crawled along the bank towards it and recognised his phone. He snatched it up and then realised that it was only the front of the phone. The back, comprising the battery, was missing.

Steven slumped down on the ground, feeling the will to live seriously weaken in him. His shivering was subsiding; the pain was fading and he was starting to feel comfortable. For the moment he would get some sleep and someone would come along in the morning...

'Get up!' warned the voice inside his head. 'Get your arse into gear, Dunbar! Move it!' It was the voice of a drill sergeant from all those years ago. The voice that had driven him on through the hell of an SAS selection course in the mountains of North Wales. 'Giving up is not an option! You go to sleep now and you'll never wake up again. Your choice!'

Steven got to his knees and found himself facing the bag of logs he'd flung on to the bank. The irony made him dissolve into maniacal laughter for a few moments. 'Nice one, God,' he spluttered but through the anger and pain and frustration and the desire to lie down and sleep his way out of it all, the image of a fire had been kindled. He started crawling up and down the bank as fast as he could in order to keep moving and he concentrated on the idea of a fire. He needed a fire...he wanted a fire...he had a bag of wet logs...the matches he'd bought would be useless too...but he hadn't bought matches! There had been a box of disposable lighters beside the till in the service station. He'd bought one of these instead!

Once again he searched through his pockets and found the lighter. He flicked the wheel with his thumb and sparks flew into the air. He tried twice more and was rewarded with a flickering flame that seemed suddenly to symbolise for him all hope on Earth.

Steven resumed crawling up and down the bank as he felt his legs go numb again. Keep moving...keep moving... must keep moving. Disjointed thoughts vied with the pain in his knees from crawling over stones. What can I burn?...no paper...the firelighters were at the bottom of the river: he'd seen them lying there...the logs were soaking wet...it would take a furnace to light them, not a bloody cigarette lighter...a furnace...a furnace...if the car's petrol tank hadn't ruptured... he had the makings of a furnace!

Steven dragged himself back to the car and unscrewed the filler cap, feeling almost nauseous with relief when petrol vapour reached his nostrils: the tank was intact. It seemed sweeter than any perfume but he needed a way to ignite it and preferably not with his face over the tank at the time.

Using what he recognised might be the last remaining ounce of strength he had left in his body, he ripped the front of his shirt and tore a strip away to dangle it in the tank. Please God it would reach! He pulled the material back out and smelt the end. It was soaked in petrol.

He suspected that he was only going to have one chance at this. He was counting on the tank not exploding because the cap was off and the contents were not confined...but on the other hand it just might. He trailed the shirt material from the cap opening along the body work and prepared to flick the lighter under it. He would do this and then dive immediately for the bank.

Steven flicked the lighter wheel and dived for the bank, doing his best to protect his injured chest by landing on his arm and side. Nothing happened. He looked back and saw the rag dangling there. At that moment, the clouds reached the moon and blackness swallowed everything up. He wanted to scream out his frustration but he steeled himself to feel his way back to the wreckage and find the end of the rag. Once again he flicked the lighter wheel and this time there was a yellow flash as he leapt back to the bank. This was followed by a second, more powerful, eruption of flame from the car as the main tank erupted.

Steven crawled away from the wall of heat that engulfed him, feeling a mixture of euphoria and pain. When the flames had died back a bit he returned and started throwing the wet logs into the cabin space in order to keep the fire going. He had a fire; he had heat. He just might survive. He was careful not to get too close, knowing of the agonising pain that comes with heating up numb limbs too quickly but after ten minutes or so he started to feel comfortable. He felt even better after another ten minutes when, through the darkness up to his left, he saw a number of flashing lights. They were an encouraging shade of blue.

*   *   *

By mid afternoon on the following day, Steven decided to sign himself out of hospital. X-rays had shown that there was no skull fracture and his 'field' diagnosis of three broken ribs had proved correct. His cuts and bruises had been cleaned and his chest strapped up. The police had visited and taken details: they had already matched them with the theft of a JCB gritter from a roads department depot about three miles from where the incident occurred. 'You wouldn't believe how much these things are worth,' the Constable had told him.

'No kidding,' Steven had replied. He was in the middle of an argument about signing himself out when Leila arrived.

'My God, I've been worried sick about you,' she said, wrapping her arms around him but immediately becoming aware of the wince he gave. 'Oh, I'm so sorry,' she said.

'My ribs are just a bit sore,' he smiled. 'It's lovely to see you.'

'I only found out when I called the police to say that you had disappeared,' said Leila. 'I tried phoning your cell phone every half hour but all I got was your answering service and then the hotel told me they hadn't heard from you...'

'Apparently I got in the way of some guy trying to steal a JCB,' said Steven. 'It turned out to be a night to remember.'

'But shouldn't you be in bed?' protested Leila when she saw that Steven was preparing to leave.

'Yes, he should,' interrupted the nursing sister who'd been watching the proceedings. 'But you just can't tell some people.'

'I really am very grateful to you and your staff, Sister,' said Steven. 'But I'm fine and I've got things to do.'

'Just tell me and I'll inform whoever it is you have to contact,' said Leila.

'No, really,' insisted Steven. 'I'm as well making myself busy as lie around here. I have to ring my sister-in-law before she reads all about this in the papers – or worse still, Jenny hears about it from some other source.'

'Jenny?' asked Leila.

'My daughter,' replied Steven, suddenly realising to his embarrassment that he hadn't mentioned Jenny before. 'She lives with my sister-in-law and her husband in Scotland.'

'I see,' said Leila. 'Well, you can make phone calls from here. What else do you have to do?'

'Get myself a car...a new phone...talk to Sci-Med...so many things.'

'As you say, Sister,' said Leila, turning to the nurse. 'You just can't tell some people.'

Later, as Leila drove Steven back to his hotel, he told her the full story of what had happened.

'It's a miracle you're still alive.'

'I think the credit goes to the tree that broke my fall,' said Steven.

'Whatever. You'll never be that lucky again.' After a short pause she added, 'You didn't tell me you had a daughter.'

Steven had been waiting for this: he had seen the brief look of surprise on Leila's face at the hospital. 'I suppose I hadn't got round to it,' he said. He told her about Lisa's death from a brain tumour and how Sue and Richard had taken Jenny in after her mother's death.

'It strikes me there's such a lot we don't know about each other,' said Leila. 'Maybe it's just as well.'

'Why?' asked Steven.

'I've decided to return to the States.'

'Oh.'

'As I said before, the chance of working with Tim Devon was what brought me here. Without him to provide the intellectual stimulation I need, I'm just marking time at the institute. They're all very nice of course…but I feel the need to get back to the university in Washington.'

'I suppose I can understand that,' said Steven. 'When will you go?'

'At the end of the month,' said Leila.

'But we can still see each other until you go?'

'Of course,' smiled Leila. 'I just thought I'd better tell you…'

'Thanks,' said Steven.

Although he returned to London two days later, Steven still managed to see Leila on a number of occasions over the next few weeks, still hoping that he might persuade her to change her mind but it became obvious that she was determined to go so in the end he accepted the situation. He spent the Easter weekend with his daughter up in Scotland instead of asking Leila to spend it with him even though it was the last before she was due to leave. He did, however, drive her to the airport, albeit with a great feeling of sadness.

'Can I call you in the States?' he asked.

Leila shook her head. 'Please Steven, don't make things more difficult for me,' she said, wiping away a tear from her cheek. 'Give me time to settle back into my life. When that happens, I'll call you.'

'Promise?'

Leila put a finger on his lips. 'I promise.'

'There's nothing I can say to make you stay?'

Leila smiled and placed the palms of her hands gently on Steven's chest. 'Please, Steven, let's not prolong this. It's agony for both of us.'

Steven conceded. He kissed her gently on the forehead and then on the lips before turning to go.

Steven joined John Macmillan for a meeting of the *Earlybird* committee at the Home Office, thinking as he entered the room that the mood of the meeting appeared to be more upbeat than his own.

'Ladies and gentlemen,' said the Home Office minister chairing the meeting, 'I don't think it's too optimistic to say that we are winning the race. Auroragen and Dubois report that the vaccine is well ahead of schedule and the security services have uncovered no evidence at all that al-Qaeda have been able to culture large amounts of virus.'

'Thank God for that,' said the Metropolitan Police Commissioner.

'And so say all of us,' said Nigel Lees.

'So, what do you think happened?' asked John Macmillan. He was looking at the people from MI5, MI6 and DIS.

'We are of the opinion that simple logistics defeated them in the end. It was just too big an undertaking for what apparently was too small a team,' said the MI6 man.

'We would agree with that,' said the woman from MI5. 'Constant vigilance stopped them getting what they needed to grow up sufficient quantities of the virus.'

'And what about DIS, Colonel, what do they think?' asked Macmillan.

'Much the same,' replied Rose. 'We failed to identify even one successful attempt to get their hands on the fertile eggs they needed to culture the virus but...'

'But what, Colonel?'

'Well, you'd think that that was something they would have planned for in advance, wouldn't you?'

You would indeed, thought Steven but he didn't say it out loud.

'Maybe they thought it would be much easier to do than it turned out to be,' suggested Lees. 'But whatever the reason, I think we owe a debt of gratitude to the police and our security services for thwarting their efforts.'

Always a crowd pleaser, thought Steven as ripples of agreement went round the room.

'We're not out of the woods yet,' said Macmillan. 'Just because we haven't found evidence of virus production does not automatically mean that such a facility doesn't exist.'

'Of course not,' agreed Lees. 'And I think we are all agreed that we must maintain the highest standards of vigilance until Dr Martin's vaccine is ready and has been deployed on both sides of the Atlantic to protect our people.'

'Of course, we have to remember that it may not work at all,' said Macmillan, much to Lees' annoyance who saw this as an attempt to rain on his victory parade. 'It's a completely untested vaccine.'

'Personally, I think we should be much more positive about things,' said Lees. 'Dr Martin did an absolutely magnificent job in doing what she did at such short notice. We are all in her debt and I for one have every confidence in her work. I'm sure her vaccine will work.'

'You *hope* it will work,' corrected Macmillan. 'Just like we all do.'

CHAPTER SEVENTEEN

'Well, what do you think?' asked Macmillan, pouring coffee when they had returned to his office.

'There's something wrong,' said Steven, starting to pace up and down. 'All that back-slapping and self-congratulation...it made me feel...nervous. They seem happy to believe that al-Qaeda were guilty of lack of foresight or bad planning. That implies that they're stupid or incompetent. They're neither.'

'Would you care to be more specific?'

'I wish I could be. I suppose it's the small team thing that worries me most. Al-Qaeda set up a big diversionary tactic involving lots of people and lots of planning to make us think that an attack was about to be made on Canary Wharf in order to throw us off the scent of what? A small team being sent in to steal Cambodia 5 virus without the back-up necessary to do anything with it? I don't think so somehow.'

'You still think they're going to use the virus?'

Steven shrugged and said, 'No point in stealing it otherwise.'

'I understand your reservations,' said Macmillan. 'But maybe the loss of three team members knocked them back?'

'The three who died were unskilled cannon fodder, totally unused to handling dangerous biological material. Their 'loss' could have been anticipated by anyone with an IQ running into treble figures.'

'But if that were the case, sending in not only a small team but a largely unskilled one would make even less sense,' said Macmillan.

'Exactly,' said Steven. 'We're not seeing something here.'

'What do you want to do?' asked Macmillan.

'Get out the file, go over everything again.'

'Let's both do that,' said Macmillan.

Steven glanced at his watch when he got in and reckoned that Leila would be back in Washington by now. She would be looking forward to seeing old colleagues at the university in the morning and getting back into the swing of her old life – her apartment was probably a far cry from a run-down old cottage in Norfolk with its one-bar electric fire. He couldn't blame her for needing or missing the intellectual stimulation she got from working at a large prestigious university but he had already started to nurture hopes that her success in designing a vaccine against the Cambodia 5 virus, when it became known, might well open up academic doors to her all over the world. England was what he really had in mind and Oxbridge would be just fine. He poured himself a gin and tonic and sat down to start working his way through the files.

Two hours and three gins later he thought he saw something that made his heart miss a beat and a thin film of sweat appear on his brow. He snatched up the phone and called Rose at Defence Intelligence. 'Tell me, Colonel, what was it exactly that made you cotton on to the fact that the hit on Canary Wharf was a red herring?'

'Hard to say when you pose the question that way,' replied Rose. 'I suppose I started to get the feeling that we were being led by the nose down a pre-charted pathway. I remember feeling pleased with our progress in the investigation and almost patting myself on the back when I suddenly realised that what we were seeing was what someone meant us to see. It didn't have anything to do with luck or skill on our part; the clues were being laid down for us. The men we were picking up were low-level nobodies who had been sacrificed for the cause. We were *meant* to track them down. They were no great loss to al-Qaeda because there was nothing they could tell us because they didn't know anything. Why do you ask?'

'Because I think I've just had exactly the same feeling,' said Steven. 'The train of events that took us to the mill house wasn't part of the big picture. It was another diversion.'

'What makes you say that?'

'Think about it: three dead men at the flat who'd been infected with Cambodia 5 virus, two of them actually murdered by their own, a vehicle parked conveniently round the back which yields a hair from a monkey and a petrol receipt. The receipt leads us to a petrol station which leads us to the mill house where we find egg cartons and a warm incubator room and then of course, the final slice of "luck", a map of all the targets they intended to hit. It's embarrassing to say it but we've been had; we've been set up. Your people couldn't find any egg supplier because none was required. It was never their intention to do what we were meant to think they were going on to do.'

There was a long silence at the end of the phone before Rose murmured, 'I wish I could argue with you...'

'Pity,' said Steven. 'I was sort of depending on you. I was hoping this was all my imagination.'

'But if the Cambodia 5 attack is nothing more than a diversion...what are they really up to?' asked Rose.

'I have absolutely no idea,' said Steven.

'Perhaps you should re-convene *Earlybird* and tell them what you've just told me?'

'And confess to everyone that we really have no idea what al-Qaeda are up to? HMG will go bananas and it'll look like sports day for headless chickens in Whitehall.'

'I suppose you're right,' agreed Rose. 'The Spanish will probably lobby Brussels to slap a quota on red herrings on the grounds that we've been over-fishing them.'

'I can't prove any of this,' said Steven. 'It's still just a feeling. I could still be wrong. Maybe the Norfolk Police were just lucky in getting to the mill house... Maybe it was just good forensic work that came up with the monkey hair and good fortune that the garage attendant remembered the Land Rover...'

'No,' interrupted Rose. 'Let me stop you there. She remembered it because it had been in to the filling station *a number of times*. We should have seen that earlier. We both know that no trained terrorist group would have returned to the same place time and time again unless...'

'They had been told to,' completed Steven. 'They *wanted* to be remembered. Of course, you're right.'

'So where do we go from here?'

'As I see it, there's nothing anyone can do that isn't already being done,' said Steven. 'All the services are already on high alert. We have to sit down and think our way out of this one.'

'So we say nothing?'

'For the moment.'

Steven saw that there was one exception he had to make and that was to tell John Macmillan. He called him and told him what he had just told Rose.

'You know,' said Macmillan, not sounding too surprised, 'I've been sitting here wondering about that petrol receipt. If it had been found among general detritus on the floor of the van, I might just have bought it, but it was the *only* thing the police found in the van apart from the monkey hair...'

'So you agree?'

'I do. I think it was a plant.'

'Did anything else strike you?' asked Steven.

'One thing,' said Macmillan. 'I see from your report that you asked about the sale of primates up and down the country?'

'I was trying to find out how the opposition got their hands on a monkey to plant in the wilds of Norfolk for the army to find,' said Steven. 'But I drew a blank. The only orders for primates placed in the previous three months came from recognised research labs.'

'That's true,' said Macmillan. 'But one of them was the Crick.'

'Professor Devon was using them to test his experimental vaccine on,' said Steven.

'The last order – for six monkeys – was placed a week after Devon died.'

'Shit, I missed that.'

'The real question is who wanted them and why?' said Macmillan. 'According to your report, Professor Devon was the only researcher using monkeys at the institute. When Dr Martin took over the work on a vaccine against Cambodia 5 there was no question of her being able to try it out on animals. Apart from there being no time, everyone had learned their lesson from the Devon debacle. Any animal tests to be carried out involving Cambodia 5 would have to be done out at Porton Down.'

'Good point,' agreed Steven. 'Maybe I'll go up to the Crick first thing tomorrow and find out who placed the order...'

Steven smiled as he put down the phone. It was good to see that John Macmillan was still as sharp as ever. He called the garage to ask why his replacement car had not turned up.

'We were promised it this morning but it didn't happen,' said Stan Silver, the owner of the small garage who'd supplied Steven's cars and who had looked after them for several years. Although they'd never served in the regiment at the same time together, Silver had also served with the SAS. 'I phoned at the back of four and they said it was 'in transit'. It's still not appeared.'

'I need a car first thing in the morning, Stan.'

'There's an old Nissan Primera you could have...rear spoiler and everything... Hello? Are you still there?'

'I assumed you were having a laugh,' said Steven coldly.

'OK, OK, look, there's a Porsche 911 I could let you have but I have to have it back by tomorrow night at the latest. A customer's coming in to see it first thing on Thursday morning and I need this sale. Definitely no cliff diving. Understood?'

'Highly amusing,' said Steven. 'I'll have it back, Stan; I promise.'

* * *

In the morning, Steven decided to drop in and see Frank Giles before driving on to the Crick Institute. As it happened, Giles was just coming out of the building as Steven was parking the Porsche.

'Bloody hell,' said Giles. 'A silver Porsche...supplied by Stan Silver Motors,' he said, reading from the rear screen. 'You've come up in the world.'

'It turns into a pumpkin at midnight,' said Steven. 'Mine for a day.'

'Bad luck. You coming to see me?'

'I was passing so I thought I'd pop in and see if you'd caught the bastard who rolled me off the bridge,' said Steven.

Giles shook his head. 'He abandoned the stolen vehicle half a mile up the road and disappeared into the night. We've absolutely nothing to go on.'

'May he rot in hell,' said Steven.

'Mustn't let a little thing like attempted murder become personal,' said Giles. 'It strikes me as odd though...'

'What does?'

'According to your statement, he reversed and deliberately pushed you off the bridge.'

'He did.'

'Why? Your car was disabled and you didn't get a look at him on the way past: you said he was all wrapped up against the cold. Why stop, reverse and try to kill you?'

'Who knows? I suppose I was pretty abusive: I shouted at him.'

'You must have really pissed him off...' said Giles. 'If a bit of road rage escalated to that...in such a short space of time...'

'Sign of the times,' said Steven.

'Maybe...'

'Well, I don't think I want to go there right now,' said Steven.

'Just a thought,' said Giles. 'Where *do* you want to go right now?'

Steven told him about going to the Crick and why.

'Let me know how you get on.'

Steven did not have much interest in cars but had to admit that the drive over to the Crick in a Porsche 911 was something to savour. He knew the car had a marvellous reputation and now he understood why. It stuck to the road like glue as he pushed it harder and harder through the corners. He was feeling quite exhilarated and more than a little disappointed that the journey was over when he reached the institute and nursed the car in through the gates to park in front of the newly rendered façade of the building.

'I didn't think we'd be seeing you again,' said Nick Cleary with a smile. He'd come along to Reception to meet Steven. 'I'd like to think this is social but I fear not.'

'There's something I need your help with,' said Steven. 'Monkeys. The Crick put in an order for six of them a week after Professor Devon died.'

'Did we? I can't think why off-hand but I can check if you like.'

'If you would.'

'It may just have been a repeat order placed after the loss of the six after the attack...' Cleary turned to the girl behind the desk and said, 'Karen, could you look out the lab animal order book?'

A few moments later a black ring binder was placed on the desk and Cleary started to leaf through it. 'Here we are... Six Rhesus monkeys ordered by... Leila.'

'Leila?'

'Like I say, she was probably replacing the ones that went missing.'

'But why? She knew she wouldn't be doing any animal testing,' said Steven.

'Good point,' agreed Cleary. 'Maybe she didn't know that at the time she placed the order.'

'Would anyone else in the institute have reason to use monkeys?'

'No.'

'So the animals will still be in the animal house?'

'I suppose so.'

'Could I see them?' asked Steven.

'Of course.'

Cleary led the way through corridors where only the smell of paint remained as a reminder of what had happened there. They finally descended two flights of stairs and came to the primate house where Cleary inserted his pass card into the lock.

'Good Morning Freda,' said Cleary to the middle aged woman who was mopping the floor. He turned to Steven. 'Freda is our new animal technician.'

Steven smiled and nodded. He wondered how Robert Smith's widow was getting on. Did she still live in the 'tied' house at the end of the drive?

'Well, there they are,' said Cleary.

Steven walked slowly past the cages and the monkeys flung

themselves at the bars, filling the air with excited screeching.

'What's all the fuss about?' demanded Freda as if she were speaking to naughty children. 'Just you stop all that nonsense...'

Steven smiled at the antics of the animals but then the smile faded from his face.

'Something wrong?' asked Cleary.

'There are only five,' said Steven.

Cleary counted. 'So there are,' he agreed, sounding puzzled. 'Freda, do you know why there are only five animals?'

'There were only five when I started,' replied Freda.

'You're sure?'

'Of course, I'm sure,' replied Freda, sounding bemused. 'You're not likely to miss a monkey...'

'Of course not,' said Cleary. 'Could I see the primate book?'

Freda propped her mop up at the side of one of the cages and went into her little office, which didn't seem to be much bigger than a shower cabinet. She returned with an A3 sized record book.

Cleary flicked through the pages and said, 'There's no recorded entry of any monkey being used but then of course, there was a bit of a hiatus after Smithy...well, you know, so perhaps records weren't kept as diligently as they should have been.'

'Six were received?' asked Steven.

'Let me see...' said Cleary, flicking back through the pages. 'No,' he said, his eyes opening wide with surprise. 'Only five have been entered in the book.

'Who made the entry?'

'Smithy. Well, I suppose that clears up the mystery – if we

only ever received five,' said Cleary.

'But six were ordered,' said Steven.

'Primates aren't as easy to obtain as other experimental animals,' said Cleary. 'Five was probably all they had. The invoice will probably confirm this but we'll have to go back upstairs.'

Once again Steven stood by while Cleary this time looked through the institutes accounts for the past two months. 'Here we are,' he announced. 'Bronington Life Sciences... Oh, that's odd, we've been charged for six animals...it must be a mistake.'

'Maybe you could ask the company to check?' said Steven, 'I presume someone would have had to sign for the animals when they arrived as well as entering the delivery in your record book downstairs?'

'Of course. I can't imagine us getting six if Smithy only entered five in the book. There has to be some mistake.'

Steven found that he could imagine only too well what had happened to the missing monkey but didn't say it.

'Let's go to my office,' said Cleary. 'I'll call from there.'

Steven looked out of the window while Cleary made the call. Looking at the institute surroundings, he found it hard to believe that such a genteel place had been at the centre of such recent violence and intrigue. He smiled wryly as he saw it as the sort of place that Agatha Christie might place a body in the library, but as for an al-Qaeda attack and the theft of lethal viruses...that was the stuff of nightmares from a different world. He heard Cleary slam the phone down and turned round.

'Bronington insists that six animals were delivered and

signed for but they can't make out the signature on the
driver's delivery note. It's a scrawl they say. Sounds to me
like the driver might have been doing a little business on his
own.'

'Maybe,' said Steven. 'I think I'll call Leila in Washington
about this before we start making any accusations.' He looked
at his watch and said, 'A bit early for the States, I'll do it later.
In the meantime, thanks for your help.'

'I'm sorry we couldn't clear this up,' said Cleary. 'Give Leila
my best when you speak to her.'

Steven decided to call in on Giles on the way back.

'I didn't expect you back,' said Giles. 'I thought you'd just
phone.'

'They ordered six monkeys but only recorded delivery of
five,' said Steven. 'Bronington Life Sciences insist they
delivered six.'

'And you think the sixth one was the monkey that was put
out for the army to find?'

'Don't you?'

'It would be stretching coincidence too far to think
anything else,' agreed Giles. 'But they must know who
ordered the monkeys?'

'Leila...Dr Martin,' replied Steven.

'Did she say why?'

'She's gone back to the States. I'm going to phone her later.'

'Who took delivery of them?'

'That's really why I came by,' said Steven. 'They say the
signature is a scrawl: they can't decipher it. There's a
possibility the driver might have done some kind of deal on

his own and hoped that the paperwork would slip through without anyone noticing...'

'But he reckoned without Sci-Med,' said Giles. 'I take it you'd like me to have a word?'

'I'd be obliged.'

'Who could say no to a man with a silver Porsche?'

Steven rang the university in Washington and asked to speak to Leila Martin in the Department of Immunology. He didn't have her direct line number because of the agreement that she would call him first.

'You're through to Immunology, caller.'

'Hello. My name is Dr Steven Dunbar. I'm calling from England. I'd like to speak to Dr Leila Martin please.'

'I'm sorry. Dr Martin is currently in Europe.'

'No, she returned to the States on Tuesday.'

'One moment please.' The minutes seemed to pass like hours before the woman came back on the line to say, 'I'm afraid that's news to everyone here, Doctor.'

'But I saw her off at the airport myself.'

'One moment please.'

Another wait.

'I've just spoken to Carla Brunner, Doctor. She's a post-doc who's been staying in Leila's apartment while she's been away. Carla hasn't heard anything about Leila's return either.'

CHAPTER EIGHTEEN

Steven put the phone down feeling utterly bemused. Leila hadn't turned up at either her apartment or the university. There had been no indication at the airport that she intended going anywhere else first so what the hell was going on? It made him wonder about her insistence that she should call him rather than the other way around. If it hadn't been for the query over the animal order she'd placed, he wouldn't even know that she wasn't back in Washington. 'Oh, Leila,' he murmured softly. 'Leila... Leila, my beautiful Leila, what are you playing at?'

Steven wondered whether Leila's apparent lack of frankness was personal and had something to do with some other relationship she might be engaged in – but maybe this was personalising the problem too much. However difficult he found it, he must try to avoid that and make his head rule his heart. It was however, possible to reconcile both with his first decision. He had to find out where she'd gone. Although her work might be over for the moment, Leila was still a major figure in the fight against any attack involving the use of Cambodia 5 virus. He called the duty man at Sci-Med and asked him to get on to Heathrow and find out as quickly as possible which flight she had boarded and where she'd gone.

While he waited for a reply, Steven called John Macmillan and told him what had happened.

'Maybe she decided to take a holiday first,' suggested Macmillan. 'She's been working round the clock for the past few months.'

'She didn't say anything about taking a holiday to me,' said Steven.

'Should she have?'

'We are friends...we had a relationship.'

'I noticed,' said Macmillan. 'Maybe you imagined that it would be on-going and she didn't?'

'Nothing like that,' Steven assured him. 'If I'm honest, I hoped that might be the case but Leila made it quite clear that her career came first and that she was going back to the States to continue it. She couldn't wait to get back to the university in Washington...she said.'

'So why not be honest about what she was planning...' mused Macmillan, as if trying to decide whether or not the deception was big enough to cause Sci-Med concern.

'I'm trying to see things objectively,' said Steven. 'But emotional involvement is getting in the way. I find myself thinking she's gone off to France or Spain to meet up with some secret lover.'

'Which, of course, would be of no concern to Sci-Med,' said Macmillan.

'Quite,' agreed Steven. 'But there may be another reason she's gone missing and that's why I need an objective view.'

Macmillan took a few moments to compose his thoughts before taking a deep breath and saying, 'Dr Martin has been – is – more than a bit player in all of this. She is the designer of our main hope of defence against a potentially disastrous biological weapon. It is essential we know exactly where she is at all times – especially if it should be somewhere other than where she said she'd be.'

'I suppose that was what I wanted to hear,' said Steven. 'I've put the wheels in motion to find out what flight she boarded and where she was going when I said goodbye to her on Tuesday.'

'Good. I have to say in any other circumstances I'd replace you with one of the others because of your personal involvement but you're in this too deep and you've already brought us a long way. You're probably still our best chance of finding out what al-Qaeda are really up to. I won't give you a lecture about steeling yourself to be objective but you must continue to think round all the angles, Steven – whoever it concerns. You're good at it, maybe the best: continue to be.'

Macmillan had already hung up but Steven murmured, 'Yes, Boss,' before switching off his phone and slumping down into his chair by the window. The light was almost gone and the traffic on the river was lit up like pearls on velvet. He concentrated on the one star he could see in the sky as he forced himself to think round all the angles where Leila was concerned. The trouble was he knew so little about her. There just hadn't been time to say much to each other about their past lives because of the demands and sense of urgency of the situation they'd found themselves in. It had been a bit like a wartime romance with no time for considerations past or future; only the 'now' had been important. This was a situation that had to be remedied. He called the duty man at Sci-Med and said, 'I've got another job for you. I need you to find out everything there is to know about Dr Leila Martin and her career. Get on to her university in Washington and see if you can get them to send a full CV. If they prove difficult, get John Macmillan to put the request through the CIA chief of station in London. If the worst comes to the worst he'll be at the meeting of the UK Joint Intelligence Committee tomorrow.'

'A CIA man at the JIC meeting?' exclaimed the duty man.

'That's normal protocol,' said Steven. 'He leaves when domestic matters are discussed. This is top priority,' he insisted. 'I need this information.'

'Understood.'

'Anything back from Heathrow yet?'

'Nothing. I'll get on to them again.'

Another hour was to pass before the duty man called back. 'Heathrow says that no one named Leila Martin left through the airport on Tuesday on any of their flights.'

'They're sure?' exclaimed Steven.

'They're positive.'

'You're telling me she never left the country?'

'No, *they're* telling you she never left the country and, like I say, they're quite sure. If you turn on your laptop, I'll forward some stuff to you that's just come in from Washington on Dr Martin. I told them we needed the CV for an article *The Times* was doing about American academics working in the UK and they sent it without question.'

'Well done,' said Steven. '"A" for initiative.'

'Mum will be pleased... Use decoder 154.'

Curiouser and curiouser, thought Steven. If Leila hadn't left the country...this could put a whole new complexion on things. He knew he shouldn't read too much into it but his spirits rose when the thought occurred to him that there was just a chance that the whole thing might be some kind of misunderstanding. Leila might have forgotten something and gone back to the cottage to get it. It had taken longer than she'd anticipated and she'd simply missed her flight! Rather than bother calling anyone, she had stayed over, made new arrangements and flew out next day or whenever they could get her on another flight! It was only a working hypothesis but he liked it. He called the duty man at Sci-Med once more and asked him to check again with the airport – this time against all departures on Wednesday or even Thursday.

'Will do. Get the CV OK?' asked the duty man.

'I'm just about to download it,' said Steven. He set up his laptop to receive and decode Leila Martin's CV and spent the next fifteen minutes going through it. He didn't feel comfortable doing it because it seemed underhand, disloyal, almost the action of a secret policeman investigating his own family but he knew it had to be done.

He read that Leila Martin was the daughter of a French father and Moroccan mother. Her late father had been a distinguished neurologist who had written several books on the subject, one of them now a widely recognised university text book. Her mother, a concert pianist who had been establishing herself as a particularly brilliant interpreter of the works of Liszt had had her career cut tragically short by arthritis in her thirties. Leila had been brought up in Paris and educated both there and at a finishing school in Berne, in Switzerland. She had returned to study biological sciences at the Pasteur Institute in Paris and had gone on to obtain a doctorate in immunology from the Seventh University of Paris before heading off to the USA to take up successive post doctoral fellowships at the University of California at Los Angeles and at Harvard Medical School in Boston. She had then moved to the World Health Organisation in Geneva to work on vaccine design for third world immunisation programmes before returning to the States to become associate professor of immunology at the university in Washington where she was currently employed.

It was clear to Steven, and anyone who read her CV, that Leila Martin was a woman of impeccable background who, in her youth, had been an exemplary student and who was now regarded by the scientific community as a gifted immunologist. Steven noted that she had picked up several academic awards and prizes along the way and had built up a formidable publication list in prestigious scientific and medical journals. There was absolutely nothing to suggest that she could be anything other than the intelligent, beautiful woman he had fallen for...so where was she and what was she doing?

Twenty minutes later, the duty man at Sci-Med rang to say that Heathrow had drawn a blank on the other days too. They were adamant that Leila Martin had not left the country through their airport.

Steven rubbed his forehead nervously with the tips of his fingers as he tried to salvage a possible scenario from the wreckage of the old one to explain why Leila was still in the country. OK, she forgot something...she went back to get it and missed her flight because...she fell ill...or had an accident! She could be lying unconscious in hospital somewhere! Worse still, she could be lying on the floor of the cottage! She could have gone back there, fallen and struck her head and no one would know she was even there!

'It was after eleven in the evening and for once Frank Giles was not still at work when Steven called. He tried his mobile number instead and got a sleepy response.

'Jesus, Dunbar, this is the first early night I've managed in yonks and you have to ruin it.'

Steven apologised but said it was important. 'Leila Martin has gone missing,' he said. 'She was supposed to get on a flight to Washington on Tuesday but it never happened. She's still in the country somewhere.'

'You mean she's been kidnapped?'

'I don't know what I mean,' confessed Steven. 'I saw her as far as the airport so I've been thinking that she may have had to go back for something and been involved in an accident but we can't rule out anything. Could you run a check on the hospitals? I'm going to drive up to her cottage.'

'I'll mobilise the troops,' said Giles. 'Just in case Ali and his pals are involved.'

Steven rushed down to the basement garage, pausing briefly when he realised that he had promised to return the Porsche to Stan Silver by the end of the day. He hated breaking a promise but this was an emergency and it was too late to arrange another car. He would call Stan from Norfolk to explain. There was still a chance he could have it back by morning.

The wheels on the 911 squealed on the compound floor of the garage as he rounded the final pillar and accelerated up the ramp where he paused briefly to look to the right before roaring off into the night.

There were moments on the journey when Steven questioned his own actions: he recognised that his emotional involvement with Leila was definitely playing a part. One moment it seemed like exactly the right action to be taking, the next an absolutely ridiculous thing to be doing when the Norfolk police could have checked out the cottage for him and probably a lot quicker. But there was no turning back now and he had cause to be grateful that the temperature was above freezing as he challenged the grip of the Porsche's fat tyres on every tight bend. At least the lateness of the hour meant that traffic was light.

The growl of the engine died away to an uneven burble as he slowed right down to turn into the lane leading to Leila's cottage, wondering why she had chosen to live here in the first place. There was no doubt that it had rural charm but, in retrospect, Leila had never even mentioned this, only the lack of heating and the jumble sale furniture. She would have been happier with a flat in the city. His heart skipped a beat when he saw that there was a car parked outside the cottage; it wasn't Leila's: this one was a dark Vauxhall Vectra estate. Surely the property couldn't have been re-let so quickly? He would have given odds against there being a queue lining up for it in winter.

The fact that there were no lights on left him with a dilemma. Should he turn around and drive off, accepting that new tenants had moved in or should he wake the household and say who he was and why he was there? He decided he had to be sure about things. He'd knock, ask and apologise if necessary.

There was no answer to either his first or second louder

knock and it made him curse under his breath but he couldn't really blame whoever was inside for not answering the door at three in the morning in the middle of nowhere. He supposed the main thing had been established and that was that Leila could not be there, lying alone and injured on the floor. He got back into the Porsche and started the engine.

When he came to do a three point turn to get back to the road his headlights swept the length of the Vectra and briefly illuminated a jacket that had been draped untidily over the back of the front passenger seat. It made him hit the brakes. It was Leila's. It was the leather blouson she'd worn over her little black number the first time they went out to dinner together. It had a distinctive, patterned collar on it. But it wasn't Leila's car… Well, it wouldn't be, you idiot, would it? his subconscious accused. Leila would have returned her car to the rental company before going to the airport on Tuesday. When she realised she'd have to come back for something she would have rented another at the airport. Vectras were among the most common hire cars around. Leila could be lying injured inside after all.

Steven cursed the fact that he wasn't driving his own car with all his bits and pieces in the boot. The Porsche didn't have a torch in it. He angled the 911 so that the headlights lit up as much of the cottage as possible and started looking for the easiest way to gain access. The front door was solid oak and had been bolted from inside – he remembered Leila doing that at night. It would have to be a window. He moved down the left side of the building, testing each of the two windows on that side but both were tightly shut and snibbed – Leila did that too in an effort to keep out the cold. He rounded the corner at the back of the house, losing any help the Porsche lights could provide, and stopped for a moment to allow his eyes to become accustomed to the inky blackness. He thought at first it was his imagination when he started to see two pencil-thin parallel lines of light in the ground but they persisted. They were very faint but definitely there. The bungalow had a cellar with a light on in it.

'Leila!' he cried, dropping to his knees, scraping at the dirt and trying to see down through one of the joints in what appeared to be an old glass brick skylight, which was largely overgrown with weeds and smeared with mud. 'Leila, can you hear me?'

There was no answer.

Steven kept altering the angle of his position on the ground, trying desperately to find an area where the joint was wide enough for him to see through. He kept calling out Leila's name but whenever he paused to listen there was just silence, apart from an owl screeching somewhere out in the surrounding forest. He was just about to give up when he found a place he could see through with one eye if he pressed his nose right up against the dirty glass. He could make out a black and white tiled floor...and two legs lying on it...female legs. The upper part of the body was obscured. 'Leila! Leila! Can you hear me?'

The legs didn't move: there was no reply.

Filled with anguish, Steven pulled out his phone, finding that all his fingers were becoming thumbs in his hurry. 'Jesus!' he exploded when he saw that there was no signal. 'Give me a break, will you!'

He ran back to the front of the house, this time along the

right side of the cottage, again checking to see if any of the windows were open. None was. Without any further delay, he picked up a heavy edging stone from the garden and used it to smash the window of the room which had been Leila's bedroom. He'd chosen that one because the car lights were shining on it.

Still calling out Leila's name, he stumbled across the floor to switch on the lights and tripped over the old electric fire sitting in the middle of the floor. His head hit the bedroom door causing him to curse before he pulled himself to his feet and clicked the switch. Nothing happened.

'What the f...' He felt his way through to the living room and to the light switch there. Still no light. How the fuck could there be light in the cellar if the power was off? he thought as he bumped and cursed his way out into the hall and along to the cellar door. He had never been down in the cottage cellar. Apart from not having any reason for doing so, Leila had told him she didn't use it and always kept the door locked. She had given him a one word reason: 'Rats'.

He pulled at the cellar door and found it unlocked. The door creaked back and cold air filled his nostrils together with the competing smells of dampness and old wood. He felt for the light switch before realising that the light should be on; this was the reason he was here; he'd seen it from outside. Surely the power couldn't have failed at the very moment he entered the cottage. Not even his luck could be that bad...the only other explanation was...that someone had turned the power off! At that moment, a blow to the back of Steven's head ended all further speculation.

* * *

Steven came round to find himself suspended by his wrists with his toes barely touching the floor. Blood from a head wound had trickled down into his eyes and crusted over them making it difficult for him to see properly but he knew he was in the cellar because of the black and white tiles on the floor. He had a blinding headache and his arms felt as if they were being torn from their sockets by the cable that secured his wrists to a beam in the ceiling. He looked for the prostrate woman he'd seen from outside but she was no longer there. Instead, he saw a bundle in the shape of a body, wrapped in black plastic, huddled at the foot of the stairs.

'Oh, please God, no,' murmured Steven, closing his eyes and railing against the agonies of body and mind that were pushing him to the very brink of endurance.

'You're awake, Dunbar.'

The man who had come from behind him was in his mid thirties and Middle Eastern in appearance. He sounded well educated and spoke without an accent but when Steven looked into his eyes he saw a cocktail of loathing and contempt there. It was being suppressed in the cause of establishing credentials of intelligence and sophistication but it was definitely there. It was a look he'd come across before and he'd always found it chilling to be regarded as something less than nothing, be it by religious zealots in their contempt for the non-believer or even in the eyes of the poor in India who could look through you as if you didn't exist. It was what the worm must see in the eye of the bird about to eat it. If it came to a choice between confronting a cold-blooded psychopath or a religious fanatic who believed that some unseen god was with him in his struggle against the infidel, it would be a close run thing.

'How do you know me?' Steven croaked.

With no change of expression, the man held up Steven's Sci-Med ID, which he'd taken from his pocket. 'A pity. Ten more minutes and I would have been gone,' he said. 'Still, as you are here, I thought I might as well make the most of it. Tell me all about *Earlybird* and what their current thinking is.' He moved across to the body lying on the floor and started to manoeuvre it into position to be dragged upstairs.

Steven felt sick in his stomach. 'Who?' he asked, fearing the answer.

The man looked amused at the question. 'Dr Leila Martin,' he said.

'You bastard! Why?'

The man stopped what he was doing and came towards Steven slowly. He didn't stop until he was only inches from his face. 'Call it collateral damage,' he said icily. 'That's what your friends, the Americans, called it when they incinerated my mother, my father and my sister.'

'There's a difference between war and cold-blooded murder,' gasped Steven.

'The difference is hypocrisy,' said the man. 'And in the end that is why you will lose. All the pretence about 'liberation' of oppressed peoples when all you ever wanted was our oil will be difficult to keep up and it will weigh you down just like the constant calls for internal investigations every time your own newspapers prints pictures that the hypocrites don't like. Pretty soon the moronic lard-arses of middle America will get it through their thick skulls that their kids' ass-kicking adventure in a place they'd never even heard of is going to come to grief. Junior's rights-of-passage romp is going to end with him coming home in a body bag with a note from Donald Rumsfeld attached.'

'While the peace-loving forces of Islam ride on to victory in the cause of truth and justice helped by ignorant kids with explosives strapped to them because they've been promised a free fuck in heaven. Do me a favour.'

The man brought the back of his hand across Steven's face in a vicious swipe that left his right ear ringing and blood pouring from his nose. 'I was beginning to think you had a point until you did that,' Steven gasped, amazed at his own attempt to take the moral high ground.

'Let's get one thing clear,' said the man as he returned to the stairs to start dragging Leila's body up them. 'I will most certainly not be doing you any favours.'

'Go screw yourself.'

The man paused on the stairs but only to give Steven a pitying look. 'Professor Devon was very 'brave' too,' he said. 'But in the end, he told me what I wanted to know...as will you. You might care to consider that while I put Dr Martin in the car.'

Waves of pain and anguish washed over Steven as he faced up to the fact that he was now in the hands of the ubiquitous 'Ali', leader of the al-Qaeda team who had tortured and murdered Timothy Devon, Robert Smith and now Leila, not to mention two of his own. He also remembered that what this man had done to Timothy Devon had turned the stomach of a hardened pathologist.

Steven tried to find rational thought through the mess of

competing emotions inside his head. His chances of getting out of this were close to zero. He supposed there was a possibility that Frank Giles might turn up eventually if it was noticed that he had been missing for some time but that would probably mean many hours and by that time he would be dead. He had no doubt of that: in fact, he had already accepted this and was concentrating on what he might have to endure before he was allowed to die.

As if having the last straw torn from his grasp, Steven suddenly realised that Frank Giles didn't even know where the cottage was! He had never had cause to tell him where Leila Martin lived and he in turn had never had reason to ask... But Ali had known and he had come calling. Why?

Poor Leila and what she must have suffered at the hands of this lunatic and after all the doubts he'd been harbouring about her. He felt guilty and ashamed. Ali must have wanted to know how far she'd progressed with the vaccine against Cambodia 5. That in itself suggested that the vaccine was still relevant to the al-Qaeda mission despite his own doubts about city centre attacks.

Leila would, of course, have told him the truth – that it was already in production, but he had probably tortured her to make sure that she wasn't lying. But what did Ali want from him? He obviously knew about *Earlybird* and that was disturbing in itself – another reminder that global terrorism was not entirely an external enemy. It was already embedded in the society it sought to destroy. Ali couldn't have anticipated his coming here tonight so it would be a case of him gleaning any extra information he could before killing him. Maybe he needed it confirmed that the trail he'd gone to so much trouble to lay had been followed by the government who had – as they were meant to do – concluded there were to be city centre attacks across the UK using Cambodia 5. The best he personally could hope to do was withstand pain long enough to make divulging this appear like a genuine admission. The only secret he must keep was the fact that he believed this to be another red herring, a view he had shared with others. But as to what the real al-Qaeda mission might be...he really had no idea. Nothing Ali could do to him could make him tell what he didn't know. A comfort? Steven thought not.

CHAPTER NINETEEN

Steven was aware that his breathing had become rapid and shallow and that cold sweat was forming on his brow. Not for the first time in his life real fear was coming to call and this time there could be only one outcome; he was going to die a painful death. If Timothy Devon's demise was anything to go by, a scalpel blade would be used to transport him to the outer reaches of agony and humiliation in a slow symphony of mutilation while all the while taking care that he remained conscious. Only he would know the final irony that there was nothing he could tell them that they didn't know already.

To all intents and purposes, al-Qaeda's bluff had worked. Neither he nor anyone in the security services knew what they were really up to. John Macmillan's faith in him had been misplaced: he had failed to come up with the truth in what must surely be his last mission and there was no comfort to be found in the knowledge that he wouldn't be around to find out just what it was that al-Qaeda had planned.

Steven's stomach cramped when he heard Ali start to come back downstairs. He was about to face hell on earth and he hoped that he could do it without letting his daughter Jenny down. He was a doctor but he had lived as a warrior and he wanted to die like one but the dice were stacked against him.

Ali knew well enough how to turn any man into a mewling, puking, jibbering wreck of his former self, a pathetic figure pleading to be put out of his misery. All the training he'd had in the past to help him resist interrogation techniques would count for nothing in this situation. This was something you could not prepare for.

'So tell me about *Earlybird*,' said Ali. His voice seemed even and calm but there was no mistaking the cold menace in it.

'It usually catches the worm,' said Steven, thinking stupidly that he sounded like Roger Moore playing James Bond.

Ali looked at him, shook his head, gave a wry smile and selected the poker from a set of fireside tools beside an old stove that appeared to have lain unused for many years. He affected an examination of it but Steven knew that he was just giving him time to think about what was to come. Physical pain was only part of the torturer's art; the other element was psychological. Steven silently prayed that Ali would hit him over the head with it so hard that either death or loss of consciousness would intervene on his behalf but, with a sudden swinging motion, Ali brought it low and horizontally into Steven's right knee cap making him cry out in pain.

'Want to try again?'

It was almost a minute before Steven was capable of speech but a movement of the poker in Ali's hand helped return the power. 'It's a committee that assesses potential threats to national security,' he gasped, fighting the waves of pain from his injured knee.

'Of course it is,' said Ali. 'You know that; I know that. So what's the latest threat to national security perceived as being?'

'You are.'

'I'm suitably flattered,' replied Ali. 'And just what am I going to do?'

'You're planning an attack on our cities using Cambodia 5 virus.'

'All on my own?' asked Ali.

'Presumably not,' said Steven. It made Ali raise the poker again and Steven gasp. 'No!'

Ali lowered the poker and said, 'How many people does *Earlybird* think we have?'

'They don't know.'

'How many do they think we'll need?'

'They don't know, quite a few, I suppose.'

'What's the estimate?'

'There isn't one.'

Ali came closer. 'No estimate?... That suggests to me that someone isn't taking us seriously,' he said, watching for Steven's reaction like a cat eyeing a cornered mouse.

'Of course they're taking you seriously,' said Steven, knowing his last answer had been a bad mistake. 'How could they not?'

'But no estimates?' Ali persisted. 'No projections from Porton Down about how many people would be required for such an operation? How much virus would be needed, wind speed, the effect of rain...'

'Of course they were done,' said Steven, trying to rescue the situation.

'One might almost think that you didn't really believe it was going to happen?' said Ali.

'It was deemed too late to try and stop your attack,' said

Steven. 'Our security people simply didn't know enough so they adopted a different strategy and put all their efforts into producing a vaccine against Cambodia 5 and tough shit, it worked: they've done it. There was no point in killing Leila. The vaccine is already in production. You've lost. You've left it too late.'

'That is a shame,' said Ali with patronising slowness. 'So how can I salvage something from the ashes? What am I going to do now that British Intelligence has out-thought me?'

Steven looked at him and saw that the question had not been rhetorical. Ali was expecting an answer. 'What do you mean?'

'Put yourself in my position. I need an alternative strategy to hit my enemy with. What am I to do?'

'How the hell should I know? I'm the last person on earth to ask that question.'

'You do yourself a disservice, Doctor and I *am* asking you the question,' said Ali who had taken a velvet pouch from inside his jacket and was unrolling it to reveal three surgical scalpels, one with a curved blade and two with different sized straight ones. He slid the plastic guards off the ends, 'Tell me, Doctor...what am I going to do now that my plans for a Cambodia 5 attack are in ruins?'

'I have no fucking idea,' exclaimed Steven, unable to take his eyes off the scalpels and feeling his imagination soar into overdrive.

'Good to hear,' said Ali. 'But you will understand that I do have to be very sure of that...'

'Why don't *you* tell *me*?' gasped Steven, mounting a last minute appeal to the man's vanity. 'Just what the fuck does al-

Qaeda think it's going to do now that we have the vaccine? Make a new video of Osama in his latest cave? Just how scary is that?'

Steven had been prepared for a sudden backlash of violence but none came. Instead, Ali smiled and said, 'Very good, Dunbar. At this point I am supposed to lose my temper and tell you everything before I kill you just like the villains always do in movies. No, I prefer my way. You...tell...me... What am I going to do?'

There was a scraping noise from above that both Ali and Steven heard at the same time and looked up. For the first time, Ali looked less than supremely confident but he didn't lose his nerve. He held a scalpel to Steven's throat to ensure his silence and then forced the velvet that the scalpels had been wrapped in inside his mouth before taping it in place with the same tape that Steven had seen used on the body bag for Leila. Ali put out the lights and started to climb the stairs. He had put down the scalpels in favour of an automatic pistol.

Steven was beginning to think that there had been nothing to the noise – just another fact of life in the country – when he heard a floorboard creak. There really was someone up there. Or something. But who? What? A burglar about to become fatally familiar with Ali's notion of reasonable force in defending his property? A tramp looking for food and shelter? Maybe even a fox had gained access through the smashed window. Depressingly, he had to admit that that was more likely than the detachment of Royal Marines he would have preferred but at least it had taken Ali's attention away from the scalpels for a few minutes.

Listening in the darkness, he sensed that Ali had reached the top of the stairs and had a hand on the cellar door handle. It gave out the tiniest of squeaks when he turned it. Almost immediately flood lighting silhouetted Ali at the head of the stairs and the air was filled with shouts of, 'Armed Police! Lay down your weapon!

Ali only managed to get off one shot and had half turned away from the door when his body was riddled with bullets and he tumbled backwards downstairs like a rag doll to lie in a heap at the foot of the stairs in almost exactly the same spot where Leila's body had been lying a short while before.

The lights came on and Steven saw Frank Giles coming downstairs. Giles looked up at the cable securing Steven's wrists and said to his sergeant, 'Wasn't I just saying the other day, Morley, that the security services seemed to spend most of their time just hanging around while the police get left to do all the work?'

Morley released Steven and he slumped to the floor to lie there for a moment before looking up at Giles and saying, 'I don't think I've ever felt like kissing a man before. How on earth did you know I was here?'

'Sheer bloody brilliance,' said Giles.

Steven removed the last of the tape from his face and mouth and rolled up his trouser to examine his injured knee. 'I'm still waiting,' he said.

'Shit, that looks nasty,' said Giles, grimacing at the sight of Steven's swollen and bloody knee. 'It was your old soldier buddy, Stan Silver. He phoned to say that you hadn't brought his Porsche back. As it was two in the morning I told him to go fuck himself but he insisted that you had both served with the SAS and you had made him a promise. The fact that you hadn't kept it suggested that you were in real trouble.'

'Bloody hell,' said Steven. 'That's true, but how did you know where I was?'

'Very nice cars like the Porsche 911s often have a satellite tracking system fitted as an anti-theft device. You got lucky. The silver Porsche told us where it was on the planet with an accuracy of plus or minus twelve feet.'

Steven felt himself go weak as all energy seemed to leave him. 'I will never,' he averred, 'never ever complain about my luck again.'

'That sounds just about right,' agreed Giles. 'I take it sonny Jim here is Ali?'

'That's your man,' said Steven, looking at the crumpled body of his would-be tormentor.

'Know anything about the woman's body in the car outside?'

'It's Leila,' said Steven, looking down at the floor to avoid Giles seeing what was in his eyes. 'Dr Leila Martin. Ali killed her.'

'I'm sorry,' said Giles. 'I got the impression maybe you and she...'

Steven nodded and further examined his knee.

'Does this mean that the al-Qaeda threat is over?' asked Giles who had walked over to watch his colleagues deal with Ali's body.

'I'd like to think so,' said Steven.

'But?'

Steven gave an uncertain shrug.

'Maybe shooting him wasn't such a good idea,' said Giles.

'Personally, I think it was a bloody excellent one,' said Steven with some feeling.

'Sounds like the ambulance,' said Giles as a distant siren sounded. 'You can't drive with your leg like that. Is the knee broken?'

'I don't think so,' said Steven. 'But there's too much swelling right now to be absolutely sure. I'll need to have it X-rayed.'

'I'll have one of my guys take your pal's Porsche back. I take it he should convey your thanks to Mr Silver?'

'And then some. Tell Stan I owe him big time.'

Steven preferred to 'walk' out to the ambulance with the aid of Giles and Sergeant Morley. As he manoeuvred himself into the back and turned round to thank them he saw that Leila's body was being transferred to a police vehicle. His first impulse was to get back out again and go over to her but Giles put a hand on his arm. 'Maybe not,' he said kindly. Steven thought about it before concurring with a nod.

Steven managed a couple of hours sleep after having been assured that his injuries – although painful – would not demand hospitalization. His face was swollen and discoloured but again nothing that wouldn't subside and heal with time or as the houseman on duty had said, 'Presumably that's what you get for calling Mike Tyson a sissy.'

The first face Steven saw when he opened his eyes was John Macmillan.

'I heard you had a pretty narrow escape. How are you feeling?'

'They don't come any narrower,' agreed Steven. 'But I'm fine.'

'Ali's dead?'

'He's dead. So is Leila.'

'I'm sorry.'

Steven nodded but added. 'You didn't come here to be sorry.'

'No, I didn't,' agreed Macmillan. 'I have to know if you managed to get anything out of Ali to confirm your suspicions about the Cambodia 5 attack being another red herring?'

'He was doing the interrogating,' replied Steven.

'Do you still think it was a false trail? I have to know. Pressure from above. HMG would like to be assured that the al-Qaeda operation has been thwarted.'

Steven put his head back on the pillow and closed his eyes. 'I can't give them that assurance,' he said. 'Ali was definitely trying to find out if I thought the Cambodia 5 attack on UK cities was a bluff and that to me suggests that it was. More than that, he was smug; smug as if something else was a done deal and there was nothing at all we could do about it.'

'Damnation,' said Macmillan. 'That is exactly what HMG don't want to hear with an election only weeks away.'

Steven swallowed the vitriolic comment that came to mind and instead said, 'Of course not.'

'You've absolutely no idea at all what he might have been planning?'

'Only that it still involves Cambodia 5, I'm pretty sure of that. They wouldn't have gone to all that trouble to get the virus just to use as a bluff.'

'Then we've still got a chance,' said Macmillan. 'Auroragen say that the accelerated vaccine production process has been going well. They should be in a position to supply the first vials in about five days time.'

'How did they manage that?' asked Steven.

'A top level decision,' replied Macmillan.

'Meaning?'

'Although the company can't have the vaccine ready for everyone, they are concentrating some of it by high speed centrifugation so that about twenty thousand doses will be ready for inoculation next week. They reckon about two million doses will follow in about three weeks time followed by up to forty million by the late summer.'

'Who gets protection first?' asked Steven.

'The intelligence communities are still of a mind that the UK and the USA are the most likely targets for al-Qaeda so the first doses will go to all key personnel in both UK and American administrations and people vital to the infrastructure of both countries, police army, fire services, health personnel and so on down the line until all citizens can be offered protection.'

Steven nodded and said, 'Leila said vaccination will be effective in two to three days so if Ali's operation is not mounted some time in the next eight days, we should be out of the woods.'

'That has a nice ring to it,' said Macmillan. 'So what do I tell our political masters meantime?

'They should keep their fingers crossed for eight days.'

'Seriously,' prompted Macmillan.

'Definitely no crowing to the Press about having smashed an al-Qaeda plot,' said Steven. 'We had enough of that rubbish last time and we haven't. Vaccine distribution must remain our number one priority and every minute counts. And of course, that old favourite of ours...'

'Heightened security measures,' said Macmillan.

'With special emphasis on confiscating nail clippers,' added Steven tongue in check. 'That should show al-Qaeda we mean business...'

'Let's not go there again,' said Macmillan. 'I know we're of a mind about that but at least in this instance it should create an impression of alertness. You need sleep. I'll talk to you later.'

'Do we know who Ali was yet?' asked Steven as Macmillan rose to leave.

'They're still working on it.'

'His mother, father and a sister died in an American air attack – collateral damage,' said Steven. 'He told me.'

'I'll pass that on.'

Steven drifted off into a fitful sleep for another few hours, a sleep which was permeated by bad dreams but above all, by feelings of great unease. Ali had sensed that he hadn't swallowed the city centre attacks story and yet he had still seemed unperturbed. He also knew that a vaccine against Cambodia 5 was entering the final stages of production and still...he exuded the air of a winner, not of someone who was still running the race. At one point, thoughts of what Ali must have done to Leila to make sure she was telling the truth started to intrude and he woke to sit bolt upright in bed, sweat running down his face, before sinking back down again and imagining Macmillan saying, 'All the angles, Steven, all the angles.'

Three days later, Steven's knee swelling had died down enough to let him drive back to London. His face still looked as if he had collided with a door at speed but in general he was feeling much better and he limped into the

Home Office to see John Macmillan.

'Ali was Mahmoud Ali Mansour,' said Macmillan. 'Iraqi father, French mother. She and his father and one of his sisters were killed in an American air attack on Baghdad – mistaken coordinates apparently. He was educated at a public school in Britain before going home to study at Baghdad University where his father was a professor of mathematics. He himself studied microbiology and got a post graduate degree from Lund University in Sweden before seeing the light – or is it the darkness in this case – and joining up with Osama in Afghanistan. He spoke four languages fluently and had been used primarily in liaison between al-Qaeda and other terrorist organisations.'

'Until this time,' said Steven.

'Until this time,' agreed Macmillan. 'He comes from a very bright family apparently.'

'So maybe this was all his idea, his big chance to impress.'

'Could well be. I take it you've had no further thoughts on the subject?'

''Fraid not.'

'Then it's still fingers crossed time. The first batch of vaccine will leave the factory in three days for distribution to key personnel. You and I are considered to fit into that category.'

'Nice to feel appreciated,' said Steven dryly.

'An RAF Hercules aircraft will leave from RAF Lyneham at noon on that day bound for Washington carrying vaccine for key US administration personnel.'

'I also thought you might like to know that, on the same day, Dr Martin's brother is due in from the USA to carry out formal identification of her body and make arrangements for her return to the United States.'

'How...traumatic is that going to be for him?'

'The Pathologist's report said that she hadn't been tortured or disfigured in any way. Death was by strangulation.'

'Strangulation,' repeated Steven, finding that the news that Leila had not been tortured was not so much a cause for relief as for puzzlement. He had been wrong again.

'You look surprised,' said Macmillan.

'Ali was the kind of person who would have to make sure that what he was hearing was the truth. If he went to the trouble of seeking out Leila, he must have wanted to know something and he wouldn't just have accepted what she told him.'

'Unless he already knew from another source,' said Macmillan.

'In which case why seek her out?'

'Good question.'

'There's something wrong here,' said Steven.

'About what?'

'Everything,' said Steven. 'I'm going back to Norfolk.'

'To do what?'

'I'm not sure,' Steven confessed. 'But I need to be there. I need to walk around the scene of the crime if you like. Drive around the area. Hope something comes to mind that I've missed before. I'll also be there to meet Leila's brother when he arrives.'

'Whatever you say,' conceded Macmillan.

'He's due at the mortuary at twelve noon,' said Frank Giles when Steven arrived in his office. 'I'll run you over.'

'Thanks,' said Steven. 'I've been feeling guilty about not saying good bye to her properly.'

Giles nodded. 'How's the war against al-Qaeda going?'

'We're sitting with our fingers crossed,' said Steven.

'A comfort,' said Giles. 'A good time for me and the missus to take a holiday in Barbados then?'

'We don't think they're going for a city centre attack any more but we're still gambling on them using Cambodia 5 virus in some way. The good news is that the vaccine starts going out today. Of course, if it should turn out not to be a Cambodia 5 attack...we'll all be left sitting in that well known creek without a paddle.'

'And on that happy note,' said Giles. 'Maybe we should start out for the mortuary.'

CHAPTER TWENTY

It was raining on the drive over to the city mortuary and the two men sat in silence – apart from Giles' occasional mutterings about roadworks and the state of the traffic. Steven sat as if mesmerised by the sweep of the wipers but he was deep in thought. He found it a perpetually annoying fact of life that it always seemed easier to predict other people's reactions and responses to given situations than his own. Lisa, his wife, had put this down to him thinking about things on too many levels at once. 'Not everyone's playing chess with you,' she had pointed out. 'Not everyone in life has an ulterior motive.'

The trouble was that in his line of work they usually had and it was unavoidable that natural suspicion would spill over into his personal life, making him 'think round all the angles' as Macmillan put it. Sometimes it was a cross that was hard to bear. It would be so good, perhaps just on occasion, to be able to react spontaneously to events, to take things at face value, to give in and display natural emotion without going through some vetting process. Right now, he was going to say a final goodbye to Leila Martin, a woman he had had feelings for. He should feel sad...and he did. He needed to feel grief...and he did...but it was not unequivocal. A day's driving around on his own, visiting all the old spots, had left him with lingering doubts and unanswered questions and he wished that this wasn't the case.

Giles parked the car in the space marked for visitors outside the mortuary and they both went inside.

'Hello, John boy,' said Marjorie Ryman. 'I see you haven't found your way back to Waltons' Mountain.'

'Still looking, Elizabeth,' said Steven. 'Still looking.'

'Dr Martin's brother isn't here yet. Would you like to take a dekko at the body first or will you wait?'

'We'll wait,' said Giles quickly.

Fearing an uncomfortable silence about to develop, Steven told Giles that he'd go back out and wait in the car park. Giles nodded.

'You could wait in my office,' suggested Marjorie Ryman. 'There's a coffee machine…'

'I'll get some air,' said Steven.

He had completed three slow laps of the car park with his hands deep in his pockets, seemingly having examined every cigarette butt lying there and flicked at every loose pebble with his toe, when he was joined by Marjorie Ryman at his elbow.

'I'm sorry, John boy. Frank just told me that you and the deceased were friends. I didn't know.'

'Don't worry about it,' said Steven.

'I naturally assumed your interest in the case was professional. I'm so sorry.'

'That's OK. Really,' said Steven. 'You weren't to know.'

At that moment, a dark Rover drew up. It was unmarked but might well have had 'Official Government Vehicle' stamped all over it. A tall man wearing a dark overcoat over a light coloured suit got out from the back and thanked the driver before listening for a few moments to details about a later pick-up. He straightened up and looked at the building. It wasn't difficult to imagine what he was thinking, thought Steven, but there was already too much going on inside his own head for him to dwell too long on the pain of others. Marjorie Ryman had gone inside as soon as the car arrived leaving Steven the only other person in the car park.

'Mr Martin?' he said, straightening up and walking towards him.

'Yes. And you?'

'Steven Dunbar. I was a close friend of your sister while she was working at the Crick Institute.'

They shook hands. 'You're a scientist too?' he asked with the same pleasant French accent that Leila had had.

'Actually, no... I'm a doctor.'

They went inside to where Martin was introduced to Giles and Marjorie Ryman who both shook hands and offered their condolences.

'If you'd care to come this way, Mr Martin,' said Marjorie in subdued tones. 'We can carry out the formal identification and then you can have some time alone with your sister if you'd like before we discuss arrangements for repatriation.'

The four of them trooped along a narrow corridor in single file to where Marjorie stopped outside a door and turned to Martin to ask, 'Ready?'

Martin nodded and she opened the door.

They entered a small, square room where some attempt had been made to soften the reality of the building with paintings on the walls depicting pastoral scenes and alluding to the possibility of an afterlife. A simple crucifix sat on a semi circular table between candlesticks and purple drapes – hung albeit on an interior wall because the room had no windows. All attention was focused on the trolley that sat in the middle of the floor with a plain white sheet draped over the body that lay on it.

Marjory Ryman went to the head of the trolley and gripped the top of the sheet with both hands. She paused to give Martin a questioning look. Martin nodded and she lowered the sheet to reveal the head and shoulders of the deceased.

'Is this your sister, Dr Leila Martin, sir?' asked Giles.

Martin took two steps forward and looked at the dead woman. He nodded slowly and with great sadness. 'Yes, this is Leila,' he replied, a sob catching in his throat. 'This is my sister.'

Steven swallowed and felt a lump come to his own throat as he waited for Martin to step back before moving forward to say his own goodbye. He made eye contact with Marjorie Ryman who gave him a small smile of encouragement tinged with residual guilt from the earlier misunderstanding. He bowed his head and closed his eyes for a moment, steeling himself to see Leila in death rather than the vibrant image of her he'd kept alive in his mind. When he opened his eyes his heart missed a beat and his stomach turned over as his subconscious railed against this latest outrage of fate. His voice sounded foreign, even to him, when he said, 'This is not Leila Martin.'

Steven was looking at the body of a woman who bore almost no resemblance to Leila at all. This woman was plain where Leila had been beautiful. This woman had a small thin mouth, a broad nose and a chin that was almost masculine and looked about ten years older than Leila.

'But you told me it was...' said Giles, obviously bemused and more than a little embarrassed. 'At the cottage...'

'Ali told me. I didn't see the body,' said Steven, still staring at the unknown woman.

Martin, looking at Steven as if in complete disbelief, spluttered out, 'Of course it's Leila, are you suggesting that I don't know my own sister? What the hell are you talking about, man?'

Wheels were spinning inside Steven's head like the machinery of a fairground ride picking up speed. He looked at Martin without really seeing him but recovered some sense of the moment and said, 'I'm sorry,' he said. 'There's been some awful misunderstanding...'

'The man's crazy,' murmured Martin.

Giles looked like a man wading in out of his depth. He said to Martin, 'I'm sorry sir, I must ask you again; are you quite certain that this woman is your sister, Dr Leila Martin.'

'Of course it's Leila,' snapped Martin, still angry at what Steven had said. 'I don't know what this idiot here is talking about.'

Giles made a gesture with his head to signify that Steven should leave the room and Steven complied.

'What the hell's going on?' hissed Giles when he came out to join him.

'That's not the Leila Martin I knew,' said Steven. 'That is not the Leila Martin who worked at Crick.'

'I just don't get this,' stormed Giles, still struggling to keep his voice down to avoid those inside hearing. 'Then who the hell is the woman lying on the trolley in there?...the woman whose own brother has just identified as being Leila Martin?'

Steven now understood the look he'd seen in Ali's eyes when he had told him whose body was in the plastic bag. He had been enjoying a joke of his own. 'I think she's Leila Martin,' he replied without emotion.

'Am I missing something here?' asked Giles, now displaying serious exasperation. 'Are you telling me there are two Leila Martins?'

Steven looked at him distantly and said, 'No, I think not. There is only one real Dr Leila Martin and I think that's her lying on the trolley in there... She must have been intercepted as soon as she entered the country... Leila took her place.'

Giles' eyes opened wide. 'An imposter?'

Steven nodded. 'Yup.'

'What the hell was she doing there?'

The awful answer to that question was becoming crystal clear to Steven as was so much else as he realised what a fool he'd been. Leila, his Leila, the beautiful woman at the Crick had encouraged their relationship just so that she could use him to keep tabs on what he and the Intelligence services were thinking so that she could report back to Ali Mansour.

When she thought she had no further use for him, it had been she who had set up the attack on his life. She had simply passed on the details of their dinner arrangements to Ali so that he could intercept him on the road to her cottage. Even the cottage now made sense where it hadn't before. Leila hated the place but it was remote and that must have been its attraction. It was a convenient, safe base for Ali – and it had an ice-cold cellar. Steven could see that Giles was waiting for an answer.

'The woman I knew as Leila Martin wasn't working on a vaccine at all. Quite the opposite; she was growing up Cambodia 5 virus. That's why we could find no trace of the eggs al-Qaeda needed for cultivation. She was growing up the virus at the Crick.'

'What's she done with it?' asked Giles.

'She gave it to Auroragen to grow up on an industrial scale. They've been filling injection vials with it for inoculation...with distribution due to start today.'

'Christ! This is a bloody nightmare.'

'If we can't stop it,' said Steven, frantically pulling his phone out, 'something like fifty million people both here and the USA are going to be injected with Cambodia 5 virus instead of vaccine.'

'Jesus!'

Steven called the duty officer at Sci-Med. 'Listen and listen carefully. This is the biggest situation you are ever going to handle. We are talking a grade-one national emergency. All supplies of flu vaccine emanating from Auroragen in Liverpool must be recalled immediately. The vials do not contain vaccine, they contain a biological weapon. All government departments must be alerted to the danger and the police and army should make recovery of the vials a first priority. Auroragen can supply the distribution schedules including the arrangements for the US consignment. The company was not part of the conspiracy. Got that?'

'Got it.'

'When you've finished with the top level alerts, all major UK cities on the Auroragen supply list should be instructed to implement their biohazard emergency procedures just in case any of the distribution vehicles should be involved in an accident.'

'Understood.'

'Any consignments in the air should be recalled and diverted to military airports away from populated areas. If they've already gone beyond the point of no return, the same goes for the other side of the Atlantic.'

'Understood.'

'Good man. Put me through to Macmillan.'

Steven confined himself to telling Macmillan quickly that the Auroragen vials contained Cambodia 5 virus, not vaccine, knowing that his boss would appreciate the urgency of the situation and want to start making calls of his own. They agreed to speak later.

By four in the afternoon all 'vaccine' production had been closed down at Auroragen and stocks placed in quarantine, pending removal to Porton Down. All production workers had been placed under virtual house arrest until the incubation time for Cambodia 5 had passed – just in case they had infected themselves during the course of their everyday work. But the fact that they had been so well trained in safe microbiological techniques in an effort to avoid 'contamination' of the vaccine after last year's fiasco worked both ways. Their skills had also protected them from infection when handling Cambodia 5. Fifteen outward bound trucks, laden with injection vials, had been intercepted and ordered to return to the pharmaceutical company under police escort and an RAF Hercules flight had been recalled when already two hours out over the Atlantic, bound for the USA, carrying emergency 'vaccine' for the Bush administration.

'I think it fair to say that the Prime Minister and the entire cabinet were astounded at the audacity of the al-Qaeda operation,' said Macmillan. 'Another few hours and it would have been too late. The UK and US governments would have been crippled within weeks and it's almost certain that a global pandemic would have ensued. They asked me to pass on their sincere thanks.'

Steven nodded. 'So, what are they going to tell the electorate about the lack of flu vaccine this year when the papers have been doing their level best to cause panic over bird flu?' he asked. 'There's no time left now to come up with a real vaccine.'

'I understand they're going to dress up the shortage as a change in strategy,' said Macmillan. 'The Health Secretary will announce that they've decided to go for stocks of an antiviral drug instead of a vaccine. Apparently a Swiss pharmaceutical company has come up with one they've had some success with.'

'In getting politicians out of a tight corner,' completed Steven.

'That might well be its main asset,' agreed Macmillan. 'But I understand that it can be effective in preventing death if it's taken quickly enough.'

'And like all anti-virals, that means at the very first sign of symptoms,' said Steven. 'And we both know the chances of that are practically zero. By the time people have actually decided they've got flu and sought help it'll be too late.'

Macmillan looked equally dubious. 'Either that or there will be a panic and people will demand the drug and take it when they haven't even got the disease, which will be no use at all in preventing it and just use up stocks.'

Both men remained silent for a moment before Macmillam shook his head and changed the subject. He asked, 'Any thoughts on who the false Leila Martin really was?'

'I'm still thinking about it,' replied Steven. 'And before you remind me, I am aware that she's still out there.'

The sun had come out and Steven walked by the Thames Embankment while he considered 'Leila's' deception. She'd obviously had enough training in microbiology for her to be able to culture the virus safely and pass herself off as a visiting research fellow at the Crick Institute although, through pressure of work, she had had the perfect excuse to avoid too much contact with fellow scientists. The deadline for the vaccine had also helped her avoid facing any questions about its design where any shortcomings about her knowledge might have been exposed. He himself, to his embarrassment, had helped her negotiate her way through the safety screens of Auroragen.

The real Leila Martin had had a French father and a Moroccan mother and had been educated in France. His Leila had the right looks for such a mix and also the right accent... It was also similar to Ali Mansour's background, thought Steven. Mansour was the son of an Iraqi father and a French mother... He was also a graduate in microbiology...

Steven pulled out his phone and called Mac Davidson at the Sci-Med lab.

'Do you remember the DNA fingerprint tests I requested a while back on the staff of the Crick Institute?' he asked.

'Of course.'

'Do you still have them?'

'I don't think we've got round to destroying them yet,' said Davidson. 'Why? There were no matches as I remember.'

'I know but I'd like you to look at them again, particularly a comparison of the woman we believed to be Leila Martin and the DNA profile taken from the safe handle – the one that was subsequently shown to be Ali Mansour's.'

'I'll get back to you.'

Two hours later an embarrassed Mac Davidson got back to Steven. 'I'm not sure how we missed this,' he said. 'Perhaps it was because we were just looking for exact matches at the time but...there are certain corresponding features about the two profiles you asked to be re-examined.'

'Let me guess,' said Steven. 'The two subjects concerned could be brother and sister.'

'That's about it,' conceded Davidson. 'Sorry.'

'Thanks, Mac,' said Steven. When it came to missing things, he didn't feel up to calling the kettle black. He called Macmillan. 'Leila was Ali Mansour's sister,' he said. 'I take it you have details of Mansour's family there?'

'I'll email them to you. Well done again!'

Fifteen minutes later, Steven was gazing at a photograph

of his Leila on the screen of his laptop, only she was, in reality, Zainab Aline Mansour. She was eight years younger than the real Leila Martin but she had a degree in microbiology like her brother and had actually worked in the real Leila Martin's lab in Washington at one time as a graduate student.

Steven called Macmillan back and gave him the details. 'If she didn't leave the country as Leila Martin,' he said. 'There's a good chance she travelled under her own name of Zainab Aline Mansour. She may still be waiting for her brother to join her somewhere.'

'I'll let loose the dogs,' said Macmillan.

'Quite a family affair,' murmured Steven. He wondered how many more Mansour families were out there with scores to settle.

Macmillan called just after seven in the evening to say that 'Leila' had been traced and detained by the French Police. She had been living in an apartment in Montrouge in Paris, having flown there directly from Heathrow on the day Steven had seen her off – travelling under her own name.

'It seems you've worked out everything,' said Macmillan.

'*They* damned nearly worked out everything,' said Steven. 'We came *that* close to disaster.'

'What was it my old Scots granny used to say?' mused Macmillan. '*Nearly* never killed a man.'

'A comfort,' said Steven.

'So what d'you think they'll do next?'

'Crystal ball time,' sighed Steven. 'One thing's for sure: it'll take time to set up another "spectacular"... On the other hand, they won't want to lose face in the short term... They could go for a direct strike.'

'A bomb?'

'Probably. They might well sacrifice a few foot soldiers... mount a suicide attack on some building in the city...or the transport system...'